THE PROVIDENT EYE

by

ALLAN STEVEN

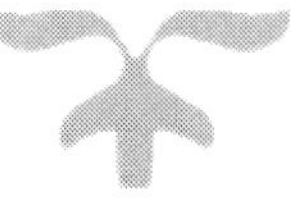

fruitymetcalfe@me.com

Cover artwork by Martin Gorst

Dedicated to Martin, who has walked beside me throughout the journey.

"Noble vengeance is the daughter of deep silence."

Italian proverb

1

"A sight to touch e'en hatred's self with pity."
'Oedipus Rex' Sophocles

The old girl had seen better days, but she still slid smoothly out of harbour under the watchful gaze of her master. She eased away into deep waters, which were remarkably quiet for a December day in the Shetlands. To all intents and purposes the retired cruise liner was undertaking a leisurely perambulation down the west coast. She would turn east below Cornwall, and head for Naples. That was the story her unwilling passengers had been told.

It was three in the afternoon when they left Fair Isle. A handful of the two thousand illegal immigrants on board had been permitted to stroll on deck. The chill winter air soon sent them scuttling down below. Scottish winters are too much for the blood of peoples used to warmer climes. Their detention on Fair Isle had been long and hard. When they learnt that they would be transported to Libya they found solace in the thought that they would no longer waste away in this freezing land. Darkness descended rapidly over the UK's northern outpost. A few stragglers on deck stared intently at the pulse of the Fair Isle South light. It receded, as the ship drove through the waves. In a desultory fashion they joined their companions below.

"Here we are my merry men!"

The Head Steward announced the buffet in the restaurant. A full complement of passengers was fed in the half dozen restaurants that once served holidaymakers. At least they were getting a good feed, something that had not been customary in the detention centres on Fair Isle. The ship's crew chattered and made jokes, showering attention on the children. It was all disarming.

Full and satisfied, nearly everyone retired to their cabins early. Soon not a whisper or movement could be detected. It was a ship of ghosts. None were cognisant of the ship manoeuvring, to head back towards the Norwegian Sea. When midnight struck, the *'Lucy Belle'* was closer to Iceland than to Cornwall.

A monumental lightning strike broke the cruise liner in two amidships, and a volcanic pillar of fire rose from her centre. Two thousand souls sank into the deep, oblivious to their fate. The opiates which laced their food would have made them thankful for small mercies, if they had known of them.

On the bridge of his freighter the skipper watched the *'Lucy Belle'* disappear. Shards of metal danced a stately gavotte, before sinking into the fathomless depths.

"All safely aboard, sir!" a voice announced from the doorway.

Master and crew from the defunct liner had been picked up from their lifeboats.

"See they get fed and watered, Johnny."

"Already under way, skip."

The freighter stole away into the night, heading for Liverpool.

Another vessel sank deeper into the waters nearby. She was two torpedoes shy of her usual complement.

A few hundred miles away in London an Admiralty clerk, with the highest security clearance, knocked on the door of a man stratospherically above his pay grade.

"Enter."

"Message reads, *'All Souls Day'* repeat *'All Souls Day'*."

2

"Never honour the gods in one breath and take the gods for fools the next."
'Oedipus Rex'

Isabel Joseph was thought to be Jewish by those who met her for the first time. Her classmates at High Heath Public School, Hampstead, knew better. When she arrived they called her Izzy. She made it known, in that gentle way of hers, that she preferred Isa. After a couple of weeks of teasing that she was named after a tax free investment bond Isa it was. Even the sarcastic Hugo terminated his persecution when one day she faced him and gazed deeply into his eyes. What he saw unnerved him. He recalled the brilliantined shimmer of the Indian Ocean, which he had plunged into on his summer holiday. It paled into insignificance compared with the light pouring from Isa. Hugo's eyes were a perfect copy of his step-uncle's; black and unyielding, full of menace.

Isa was keen to retain her name because it had been her father's; an acceptable form whether masculine or feminine. Being Coptic Christian induced her to hold to her origins. Her birth name was Isa Yusuf. Anglicising your name has a long history in Hampstead, especially with Jewish immigrants. German Jews cultivated a rich harvest; Grunewalds became Greenwoods, Weismann transposed itself to Whiteman and Stein, as if by alchemy, turned to Stone.

The family arrived in England when she was a baby. Since then, the persecution of Christians in the Middle East had gone from bad to worse. Events in the United Kingdom accelerated the process. In Arab states, churches were bombed with frightful regularity, and kidnappings and beheadings were commonplace. It was with relief that the Yusufs looked back upon their flight from Egypt as opportune. They came to a country ruled by Parliamentary Democracy, then Martial Law had been declared. The massacre of a Christian congregation in St. George's Church Banksmore, a small Buckinghamshire village, and the ensuing civil disorder was the catalyst for draconian measures. A cabal of government and opposition M. P.'s, in cahoots with the military top brass, despatched troops into the House and suspended Parliament. From January to August a coalition Rump Parliament, assisted by the military, had ruled the country with crisp severity. The Middle East boiled more fervently than usual when ghettoes and identity cards were created for Muslims. The opening of internment camps, on remote Scottish Islands, for illegal immigrants stirred the pot. Military trials and summary executions of those foolish enough to commit terrorist acts on the British mainland just about put the tin lid on it.

The Conservatives won a landslide in the August General Election. Former Marxist Prime Minister Tommy O'Donnell was confined to the dustbin of history. He slunk back to his hometown of Liverpool, and the obscurity he richly deserved. His former Home Secretary Henry Longfellow, who served as interim Prime Minister, was elevated to the House of Lords, to become *'special adviser'* to the new incumbent at the Home Office.

When the year drew to a close the new government came under pressure to resettle Christians from the Middle East in the United Kingdom. There had been considerable resistance from within Cabinet. Some objected to the voluntary intake of their darker brethren, Christians or not.

The Prime Minister, Julian Marlborough, was adamant. His acolytes deferred to his chill authority. Julian spoke to the Cabinet with an apparent sincerity about their duty and responsibility. It would have astonished his former acquaintances who knew only too well his virulent racist views. However, a few thousand people wouldn't make any difference to his long term intentions, and it would do wonders for his image.

Over drinks with Andrew 'Freddie' Forbes, now Earl of Seaforth, a brilliant idea emerged, which appealed mightily to Julian's ego. He laughed like a drain when 'Freddie' outlined the plan for presenting the potentially explosive proposal to the nation.

On Christmas Eve the usual service was held in Westminster Abbey. It also commemorated the horror perpetrated in Banksmore exactly a year before. The government made a big issue of it in the run up to Christmas, with adverts on television, and a social media campaign. The nation was urged to watch the service, and to remember that the deaths of their fellow citizens had caused a seismic shift in the life of the nation. Drink in hand, millions paused in celebration and tuned into the live broadcast.

The mandate of the Archbishop of Canterbury does not run in Westminster Abbey. The old place is a Royal Peculiar, as such the Dean of Westminster is the guvnor. She wasn't best pleased at having the occasion rearranged a little, but acquiesced. Julian Marlborough chose the boy himself from the village of Banksmore. A little fellow of nine whose grandmother died in the raking fire from Uzi submachine guns in St. George's Church. His angelic and Aryan looks would have made Heinrich Himmler weep. Edward Fisher's voice tinkled with the magical clarity of wind chimes pattering in an English summer breeze:

"...When Herod realised that he had been outwitted by the Magi, he was furious, and he gave orders to kill all the boys in Bethlehem and its vicinity who were two years old and under...Then what was said through the prophet Jeremiah was fulfilled:
'A voice is heard in Ramah, weeping and great mourning, Rachel weeping for her children and refusing to be comforted, because they are no more.'"

The Prime Minister commandeered the pulpit from the Dean, an act of arrogance that surprised everyone but his mother. He held the congregation and nation by their collective sweetbreads. Julian spoke movingly of past

events, cautiously about the present, and with hope for the future. Then he referred to the reading they had heard. Some thought they discerned a tremor of emotion in his voice as he spoke of the plight of Middle Eastern Christians. He recovered himself, and in ringing tones announced his plan to admit some as refugees, because *"they share our beliefs and values."* The nation took it on the chin, and got back to serious drinking.

3

"I was born to join in love, not hate – that is my nature."
'Antigone' Sophocles.

High Heath School lies on the edge of the Heath along Hampstead Lane, not far from the Spaniard's Inn; a convenient watering hole for generations of masters and mistresses. Speech Day repeated the pattern of the ages; not so much a 'Day' as an Evening held at the beginning of June. Arthur the Caretaker was on gate duty, directing the Headmaster's guests to parking spots. A glitzy Maserati edged through the opening, and Arthur hove alongside to make enquiries.

"Good evening sir, good evening madam," he oozed his version of charm. "May I ask if you are de Headmaster's guests?"

Arthur's fruity tones and accent revealed East End origins from a bygone age.

The Maserati's occupants were imperious, "No, but it's a bugger to park around here. Now let us through."

During thirty-five years in post, Arthur had dealt with numerous parents trying it on.

"I'm sorry sir, only those wiv a Headmaster's invitation can park 'ere."

The wife leant across her husband, "Do you know who we are?"

Arthur sniffed the air, and with impeccable timing, and a wink to his assistant Joey, exclaimed, "Why, 'ave you got amnesia?" He snuffled at his own wit.

The driver exploded, "How dare you. I pay twenty-five thousand pounds a year for my son to come to High Heath..."

Arthur halted him mid-sentence, "I don't care wot you pay. If you aint one of de Headmaster's guests, you can fuck off!"

"I shall report your insolence to..."

Arthur thrust his face into the car, "You are holdin' up de Prime Minister."

The Maserati owner looked over his shoulder and saw a grand limousine waiting on the road.

"Nah, put it in reverse, an' fuck off!"

The rejected, and dejected, parents were soon out of the way. Arthur waved the limo through, but it halted as it came abreast of him. A powerful and amused voice thrust itself through the open window.

"Good God Arthur, haven't they sent you to the knacker's yard yet?"

"Good evening, Prime Minister. No sir, de Headmaster sez I'm indispensable."

Laughter bounced around the interior of the limo, "You're a legend Arthur," as an afterthought the P.M. added, "King Arthur of High Heath!" The limo glided to its reserved spot at the front of the school.

Arthur watched it drift slowly up the drive, his face unfathomable. "Cunt!" he murmured.

Joey, his partner in crime sidled closer, "Didn't vote for 'im then, Arthur?"

"Wot, for that fucker? Let me tell you wot 'e did when 'e was eighteen..."

An Aston Martin pulled up, "Good evenin' madam. Are you one of de Headmaster's guests?"

"No, but..."

Arthur put her straight, and the wheel of life turned another obscene notch.

Hugo pleaded, not something his step-uncle would have approved of but he was enamoured of her.

"Come on Izzy, I'll introduce you to him."

She faced her fellow sixth former in the cavernous waste of the Great Hall.

"Isa please, Hugo," she said not unkindly.

"I've told him all about you, Isa. He says he'd be delighted to meet you."

She smiled, "I'll look forward to meeting him later, Hugo, but we have duties towards all of our guests."

The squadron of sixth form monitors was deployed to meet, greet and mingle.

Hugo's tone became harsher. "I rather think that my uncle takes precedence. Now come on, I promised him that I'd introduce you the moment he arrived." He grasped Isa by the elbow.

She was about to ask him to release his grip when the tall young man who had been observing from a distance strode over.

"Let her be, you're always bothering her."

Hugo blushed to the roots. Other students meandered over to watch the confrontation.

"Go and fuck yourself Andrews!"

A guffaw spilt from a huge lad at Jacob Andrews' shoulder.

"At least he can, Marlborough. Have you seen him in the showers? Now as for you..." The boy flexed his little finger in the air, and added for good measure, "How is Mr. Winky Pinky these days? Still playing with his friend Mr. Palm?"

Isa remained motionless and serene, whilst the others shook with glee.

"Sod off Peters," Hugo muttered.

Simon Peters closed in on Hugo Melton.

"Or you'll what badger breath?"

Hugo bore most of Julian's traits, but courage wasn't one of them. A beautiful hand rested on Simon's shoulder and the anger went out of him. The mountainous lad looked shamefaced.

"Sorry Isa, sorry."

The deputy head bounded up. "Come on chaps and chappesses," he declared cheerily, "would you mind awfully getting about your business? The Prime Minister has arrived. Hugo, you may join your uncle in the Headmaster's study." He frowned. "I must go and have a cautionary word with Arthur."

4

"The dead alone feel no pain."
'Oedipus at Colonus' Sophocles

Anna Wilbey and her mother, Alex, knew the footpaths and byways of the Chiltern Hills intimately. They relished the rare opportunity to be together for fresh air and exercise. Alex marvelled at her daughter, and never ceased to feel humble before God when she could walk beside her through the wonders of creation.

They approached the stile in unison.

"Oops, bootlace undone again. You carry on Mum."

Anna lifted a foot onto the stile to retie her lace. The early June evening was still warm. Soon they would be back at her car, and off into Great Missenden for a pub meal and a glass of bubbles.

Rignall Road runs out of Great Missenden, and flows into Missenden Road. It's a lengthy country road with winding bends and long straight stretches. What makes it noteworthy is that it leads directly to Chequers, the country residence of prime ministers since 1921. For over one hundred years an array of expensive vehicles and cavalcades conveyed prime ministers and their mighty guests along this highway.

Julian Marlborough was accompanied by police and security, but he liked to drive himself in a top spec car. The High Heath Speech Day had been a necessary bore. He hit the long straight at ninety miles per hour. His personal bodyguard sat beside him. Fiona's squeal of delight was sexual, and a musk rose from her. The police outriders kept pace with the Aston Martin, whilst the car behind maintained a sensible gap from the beast in front. Julian knew the curves of the highway with his eyes closed, and he didn't slow as a sweeping bend rushed furiously towards them.

Anna heard the car a second or two after her mother. For Alex it was far too late. The Aston ploughed straight through her. She flew over the bonnet, landing in the middle of the road broken and lifeless. Fiona saved them from careening off the road and into the dense woodland. She leant over Julian, knocking his hands from the steering wheel and barking instructions at him. The flash motor halted one hundred and twenty metres on from Alex Wilbey's wrecked body. The motorcycle outriders swept a circle, growling in stately fashion towards the dead woman. Security operatives stepped from their vehicle, obscuring the accident from behind. Astonishingly, the Aston Martin coolly reversed until it masked the incident from in front.

The Reverend Anna Wilbey knelt beside her beloved mother, and beseeched God to spare her. Hard men looked down. They blanched as they saw her hands turn this way and that searching for a tender way to take her mother into her arms.

A young motorcycle cop broke the spell, placing a hand on Anna's shoulder.

"The ambulance is on its way, madam. Come with me. We'll look after her."

Perseverance had been both a profitable stimulus and a bugbear for Anna all her life. Now it reflected the depth of her love.

"This is my place...until they come for her."

Commander Guy Grosvenor eased the young constable to one side. Every head lifted to taste the air. The faint sound of a siren carried across the adjacent hills. Guy came abreast of the Aston Martin. A rictus of disgust spread across his face when he saw Fiona sitting in the driver's seat. The Prime Minister sat upright in the passenger seat looking like butter wouldn't melt in his mouth. Arse covering already under way.

Julian's voice carried on the light summer breeze.

"Is this going to take long, Guy? Rather pressing business waiting."

As Head of Counter Terrorism, Guy Grosvenor knew a great deal about his boss. His predecessor, Giles Wentmore, had given him chapter and verse before he retired. All except the Banksmore affair, which lay bunkered in the recesses of Giles' mind. Guy knew better than to say anything that would affront Marlborough's sense of his own importance. Simply, he said,

"The lady is dead, sir."

Julian Marlborough's loud exclamation reverberated with the force of a hammer striking iron.

"Don't bleed on me!"

Anna's head began to spin, and the words drummed ever louder in her skull. She knew those words; she had heard them before. The realisation hit her with the force of a landslide. Of course. Her grandfather Adam. She had listened to his story, far away in the Nilgiri Hills. *"Don't bleed on me!"* Words he had once overheard, and which changed the course of his life.

She looked upwards in cautious dignity. Sharp-suited men loomed over her, and she knew instantly who had taken the life of her loving mother. Anna wrapped her mum in her arms, and as she gazed into her black unknowing eyes she thought, *"I will lift up mine eyes unto the hills, from whence cometh my help..."*

"Madam...madam, we'll take care of her now."

Anna hadn't heard the ambulance arrive.

They helped her to her feet, and she assured them that she was alright. The paramedics didn't waste time. It wasn't difficult to ascertain that life was extinct, and soon Alex was safely inside the ambulance.

"What's her name, madam?"

Anna was distracted, staring at the Aston Martin in front of her. She took three strides towards it, but Guy Grosvenor intercepted her.

"Sorry ma'am, can't let you approach the vehicle...," and he lied, "...evidence and all that."

The paramedic had followed.

"What's the lady's name, love?"

"My mother, she's my mother. Alex, Alexandra Wilbey." Her face was stone, as she looked at Grosvenor.

“My father, her husband, is Deputy Chief Constable David Wilbey.”

Guy Grosvenor mastered his desire to exclaim, “Oh shit!” to the verdant hills. He wanted this lady out of the way.

“You can go with her, if you’d like to. The motorcycle lads will accompany you, and we can sort out all of the formalities later. Do you mind me asking your name?”

Anna was about to respond when she glanced at the rear window of the Aston Martin. Her eyes met those of Julian Marlborough, only for seconds before the P.M. turned away. An anonymous woman in early middle-age; not bad looking.

“Anna, my name is Anna.” She saw no reason to disclose her profession.

“Thank you Anna, I’m Guy. Can’t say how sorry we all are about this dreadful accident…”

Anna interrupted tersely, “Accident Guy? Yes, I suppose that’s what *you* would call it.”

She turned on her heel, to sit beside her mother in the ambulance. The local police had arrived. They went about their business, redirecting traffic and conferring over the scene of the accident.

When Anna’s voice shattered the dusk like a shockwave, police and security men alike looked at her. She stood tall between the open doors of the ambulance.

“Guy! Are you sure that *everyone* is sorry?”

The doors closed, and the ambulance pulled away. A severely dented Aston Martin drove sedately towards

Chequers with Fiona at the wheel. Julian sat in silence, a faint look of puzzlement on his face.

"What is it Jules?"

"That voice..."

"Whose?"

"The woman's. Could swear I've heard it before...?

Anna had heard his voice many times, on the television; he had heard hers but once, through the same medium. Now they had come face to face.

"What?"

"I said, not likely, darling. You've had a massive shock, poor thing. Let's get you home, and I'll take all the stress out of your day," she purred.

They looked at each other in solemn complicity, and then they laughed...and they laughed.

5

"I could not turn away from anyone like you, a stranger,
or refuse to help him.
I know well, being mortal, that my claim upon the future
is no more than yours."
'Oedipus at Colonus'

Gales of laughter shook the tent. Paul Baxter rolled around whilst his three-year old daughter Lucy tried to tickle him, aided and abetted by his wife Samantha. They had pitched camp in an abandoned crofter's cottage, set back a couple of hundred metres from the shoreline. The sheltered inlet of Uig Bay sparkled each and every day of their summer holiday. For once, the Isle of Skye behaved, and excelled itself with wonderful weather, midges excepted. The Baxters always travelled northwards for holidays; never southwards from their Cumbrian home in Cartmel. Old and dangerous relationships lay in wait in the southlands. Sam and Paul were quite content with their lives, even if Sam shivered her way through northern winters.

"Time for bed, my girl."

"Oh mummy!" She appealed to her old dad. "Five more minutes, daddy!"

The old soldier had become soft as butter. His life of contented solitude with his wife and child was bliss, but when it was bedtime he always acquiesced to Sam's wishes.

"Sailing tomorrow, darling!" he exclaimed. Paul bounced Lucy up and down to a raucous rendition of "A life on the ocean wave..."

Samantha screamed, and clamped her hands over her ears.

"Quick Lucy, daddy's singing, cover your ears!"

The laughter of true love beat against the sides of the tent.

Stars burnished the midnight sky providing the Baxters with light, to supplement the glow from their campfire. They sat in front of it, arms around each other's shoulders. Little Lucy lay fast asleep in the tent burbling away, and occasionally giggling.

"What a funny little scrap she is," Sam said. "I wonder what her dreams are?"

Paul smiled, "Very happy ones by the sound of it. I..." He became very still, and gently placed his hand across Sam's mouth.

From the stygian darkness of the sea loch two sounds alternated. First the phut, phut of a dying outboard motor, then a groan of pain. It came closer and closer. Stealthily, Paul led Sam to the tent and made her go inside. He crouched behind a ruined wall of the cottage, gripping the carving knife they'd used during their *al fresco* supper. Paul hurriedly extinguished the fire with sand, but embers glowed like watchful eyes.

A scraping noise creased the night air, the sound of a boat being dragged onto the beach. Silence. A low moaning increased the tension Paul felt. He stood ready to defend his family from God knows what. Smugglers? Gun runners? Drugs? A heavy thump resounded, and a cry of pain came hard on its heels. It sounded as though someone was being hauled across the beach. Whimpering moans accompanied its progress.

"Help me, please."

Paul remained rigid.

"I know there's someone there," the voice came through gasps. "Your fire's not quite out. Please, I really need your help."

Samantha had crept out of the tent, and was at Paul's shoulder.

"Look," she whispered.

A faint silhouette, visible by the remnants of the fire, became clearer and clearer. A man was crawling across the sand with great effort, and pitiful cries revealed his extremis. Sam didn't hesitate, breaking cover and racing towards him with Paul chasing her frantically, his knife ever ready.

"Thank God!"

The exclamation rose in relief from the mouth of a man flat on his back. A torn and dishevelled rust-coloured uniform covered his body. It didn't hide the blood and bruises on his torso, and his swollen face told a similar story.

"Fetch some water, Paul."

Sam had to face down his uncertainty about leaving her alone with the stranger before he walked briskly to their camp.

"I'm Sam." The stranger looked as though he might drift into sleep at any moment. "That's my husband Paul. Where on earth have you come from?"

Suddenly, the bloodied figure was alert; he didn't move, but you could see the wariness in his eyes. Instead of an answer a question came.

"Where am I?"

"You've come ashore on the Isle of Skye. What on earth happened to you?"

Paul reappeared at her elbow. Whilst Sam cradled the man's head, he dribbled water into his mouth slowly. After a few moments the stranger seemed to gather himself, and he sat upright.

"Thank you. Thank you. You're very kind."

Paul took a decision. "Come on mate, we'll build up the fire and get you warm."

They got him to his feet and led him the last few metres to the dying fire. Once he was seated on a camping chair, Paul eyed him closely. He adjudged correctly that his injuries were rather superficial. It was more likely that he was exhausted from being adrift in an open boat for God knows how long. Paul stoked the fire. It was still only twenty minutes past midnight.

"Are you hungry?"

The taciturn 'sailor' nodded, and said, "Yes, very."

By the time she returned from the abandoned cottage the fire was blazing, and the Baxters could study their unexpected guest with ease. Beneath the grime and the swelling, they discerned a handsome young man, perhaps in his late-twenties. A shock of red hair topped off a strong and rugged physique. Sam handed him a plate of cheese, ham and bread.

"Here we are friend," she said with a smile. "Take it slowly. Would a bottle of beer go amiss?"

Paul interjected, "That might not be a good idea at this stage. How long were you adrift, my friend?" He echoed Sam's generous word deliberately.

The food was chewed with care, whilst a pair of troubled eyes looked intently at their saviours.

Half an hour ago the calm of untroubled nature had bathed man, wife and child in rays of peace; now the sound of the waves slapped the seashore like pistol shots. All sense of ease was lost to them.

Sam took the plunge. "It's okay, you don't have to say anything. You don't have to tell us anything...if you don't want to."

She gave him time to eat and sip his water, before seeing if a little circumlocution might encourage him to speak.

"We're on holiday. This is Paul and I'm Sam, our little girl Lucy is asleep in the tent. She's three years old."

The faintest of smiles played across the man's lips, and there was a perceptible softening of his features beneath the bumps and bruises.

"The weather's been fabulous, hasn't it Paul? Strange you coming ashore like this, cos we're going sailing tomorrow. Only two days of the hols left. We thought it was about time Lucy took to the high seas."

He held her gaze, and then proffered the empty plate.

"Thank you for that, I needed it. My first food in three days."

A Scottish accent rang as clear as a bell.

"You seem to be close to home, friend," Paul ventured.

The wary look crept into his eyes once more.

"Aye, and you sound as if you're quite a way from hame. Scouser is it?"

Paul and Sam exchanged a glance.

"He is," she said with a grin, "originally."

"You've a good ear son. Thought I'd lost the accent long ago."

"And the lady? You're no from these parts, and you're no from Liverpool."

Sam's delightful open laugh lightened the mood.

"A long, long way south. A long time ago."

For the first time there was something resembling a companionable silence.

"You can call me Tom," the tired stranger announced. "Would you mind if I bedded down here the night? I'll no be any trouble to you. I can kip in the boat."

Sam wouldn't hear of it. "No you won't," she asserted authoritatively. "We can put something together for you just outside our tent in the lee of the cottage walls. Isn't that right Paul?"

Paul looked a mite dubious, but he went along with the suggestion.

Tom gave a nod of acquiescence; he was too tired to argue.

"I'm afraid I might wake you early Tom. Penalty of being an old soldier; early riser. Still, it means I can get breakfast on the go, and we can give you a good feed before you get on your way."

"Paul," Sam admonished, "I'd say Tom needs a little rest and recuperation before he goes anywhere. You stay with us Tom, and when you're fit and well we'll drop you back in civilisation. Okay?"

The question was aimed at both husband and newly-found friend. Paul shrugged his agreement, and Tom was thoughtful before replying.

"Aye...aye, that'll be grand. My thanks to you both. You're very kind. Ex-military is it? Who did you serve with?"

Paul had no reason to be mysterious.

"With the Rifles, many moons ago."

"He was a sergeant," Sam added with pride.

Paul looked Tom up and down, taking in the tattered and indistinct remnants of the clothes he wore.

"What sort of uniform is that you're wearing, Tom?"

Adroitly, he sidestepped the question. "I used to be with the Territorials, Paul. Paratroopers. Would you mind if I got ma head doon now? I'm no feeling ma best."

Neither party saw any sense in pursuing the issue. Before long all was still around the loch. Tom drifted into a deep sleep, as did Samantha. Paul lay beside her dozing lightly, the carving knife not far from his grasp.

6

"...the present hour hath pain, crime, ruin: whatso'er of ill Mankind have named, not one is absent here."
'Oedipus Rex'

Frank Steen drew on his pipe. He gazed lovingly upon his son, Frank junior, playing amidst the fading blooms of summer. Home was bliss, but Frank acceded to duty, and travelled frequently. He had said his goodbyes to wife and child. Picking up his overnight bag, he gave thanks that he would only be away for one night from his precious family.

The day was warm, and he decided to walk to the train station. The odd greeting from neighbours was returned with modesty, and a taciturn smile. The Steens were well-thought of by those who knew them, but none knew them intimately. If pressed Frank, and his wife Sylvia, would admit to his job as some sort of civil servant, based in Southampton. Sylvia was most adept at redirecting the conversation if someone tried to pry further. The good burghers of Lymington liked the Steens, and accepted them into the community as discreet folk of the old school.

It was tiresome having to take a longer route, but Frank never demurred from doing his duty properly. He could have boarded a ferry at Lymington, and been on the Isle of Wight in no time. Instead he took the train to Portsmouth, and from thence the hovercraft from Southsea to Ryde. Just a middle-aged man in nondescript clothing. Frank was a stickler for timing, and his wait for the bus was brief. He enjoyed the ride through the undulating countryside, and deflected the attempt at conversation by the woman sitting next to him. They disembarked at the same stop, and she knew why the man had been reluctant to talk. They were on the same journey.

The queue to enter HMP Parkhurst wasn't that long, for once. Frank was processed, along with others visiting their incarcerated loved ones. A murmur passed down the line when a voice said,

"Would you step this way sir?"

"Why?"

"Random search, sir."

"Oh, sorry. My first time."

The queue resumed its apathy, and Frank trailed the prison officer.

"Good morning sir."

The prison governor gave a fair impression of standing to attention before Frank.

"Has my colleague arrived?"

"She's waiting for you in the gym."

Pleasantries were not exchanged. There was a job to do. Frank never wasted time on fripperies. When he entered the gym Fiona was entertaining the 'troops'. Twenty men from the *'Defence of the Realm Corps'* were gathered around her. Their russet-coloured uniforms did not bear insignia. They resembled the tattered remains worn by a man washed up on the shore of the Isle of Skye, but theirs were pristine. Banter and innuendo crackled in the air.

Frank stood immobile in the doorway, watching. An uncomfortable air settled on the room, like a miasma entrapping an Irish bog. The men caught sight of the figure. First one-by-one, and then by nudges from their mates they became silent. They were awestruck. None had met him before, but his codename was legendary.

Fiona turned. “Oh hi!”

Her breezy demeanour did not elicit a response. Frank Steen and Fiona Hudson did not hate each other; they held each other in contempt. They worked for the same man, and each was intimate with him in quite separate ways. She divined early on that he disliked her, and was intelligent enough to understand why. Frank justified his distasteful work as a national necessity; however reprehensible, an act of patriotism. From their first mission together he knew that Fiona took a primitive and sadistic delight in the work. Frank was a Roman Catholic, and sought forgiveness in the Confessional Box. To kill and destroy for pleasure was beyond his ken.

She became professional.

“Gentlemen, resume your seats, please.”

Frank stood beside her, and she continued.

“You have been briefed about the nature of your mission. Now for the details. *‘Harbinger’*, would you care to enlighten them?”

Frank's face stayed in repose, and his voice did not carry to the seated men. They eyed him with curiosity, as he spoke quietly into Fiona's ear. He looked so ordinary, yet it was he who had planned and fronted many 'retributive' missions. It had been made known, throughout the so-called defence force, that he provided the idea for resolving the illegal immigrant crisis. None knew that he had actually been on board the freighter, watching two thousand souls plummeting into frozen waters. Silence was golden, in the presence of this man. Not one of them stirred a muscle.

Fiona nodded, and recommenced her peroration.

"The *'cleansing'* will commence at midnight, and continue without respite until it is completed. There are twelve-hundred *'units'* to be despatched. My arithmetic makes that sixty each. Upon completion you will depart. Any questions?"

A tentative hand appeared.

"Yes?"

"What happens to the remains?"

Frank's voice barely carried.

"That need not concern you. Suffice to say, relocation has been arranged."

Fiona's tone bore a note of devil-may-care.

"Sorry you have to remain in here all day, chaps. Plenty of food and drink laid on, and you can use the gym facilities to your heart's content. Good hunting."

Her attempt at whimsy, accompanied by a pitiless laugh, failed to elicit a response. You could go off a woman.

The day dribbled by in desultory fashion. Some prisoners complained about not having access to the gym. Officers reassured them that all would be normal in the morning. Safety checks on equipment in progress.

Evening meal passed peacefully, and golden slumber fell upon the prison by ten p.m. The tried and tested method of lacing food with opiates proved itself once more. At precisely midnight the executions began. Each man was assigned a number of cells. The pistols had been silenced unnecessarily. Over previous months, all prisoners, except those convicted for murder and child sex offences, had been transferred. Their places filled with murderers and nonces from other prisons.

Frank passed along corridors, checking randomly that the neck shots were being administered efficiently. He stepped into one doorway just as Fiona held the muzzle of a gun to the drugged neck of a prisoner. She fired and gasped simultaneously. Frank detected the savage and primeval glitter in her eyes and the wetness of her lips, as she turned to the 'soldier' whose pistol she had borrowed. She caught Frank's gaze, and held it in defiance. He gave an almost imperceptible twitch of his head. Fiona returned the pistol, and joined him outside the cell.

"Going well, Frank!"

His glacial look chilled her.

"All under control *'Harbinger'*."

"Thank you, *'Omen'*. I'm leaving now. Disposal of remains as agreed. No deviations from procedure. I want to report to the guvnor that all went smoothly."

Fiona smirked. "I'll be seeing him on Wednesday evening." She couldn't resist it, "Dinner date, you know."

An unseasonal smile played on Frank's lips. "I'll be seeing him today. Lunch you know!"

She watched his measured tread, as he departed. She believed hatred to be a waste of energy. There might be an exception. With a shrug she strode away in the opposite direction. This was turning into a fun evening.

7

"All men make mistakes, but a good man yields when he knows his course is wrong, and repairs the evil. The only crime is pride."
'Antigone'

Samantha drove their Volvo XC90. By the time they had followed the A87 down from Uig, and crossed the bridge into mainland Scotland via the Kyle of Lochalsh, Paul was asleep beside her. Their daughter Lucy slumbered in the back, but her companion remained alert. *'Tom from the Sea'*, as Lucy called him, had rested with them for two days. For most of the time he stayed silent and watchful; fear never far from his eyes. They persuaded him to accept a lift. Happenstance kicked in when he requested Edinburgh. Their final port of call before the holiday ended, and they returned to Cartmel. Tom's initial reluctance was rooted in his tatty clothes.

"We'll get you some new threads in Portree, mate."

"Thanks Paul." He stroked his chin warily. "You wouldn't have a spare pair of trousers?"

"Sure. You're a bit taller than me. They'll be at half-mast, but you being a sailor an' all that...I'll get 'em for you."

Tom changed immediately, and strode away along the beach with his tattered jacket and trousers in hand, and a glowing brand from the breakfast fire. Sam and Paul watched the smoke drift into the sky.

The Sat Nav directed her from the A87 to the A9. They were just beyond Perth, approaching the small town called Bridge of Earn. She kept glancing at Tom in her rear view mirror. His features never changed; his thoughts remote and unassailable. Her fascination with him nearly brought them to grief. The tiny figure by the side of the narrow road stepped towards the moving vehicle. Sam slammed the brakes on so hard that Paul erupted from his doze exclaiming, "What the f...?" Tom had thrown an arm across the still sleeping Lucy.

The hitchhiker calmly walked past the bonnet, and came abreast of the driver's window. Sam, in her fright and fury, had already opened it.

"You bl....!"

The angry expletive froze on her lips. She beheld a serene and smiling face. Eyes lit up an overcast day. Sam was puzzled momentarily, and then she smiled in return.

"Where are you headed?"

"Edinburgh."

Paul leant across his wife. He too was captivated.

"Your lucky day, young lady. Hop in."

The young woman sat behind Sam, her small rucksack in the well. Lucy slept on in her child seat. Only Tom remained disinterested, looking straight ahead; his thoughts a brooding storm of anguish.

Paul looked over his shoulder, and saw a delicate hand resting on his daughter's podgy fingers. The child awoke, and stared into the eyes of her companion.

"What's your name?"

"I'm Isa."

"That's a funny name, but I still like you." Lucy was up-and-running. "They're my mummy and daddy, and this is *'Tom from the Sea'*."

Names were exchanged, but Tom did not speak. As they settled down to the journey, Isa reached across Lucy.

"Hello, *'Tom from the Sea'*." Her hand lay across his shoulder.

He shook to begin with, and then sobs roared from him, like breakers upon a reef.

The child reached out to him. "Don't cry Tom, we'll make it better..."

"Lucy is right, Tom. We can make it better."

Two muted voices exchanged confidences in the rear of the Volvo. Even Lucy, seated between them, found it difficult to hear what was said. A torrent of words and emotions spilt from Tom. Occasionally, Isa soothed him with words, but he was calmed more by the light of compassion that flowed like a revelation from her.

"Sam...Paul. Tom and I would like to beg a favour from you. Could we take a break at Dunfermline? It's on the route. Perhaps we could visit the Abbey. Kings of Scotland are buried there, including Robert the Bruce. I'm sure you'd find it interesting. Then it's just a short hop into Edinburgh."

Husband and wife exchanged a look, and shrugged.

"Yeh, reckon we could do with a brew."

Sam chimed in with, "Would you like to meet some kings, bear?"

The little girl chirruped with excitement.

Coffee and cake were consumed with relish before sightseeing. The current building is a parish church of the Church of Scotland, on the site of the choir of the old Abbey. Robert the Bruce's heart rests in Melrose, but his bones lie in Dunfermline Abbey. A monumental brass in the floor indicates the royal vault.

Isa and Lucy walked hand in hand, whilst Paul and Sam sat beside Tom, and listened to his story.

"Two thousand people, lost in the waters..."

"...and you say it's not the first time?"

Tom nodded. "It's not the half of what's going on in secret. The nation is being 'cleansed', and we're responsible."

"Steady lad," Paul put an arm about him. "Who's we?"

"Defence of the Realm Corps."

"Never heard of them, mate."

"No-one has Paul. That was the uniform I burnt."

"How can they be so secret, Tom?"

"A clique within the security service recruits them, Sam. Pubs and clubs, and Rugby and Football grounds. Taken from every right and left wing group in the U.K. Once chosen they leave their homes discreetly for remote camps. After indoctrination and training they are stationed around Britain. They travel at night only, and in civilian clothes."

"Listen mate, I still don't get what they're after..."

Tom's voice was filled with rage and horror.

"I've told you, Paul. Cleansing! Not just ethnic, but the destruction of anyone who falls outside the credo of our lord and master."

Paul shook his head in bewilderment. "Who the hell is he?"

Samantha trembled in recognition, and two words vomited from her throat.

"Julian Marlborough!"

Tom nodded at Paul's disbelieving face.

"I met him once.... he came to our training camp...I never want to see his face again, not even on television..."

"Time to go, I think. Tom needs to get to his sister's. Thank you for the lift. I'm going to stay here for a while. See you tomorrow, Tom."

Isa shook hands with the three adults, and she swept Lucy into her arms.

"Bless you Lucy Baxter. We will meet again."

They watched her walk the length of the Romanesque nave, and exit.

Tom left them near the Royal Botanic Garden, in Edinburgh. The Baxters drove on a couple of miles to their hotel in Leith.

Lucy was tucked up in bed. A babysitter would be with them in half an hour. Husband and wife were looking forward to a special meal in the famous Michelin starred restaurant 'The Kitchin', located on Leith waterfront. Sam stepped into their bedroom, naked from her shower. Paul dropped his towel, and embraced her skin to skin.

"Down boy!" she growled in amusement. "Oh go on then, as it's your birthday."

They lay in each other's arms, and kissed lovingly. A startled Sam sat upright.

"What is it?"

"She called her Lucy!"

Paul reached out to drag her back down. "That's my little bear."

"Yes, but Isa had only been in the car five minutes. Nobody used Lucy's name."

8

"I have nothing but contempt for the kind of governor who is afraid, for whatever reason, to follow the course that he knows is best..."
'Antigone'

The bearded figure resembled an ill-formed creature skulking in the north-west transept of Canterbury Cathedral. His mind skipped to-and-fro, it always had done. He recollected that the transept is known to aficionados as the *'Martyrdom'*. This was the spot were four knights murdered Archbishop Thomas Becket on Tuesday, December 29th 1170. His thoughts turned to the plaintive appeal of the knights' master, King Henry II.

"Will no one rid me of this turbulent priest?"

Arthur Cantwell was perceptive enough to recognise the irony. He shared the sentiment. He shook it from himself. It was not fitting that he, the present incumbent of the See of Canterbury, should think like that. It tarnished his office, as leader of the Church of England and symbolic head of the worldwide Anglican Communion. An outsider, privy to the Archbishop's reflections, might have raised an eyebrow. Arthur's first recourse was to the reflective glory of his own image, not the shining armour of God and the lustrous wonder of the Prince of Peace.

His Grace sighed. Why had Julian Marlborough insisted that he was the only acceptable candidate for the highest office? Arthur knew the answer. He would re-establish the Church of England as the Tory Party at prayer. A model of restraint; always prepared to accept and support the status quo. The Prime Minister had made it clear to Arthur that he was fed up to the back teeth of equivocation.

"You're not there to be the religious arm of the bloody Lib Dems, Arthur!"

He winced at the P.M.'s next words.

"Arthur, you will be the rock upon which I will rebuild this country."

Ambition... No, he wouldn't go there. His Chaplain approached.

"Your Grace, the lady has arrived."

Anna Wilbey gave due deference to the Archbishop when invited into his office. They prayed for guidance before venturing into the troubled waters of the interview.

"Anna, may I express my deepest sympathy to you and your father for the loss of your mother in so tragic an accident."

Reverend Wilbey slowed her breathing. She didn't want to launch straight into an attack. Anna recognised the authority of the man before her. It was her deepest desire that she would be able to submit to that authority, and be obedient.

"Thank you, Your Grace. It has been a most difficult time. First my grandfather, then my mother..."

"Your grandfather? I didn't know about that."

"It was when I visited him in India. You recall that I had to leave the country suddenly?"

The first salvo had been fired.

Arthur cleared his throat. "Yes, yes, of course..." He had no wish to go over old ground, and examine the causes for Anna fleeing England. His inaction, if not dereliction of duty, had played a part in that.

"Are you an Anglo-Indian family, Anna?"

"No, Your Grace. Adam, my grandfather, was English through and through."

"What was he doing in India?"

"He worked with Dalit children in an orphanage, and..."

"Yes, Anna?"

"He was forging his Christian life in the perpetual fire of those trials and tribulations that beset us all. Adam Sampson was a remarkable Christian man. He was my grandfather, and I love him."

She trembled briefly, but mastered her emotions.

"Indeed, indeed...remarkable, as you say. No doubt a man who understood the complexity of the world, and the compromises it urges us to make."

Cantuar was not a stupid man. His keen academic intellect served him well in the task of directing a conversation to where he wanted it to go.

Neither was Anna short of *"ze little grey cells."*

"Oh no, Your Grace. The one thing Adam would not compromise with was the face of evil. Forgive my pun, but he was adamant that we must be resolute in the face of all that is destructive." She played a risky gambit. "No matter the power that resides in the hands of the bearer of that face."

"Indeed, indeed. Your grandfather might have made a fine priest. I can see where you get it from." A benign, and insipid smile reached out...for compromise. He received none.

"No, Your Grace, he would not have been suited to priesthood. He served those Dalit children faithfully, to the point of death. No, he was *of* this world, but not *in* the world."

Arthur was perfectly aware of the stricture from John's Gospel. He was not angry at the insult he had just received; he was aghast at the knowledge that this woman saw right through him.

"Anna," he pleaded, "I had hoped that our meeting might resolve the difficulties your activism is causing. Your movement is making waves at the very highest levels of power." He could not look her in the eye. "There are pressures..." he murmured. "Anna, you are making a considerable impact in communities far and wide. I cannot tell you how excited we are to know that the message of Christ is reaching into communities where many of us have found stony ground." He paused, searching for those last words that might persuade her to moderate her activities. "Can you not, perhaps, be less critical of those whose onerous task it is to administer the life of the nation?"

She looked down, her hands folded in her lap. Anna raised her head, not in defiance, but in the prayerful hope that her words would not fall on deaf ears.

"The message of Christ? We speak of Him, Your Grace, but we listen more than we talk. Whilst we feed the hungry, clothe the naked and visit the prisoners we listen. We are sounding boards for the voiceless. They reveal their griefs and sorrows; their bitterness and their anger. Most of all they speak of fear. Do you know who they are afraid of, Your Grace?" He shook his head. "Their neighbours! Why, why? Because they are encouraged to condemn others; for the colour of their skin; their sexuality, because they are young, because they are old...the list is endless. And they are encouraged to be afraid, aided and abetted in their malicious responses to one another by those '...whose onerous task it is to administer the life of the nation.' "

The Archbishop of Canterbury sat in less than majesty. His reaction was inert.

"Anna, we have known each other such a long time. Might I ask you to do one thing?"

She waited.

"These broadcasts on radio, the newspaper articles, the torrent on social media...could you not moderate their tone, and perhaps do fewer of them?"

The breath that God had given her exclaimed an extended "Ahhhh!" into the air.

To begin with, Arthur was not certain if she was being serious.

"Would it be preferable for me to host a chatty little show on Radio 4? Or perhaps I could be a contestant on *'Strictly Come Dancing'*? A celebrity vicar who accomplishes...absolutely nothing; for Christ or his people." She glanced at the clock on the wall. "I don't wish to be rude, Your Grace, but I have a long journey to make. I'm appearing on *'Question Time'* in Liverpool."

Arthur doodled on a scrap of paper.

"I know."

Anna rose to her feet.

"Your Grace. I shall continue to act as Rector in the Benefice to which I was appointed, but it is my intention to leave the priesthood. Would you accept this letter, please?"

He came to his feet, and took the envelope gingerly. There would be no attempt to dissuade her.

"I am sorry, Anna."

"Be assured, Your Grace, I shall continue to live a Christian life, and I will listen for the voice of God. He will instruct me in the work he wants done, to the glory of His Son, our Saviour, Jesus Christ."

When she had gone, Arthur closed his eyes and prayed, but he knew not to whom, or for what, he prayed. The telephone startled him.

"Yes, put him through. Good morning Julian. No...no, immoveable I'm afraid. One thing, she has decided to give up her vocation. I have her letter of resignation in front of me. Yes, yes it may well lessen her impact. Goodbye."

The Archbishop of Canterbury was wrong. Anna had discovered where her vocation was best served.

9

"Nobody has a more sacred obligation to obey the law than those who make the law."
'Antigone'

When Frank informed Fiona about his lunch date with Julian he had exaggerated somewhat. True, they would share a cuppa together, but that was a few days away. Still, it amused Frank's sardonic side to see Fiona's miffed face, before he strolled away.

Julian kept a property in Gloucestershire; the heart of England. The village and civil parish of Saintbury is a short distance from the chocolate box town of Broadway. The Prime Minister's fun palace lay on the outskirts in splendid isolation. In privacy, nymphs and satyrs could frolic to their hearts content. A more remote building sat snug amidst woodland, reached on foot by striding across the fields from Saintbury. On Sunday mornings, whilst the bright young things slept on, dreaming of the carnal pleasures of the previous day, Julian consumed the land to reach the safe house. Chief of Security, and Head of Counter Terrorism, Guy Grosvenor was in despair whenever these weekends took place. The Prime Minister would forgo his bodyguards. Julian had put on weight in recent years, but he was still fitter than the average man of his age. Significantly, he was far more deadly. Come hail or shine, he adhered to his Krav Maga training. As a concession to Guy, he carried a sidearm during his jaunts.

Frank eschewed such pleasures, and was faithful to his wife. Their neighbours, also safe in their beds, were accustomed to his motorbike firing up at five a.m. On the occasional Sunday the roar disturbed them much earlier. There was old Frank off on his Sunday constitutional again. Blowing away the cobwebs of his dull working week astride his Vincent Black Shadow. It was an original. One of the first produced in 1948. The route from Lymington to the Midlands was a joy to Frank. For preference, he would skirt Salisbury and the Army garrison at Tidworth, bypass Swindon and Cirencester and head for the pretty Cotswold town of Bourton-on-the-Water. Even at that early hour the odd Japanese tourist could be seen. Frank never failed to cock a wry eyebrow, when the signs for Upper and Lower Slaughter came into view. At Stow-on-the-Wold he would turn left onto the A424, which runs into the A44. Before long he would enter the back lanes, and shortly afterwards his lovely beast would be secreted amongst the trees. On foot he would reach his master within ten minutes.

“Morning Frank.”

“Good morning, sir.”

“Here we go. Black tea, English breakfast, as per usual. Help yourself to a sausage sarnie, or bacon if you prefer.”

Julian’s invitation to breakfast always met with the same response.

"Good cup of char, sir. I'll decline the temptation of your baps. Sylvia will have a roast ready when I get back. Nothing like the traditional family lunch. Thanks all the same, sir."

Julian respected Frank. He approved of his discipline, and firmness of mind and principle. Momentarily, his mind was distracted by the previous evening. Sipping his coffee, he visualised Fiona's 'baps' which he had fondled during their fun and games. He frowned at the image. "Yes," he thought, "they're getting a bit floppy these days."

"Would you like the report now, sir?"

"What? Oh yes, keep it brief. I have every confidence in you, Frank."

A summary of events in HMP Parkhurst was given.

"The procedure will be repeated a further four times. That should enable us to remove all of those who are *'on the books'* at present."

"What about disposal?"

"A little more time consuming, but with the coast nearby it's not too much of a faff. Hope we aren't going to run out of decommissioned liners, sir?"

Julian waved a hand in dismissal of a minor matter.

"Something troubling you, sir?"

"Perceptive bugger, Frank. You should have been a priest, or a social worker."

Frank took no offence. He rather enjoyed the boss' mordant wit.

"Watch *'Question Time'*, Frank?"

He shook his head.

“Not for me, sir. Talking shop for the vainglorious.”

“Never mind. Let me show you this.”

Externally, their hideaway looked quaint, but every mod con had been installed; including comprehensive communication equipment. Julian had his Ipad open, and they sat side-by-side to watch the television clip. Frank recognised the Minister for Culture straight away. He was, himself, a cultured man with a particular penchant for Opera and live theatre. However, as far as Frank was concerned, the Minister for Culture was so bloody wet you could shoot snipe off him. The P.M. laughed like a drain when Frank inadvertently expressed this view at a previous rendezvous.

“A soppy sop to the tender-hearted, Frank. Window dressing.”

The unctuous tones of Sir Ken Burke drawled like dense treacle, as his brown suede shoes Jazz-danced beneath the table.

“You see, my dear, we must have discipline. Take my field, the Arts. Nothing is achieved without discipline except mediocrity and disorder...”

“With all due respect, Minister, I don’t think the lives of millions are analogous to the activities of a few. Especially, when many of those in *‘your field’* are drawn from the more privileged end of society...”

Ken waved his hand airily. The look on his face had been chiselled forty-six years ago; it hovered between a smile and a sneer.

“Oh I see, the old politics of envy...”

Anna leapt in. "Not politics, not envy. Common decency that reaches out a helping hand to people, not to beat them into submission. Common decency, which is so sadly lacking in this Prime Minister, and the government which you are part of. Good neighbourliness, Minister..."

"I'm all in favour of good neighbours, but when they become bad neighbours a firm hand is needed..."

The aging glamour puss, who fronted *'Question Time'*, shifted her long legs under the table.

"Sir Ken," she intoned, "were you a good neighbour when you tried to close an ancient right of way across your property?"

"I, I..."

"There were also questions in the House about your involvement in blocking a proposal for social housing adjacent to your village. Would you care to comment?"

Ken shifted uncomfortably in his chair. He was too old a hand to be sand-bagged.

"I rather think your viewers would prefer to return to the question in hand. The Prime Minister is leading a government of all the talents to regenerate our country, and to return us to a golden age of civility. We will not tolerate hooligans, criminals and ne'er-do-wells who sponge off the hardworking citizens of Britain."

The old authoritarian mantra received applause.

Anna spoke quietly.

"Is it true, Minister, that the Government will reintroduce birching for young offenders, and that Capital Punishment will return to the statute books?"

Ken laughed heartily, "My dear Miss Wilbey..."

"I believe she is the Reverend Wilbey, Sir Ken."

"And I am certain that she is not, Ms. Bray." His look of triumph was unbearable.

Felicity Bray raised a quizzical eyebrow in Anna's direction.

"I have decided that I can no longer minister within the Church of England. For the moment it remains Reverend, in three months' time it will be plain 'Miss'." She wondered how he knew.

The aging lothario leant across. "Hardly plain, Anna." The audience squirmed.

Felicity studiously ignored him. "May I ask why you've taken this decision, Anna?"

The tension was palpable throughout the studio. Anna clutched for words, and then she saw her Gramps in front of her. No compromise.

"From my perspective, the hierarchy of the Church of England is hand-in-glove with the Government. If it is complicit in their plans to return our country to a time of unwonted deference and fear, then it is no longer the Church of Christ."

The audience buzzed, and Anna gathered herself.

"Minister, is it true that the laws governing hate speech towards those of other religions, gender and sexuality will be removed from the statute books?"

"Where do you get these fanciful ideas from...?

"From this!" Anna held a piece of paper aloft. "A briefing document, which I'm sure you've already seen..."

Julian slammed the Ipad shut.

“Won’t waste your time, Frank. One: find the bastard who leaked the document, and make his mother cry. Two: I want people on the inside of this ‘SANITAS’ organisation. I especially want all there is to know about our Miss Wilbey. ‘SANITAS’? What crap sort of name is that? Sounds like a brand of douche bag.”

Frank had attended grammar school. He was a good student, and he enjoyed Latin classes.

“It’s a Latin feminine noun: sanity, reason, health – that sort of thing.”

Julian grinned, “Here endeth the first lesson. Knew you should have been a priest. Thanks Frank. Go and get your lunch.” His demeanour changed. “Then attend to business. Want this nipped in the bud. Important Frank, important.”

10

"Know'st not whate'er we do is done in love?"
'Antigone'

Edinburgh is a magnificent city, triumphantly known as *'The Athens of the North'*. Stroll eastward down the famous Princes Street, and look upon the gardens below. A little further on bear left, and you find yourself in Leith Walk. Fine and elegant buildings abound. A roundabout will appear, ere long. Instead of going straight on, into Picardy Place, take the first exit. Be sure not to double back on yourself into York Place. Take the fork to the right into Broughton Street. The houses retain a certain grandeur. Head down the slope, and you will pass the building once occupied by the Rifle Lodge 405. The Provincial Grand Lodge of Edinburgh is now quartered elsewhere. A little further down the street is the Headquarters of SANITAS, Scotland.

Abir Hussain was engrossed in a telephone call when the door opened. She held up a hand.

"Yes Anna...yes. See you on the 28th in Liverpool. Bye."

The young man who entered gazed at his boss admiringly; all the young men did. She had been a stunner when her husband Faisal was alive. As the years clicked by, her beauty flourished with maturity.

"We're ready to leave, Abi."

"Thank you Jamie. I'll be with you in two minutes. A few reminders before we march."

Jamie left her alone, and she sat with her face in her hands. Then she reached out, and lifted the photo frame. Faisal never changed; still the same loving and best of men of cherished memory. Branded a terrorist. She had tried and tried to clear his name, without success. To the nation, he remained one of the gang of Muslims who were said to have massacred a Christian congregation on Christmas Eve. She held his portrait to her bosom, and then kissed his unchanging face. Right, time to get the show on the road. Get this one out of the way, and then a big one in Liverpool. Protest marches were programmed for major provincial cities; a build-up to the great day in London.

"Okay," she addressed the packed room. "You are the marshals. Get among our people. Remind them, our act is non-violent. We engage in civil disobedience. There will be provocation. We don't respond. Let's do it."

"Wow!" Abi was thrilled. She looked down Broughton Street. To the horizon, and beyond, it was jam-packed. Only your shoes reminded you that there was tarmac beneath you. She stepped into the road, and a stupendous roar shook the ancient buildings. Abir Hussain was as well-known in Scotland, as Anna Wilbey in England, for her championing of the poor, the dispossessed, and the marginalised.

The procession moved off. Pairs of marshals inserted themselves into the throng, every hundred metres or so.

Slogans on banners were chanted, and song danced merrily on the air; old Beatles numbers, hymns, and protest songs revived from the 1960's.

Protestors were all ages and genders; ethnically diverse and classless. That worried the government. The old trendy middle class, who normally led and peopled these demonstrations, had been joined by the working class. More concerning was that SANITAS attracted the down-at-heel, the unemployed, the long-settled immigrants. They took their troubles to Abi and her colleagues, in branches across the country. It became known that you didn't just get a sandwich and a cup of tea. SANITAS stood by you, and represented you in the face of intransigent and fierce authority.

It took two hours before Princes Street, and the gardens below, were occupied from end-to-end. In co-operation with the Scottish police, a temporary stage had been erected. Abi scanned the sea of expectant faces. There was no preamble.

"My brothers and sisters in peace, the hands of history can never be turned backwards. Time moves inexorably forwards. Britain has come far from the days of deference to the iron fist of authority..."

The Baxters hadn't known that a demonstration was to take place when they sat with their ice creams in Princes Street Gardens. Paul had noted that it was uncommonly full, but Sam put it down to the Edinburgh Festival being in full swing. Lucy sat astride Paul's shoulders in the crush.

"Excuse me." Sam spoke to the young man beside her.

"Yeh?"

"What's this all about?"

"Protest against government policies."

"Who's the lady up there?"

The young man's eyes glittered with adoration.

"That's Abi Hussain." He looked at Sam expectantly, but she only shrugged. "Head of SANITAS in Scotland." He raised a quizzical eyebrow at her. She smiled and nodded acknowledgement of the organisation.

"She sounds English."

"She is, but she don't live there no more. Moved up here when her old man got killed."

"Oh, I'm sorry to hear that. Was it an accident?"

He stared at Sam, as if she was taking the piss.

"You gotta be kiddin' me. He was one of them Muslim geezers who slaughtered all them people on Christmas Eve. Local schoolteacher or sumfin...in Hertforshire weren't it?"

"Buckinghamshire!" Paul blurted it involuntarily.

Their informant didn't break stride.

"She reckons he weren't involved. Been trying for ages to clear his name. Even written to that git of a Prime Minister. You'd think he'd at least give her a hearing..."

The sole cloud in a matchless sky blotted out the sun. Sam and Paul's hands sought each other in the packed crowd. The look they exchanged was brief. Silently they gazed upwards to a woman inseparable from them; a shared grief bound them. When she spoke they thought she had only eyes for them.

"So it is that we must link our arms in an immoveable chain of protest. We protest against racism...we protest against judicial murder...we protest against violence...most of all, we protest against fear, and the incitement of fear and division..."

The almighty roar drowned Abi's voice. She rode the wave, and then raised her hands on high. A breathless hush descended on the thousands.

"We must be unceasing in taking the fight to the enemies..."

The bearer of the voice had been chosen especially. His basso profundo echoed off the great stone walls of the hotels.

"Like your husband did? Murderer."

This wasn't the first time Abi had been heckled in this way, but the unusual silence knocked her out of kilter. Another voice picked up the theme.

"You're frontin' for ISIS like your killer husband. Go on, admit it, Paki bitch!"

She tried to respond, but more voices drowned her in accusations and abuse. Then sections of the crowd moved towards the stage from all points. Groups of men and women who travelled at night, their russet uniforms exchanged for casual clothing. The temporary stage began to rock. A man in borrowed trousers, a little too short in the leg, took hold of Abi and led her down the steps at the rear of the stage. The forces of the Edinburgh Police moved in number to quell the disturbance. Oddly, a channel seemed to open voluntarily for them, and within minutes they had corralled the disturbers of the peace.

Abi, and her protectors, passed through the corridor created by the police, braving the faces of seething hatred either side. Not only did they abuse her, on her passage to safety, but also insulted the tall ginger-haired man holding her hand. Strangely, they fell silent when the gaze of the young girl, holding Abi's other hand, fell upon them. Soon the three of them were swallowed up amongst their own supporters.

"To your satisfaction, sir?"

Frank Steen looked down from the eyrie of his hotel room.

"Nicely done. A good trial run. We might make it a little more exciting for them in Liverpool."

A knock at the door disturbed their exchange. With Frank's permission, the Deputy Chief Constable went outside. He re-entered, like a penitent approaching the Father Confessor.

"One of your people..."

"Thank you. Cheerio! Oh, Dougie! Won't be long now, and we'll have you in the comfy chair. Your present guvnor's just about shot his bolt..."

"Not on the square, sir?"

"Positively oblong, Dougie. My thanks, again. I'll let my guvnor know that you and your boys did splendidly."

Frank lifted the telephone receiver, and dialled the room next door.

"Ready."

His aide ushered the waiting visitor in immediately. He stood to attention before Frank, who eyed him coldly.

"Better be good. Your instructions were 'no contact'. Get on with it, spit it out Jenkins."

Tom Jenkins gulped nervously. He had been the Operations Leader on the ground disrupting the SANITAS protest. He was agitated that such an august person should know his name.

"Saw something, sir. Thought you should know immediately."

Frank's icy tone chilled the hotel room.

"SomeTHING?"

"Someone, sir."

Frank passed him a glass of Scotch. He sat in an armchair, and savoured his mineral water.

"Thank you, sir. It was him, sir, the one you've been looking for. The deserter from the Isles. Walking beside the Hussain woman, like her bloody bodyguard."

"Sure?"

"Certain, sir. We trained together, and buddied up on exercise. Know him like my own brother, sir."

Frank walked to the window, where the shafts of sunlight played upon the crystal of his glass.

"Did right to let me know. Off you go now...oh, and well done. Pass on my congratulations to your men."

Frank exchanged his mineral water for a small Scotch, and returned to the window. He sighed at the thought that so many strands were held in his hands, for him to manipulate according to his judgement.

He scanned the thinning crowds through binoculars, and settled upon a couple and their little girl. The child bounced merrily upon her father's shoulders. They were an odd couple, he thought. Dad was clearly older than mum, and somewhat grizzled. Frank was blissfully content with his wife, Sylvia, but he recognised a beautiful woman when he saw one. He puzzled. Adjusting his binoculars, he drew their image closer to him. The child was a delight, but they looked so solemn. He put the bino's down. Maybe they'd had a bit of a domestic? Frank raised his glass to them, wishing them well and reconciliation to one another.

Rays of sunlight played upon the glass, and random patterns splintered around the room. Frank was in thrall to them. A smile as cold as Edinburgh in February cracked his lips, as he murmured:

"Oh what a tangled web we weave, when first we practice to deceive..."

Sir Walter Scott's poem, *'Marmion'*, was a favourite of his. Now was not the time, however, to be dwelling on honour lost and honour regained in battle. Decisively, he picked up his hand luggage, and headed for Waverley Station.

11

"Long, long ago; her thought was of that child
By him begot, the son by whom the sire was murdered..."
'Oedipus Rex'

Lady Deborah Marlborough eschewed visible passion. She scorned the emotional flood plains of the lower orders, and despised the torrents of celebrity confession that bequeathed to the nation the stench of an overflowed cess pit. Her patrician upbringing ensured that she never gave the game away. Behind her glacial smile was hidden the boiling cauldron of her loves and hates. To be precise, she possessed but one love and one hate. The object of her hatred was driving the vehicle she sat in, descending the hill from her house in Banksmore. Fiona Hudson was chauffeuring her to Chequers for her monthly meeting with her son, Julian. She quite appreciated that he was a busy man, but to her unbearably grieving heart she knew he was becoming more and more distant from her. He retained a certain filial duty, but pared to the bone.

Using peripheral vision, she glanced at her driver. Debs knew that her son was consumed with the woman, as he had been with the girl he'd brought home for Christmas. She startled herself. What was that young woman's name? Deborah prided herself on her memory, and she felt a tremor pass through her. She had turned seventy earlier in the year. Despite her trim figure, and well-groomed looks, fear gripped her at the thought of senility clutching her in a skeletal embrace. Angela, that was it, Angela something. They skirted the village green. She felt almost relieved when she saw Derek Fisher opening the gate to the church path. He bore a large bouquet of flowers. She knew that their destination was the grave of his wife; one of the many murdered by her son and Fiona Hudson with their unknown companion from the security services. A wry thought flitted through her mind. On that Christmas Eve of insanity Julian, in his act of terrorism, had accomplished a good deed. Derek Fisher was now a reformed alcoholic.

They approached Chequers at some speed. Fiona always raced along the approach road at a rate of knots, as Julian had done on the day he'd knocked down some woman. She did it deliberately in an attempt to put the wind up Debs. To her chagrin she never succeeded. Her ladyship sat there quite composed.

Fiona was keenly aware that she was loathed by her passenger. Deb's possessive and obsessive yearning for her son, was beyond her ken. That alone was sufficient to attract her ire, but Fiona had inadvertently put some very tasteless icing on the cake. On a previous visit to Chequers Deborah had to be ushered from the room when Julian's confidential line rang. Fiona had been in the corridor conferring with Frank Steen. The latter had glanced at his watch, and wondered how long he'd have to wait for his interview with the boss. Fiona laughed uproariously.

"Could be a while Frank. When mummy gets a hold of him he has to be prised away from her with a tyre wrench. My God, when Julian walks into a room you can hear her ovaries rattling!"

She had not noticed Deborah standing in the doorway.

"I say, Ma, give it a rest!"

Deborah blanched. Not so long ago Julian would never have dreamed of speaking to her in that fashion.

"You do know I'm trying to put this country back on its feet. Sixty-odd years of cock- ups and catastrophes to sort out. You don't know the half of it."

Her appeal was plaintive. "Perhaps I could help, in some way..."

"Give over, Ma. This is a young man's game."

Deb's eyes drooped, and her head hung downwards ever so slightly. Julian was astonished. He had never seen weakness in his Mother before. It thrilled him. With sublime calculation he put his arms around her.

"Steady on, Ma. Tell you what. I've got some pretty big announcements to make to the country – on the Beeb tonight. Then I'm tied up for a while implementing the necessary actions. Six to eight weeks, maybe ten, and then you can throw a big party at the old place, and we'll invite the great and the good of Buckinghamshire to meet a few celeb friends of mine. Send your stock soaring in the old neighbourhood. Make a weekend of it. What do you say?"

Her spirits lifted a mite. "Wonderful darling. I'll start planning as soon as I'm home..."

"Oh yes, home. Afraid I can't let you have Fiona for the return journey. Need her beside me."

He observed the ever so slight wince.

"Guy Grosvenor will drive you. Have you met Guy?"

"Once."

"My top security wallah. Great guy!" He laughed at his ponderous pun. "Off you go then, Ma. See you in a couple of weeks."

Her embrace was an extended cling, and Julian had to loosen himself from her grasp. His voice rang out, as she stepped into the open doorway.

"Don't forget to watch me on the 'box' tonight."

Framed in profile, she replied. "I always do. I record everything about you."

She exited the room, and strode past Fiona Hudson without a glance. The waiting Guy Grosvenor wasn't best pleased at being used as a chauffeur. His charming smile didn't betray his true feelings. Deborah returned the smile, and she thought him a very handsome man in early middle age.

Fiona closed the door behind her. Julian was staring down at his desk.

"Trouble Jules?"

"No...no."

His mother's last comment had taken him aback. *"I record everything about you."* His keen ear had detected what sounded like a threat. Fiona waited, and then he shook his head and came upright. "Imagining bloody things," he thought, and dismissed it from his mind.

"Right, let's give the broadcast details one more going over, and then..." he drew close to her, and slipped a hand inside her blouse. "Then I'll give you a going over!"

Guy and Deborah reached Great Missenden before any real conversation took place. Gradually, they discovered mutual interests in art and theatre, and their conversation flowed easily. The car swept onto the drive of the house in Banksmore.

"Safely home, Lady Deborah."

The engine was still running, but Debs had made her mind up some miles back. She reached across him, and removed the key from the ignition. Looking him straight in the eye, her free hand caressed his groin, and she felt him stiffening. His zip opened easily, and she took him in hand. Ever so slowly, she slid to her knees in the well, and took him in her mouth. Guy lay back, and luxuriated in the wet lips, and the depth to which she took him. She raised herself to her seat.

"Just a taster, Guy. Shall we go in?"

12

"Best of children, sisters arm-in-arm, we must bear what the gods give us to bear…"
'Oedipus at Colonus'

The exhalation of breath, from thousands of Scousers and unnumbered visitors to the city of Liverpool, despatched flocks of seagulls in search of fresh air high above the River Mersey. Julian stood at a fourth floor window in the old Cunard Building, his entourage craning over his shoulder for a clearer view. They gazed through their binoculars at the assembled masses on the Pier Head. Sir Ken Burke, the Minister for Culture, first broached the idea.

"That sexy vicar and her sanitary crew have arranged a demo in the *'Land of Malcontents'* in a fortnight. Why not do it there, and bollocks up their day?"

Julian eyed the old boy, over his highly-polished shoes. His feet were on his desk, and he was leaning back in his capacious chair.

"*'The Land of Malcontents'*, Burkey?"

"Liverpool!"

The Prime Minister exploded into hysterical laughter, leapt to his feet and threw an arm around old Ken.

"Marvellous Burkey, bloody marvellous. Now I know why I keep you around."

A chill consumed Sir Ken's bones. He knew he was on borrowed time.

"We'll do it, Burkey, we'll do it!"

On a bright September day SANITAS held its demonstration in Liverpool. Following the P.M.'s television broadcast one of his new laws was about to be enacted. Thousands of ghoulish onlookers had assembled peaceably, but excitedly, to witness the first public birching in God knows when. Two bodies of people, with differing ideas, were jumbled together as one.

The gasp that arose from the crowd occurred when the line of six convicted prisoners, escorted by police, came into view. At its head was a distinctly-aged and cowed Tommy O'Donnell. Almost everyone recognised the former Marxist Prime Minister. He and his acolytes mounted the podium, where the birching block squatted. A tall and well-muscled man stood erect beside it; the birch held lightly in both hands. An anonymous official stepped to the microphone.

"Thomas Patrick O'Donnell has been convicted of being drunk and disorderly, of vandalism and theft."

On a lad's night out, Tommy and his mates had crashed down Lord Street pissed as farts. An empty wine bottle sailed through a jeweller's window, and Tommy helped himself.

"A necklace for the missus, an' I 'ope it fuckin' chokes her!"

Since his enforced retirement from office he'd been in numerous scrapes. The local bizzies always covered up his misdemeanours. Julian's new Chief Constable made it clear to his force that no-one was above the law.

"By sentence of Liverpool Magistrate's Court, Thomas Patrick O'Donnell will receive twelve strokes of the birch."

A murmur of anticipation rippled through the crowd. Liverpudlians will generally side with their own, especially against authority. This was different. The novel sight of a public flogging dredged atavistic instincts, as if from the depths of the nearby river.

Black silence fell upon fifteen thousand people. They stared upwards at an elderly man stripped to the waist, stretched across the birching block. It happened simultaneously. The birch-bearer moved into position, and a delicate girl stepped forward towards the podium. Trouble had not been anticipated. The Chief Constable had thought otherwise, and suggested a heavy police presence.

"Read some fucking history on your day off, Nigel. They'll love it, like they've always done. Just enough men for general policing of a large crowd. There won't be any bother when we flog the bastard." Julian was confident of untroubled success.

The few officers stationed around the platform were startled to see such a frail looking girl coming towards them. Before they knew it her foot was on the bottom step. Two of them moved to detain her. They stood rooted, as she smiled warmly at them and continued her upward journey. The officials above were no less bemused. She looked so vulnerable, and clearly bore no threat. The announcer of O'Donnell's crime and sentence was the only one prepared to intercept her. He barely moved a pace before he caught the eye of the Chief-Superintendent at ground level. The senior officer shook his head. He had already assessed the potential disaster. If they laid a finger on this child there would be a riot.

Isa Joseph moved serenely towards the half-naked and prone figure of Tommy O'Donnell. She stopped on the far side of the birching block. Every one of the thousands watching felt that she was looking directly at them. She raised her arms, bent her torso and lay across the body of the prisoner. If Thomas Patrick O'Donnell were to be thrashed, then Isa Joseph must also be beaten mercilessly. Before the eyes of the paralysed police three more women emerged from the crowd, and ascended the platform. Anna Wilbey's dog collar flashed in the sunlight, and Abi Hussain held her hand. There was a slight murmuring as a striking blonde woman joined them. Without warning they stretched themselves above Isa and Tommy.

Eternity flowed uninterrupted, until the crackle of a radio broke the stillness. Chief Superintendent Malcolm Clarke acknowledged the instructions barked into his ear. Cautiously, he climbed the steps. Other officials moved to join him, and the growl of the crowd stirred the air with menace. Clarke held out his hands for the men to stay where they were.

The first to leave the platform was the birch bearer. He retreated towards the Cunard Building, until he was out of sight. The women heard the whispered words of the senior officer, and stood upright. Isa undid the straps binding O'Donnell. She held his hand and led him to stand beside his fellow prisoners. His tears were visible to all.

"Would you speak to them?" Clarke's words were whispered to Anna, and she nodded.

"Ladies and gentlemen, we....", and she gestured to the two other women and to Isa, "are going with this officer into the Cunard Building..."

Menace throttled the air once more, and thousands of people rippled, like an enthusiastic football crowd swaying on the terraces. A voice shouted.

"We won't let them take you!"

The ensuing sound resembled the Kop giving full voice to the scoring of a goal. Anna raised her arms, pleading for silence.

"Please, please, there is no cause for alarm. We are not under arrest. There is simply to be a meeting..."

Anna felt an electric pulse pass through her, and she was jolted sideways. Isa addressed the crowd.

"We will not be harmed; I give you my promise. Shalom...peace be with you."

She moved quickly to the steps, and the Chief Super' scurried after her. Anna, Abi, and their blonde companion followed. Soon, they too, vanished from sight. A puzzled, but exhilarated, crowd dispersed slowly in search of a drink and a bite to eat.

Doors open, and consequences can become finite. Anna walked into the plush, if faded room. Along with her companions, she recognised the Prime Minister. The pervading air was agitated, with a *soupçon* of the sardonic. Julian was privately wailing and gnashing his teeth, but his exterior mirrored that of his mother; patrician and controlled.

"My dear Ms Wilbey, or is it Reverend, or may I call you Anna?"

"Anna will be fine...Julian."

A facial muscle twitched in response to his offended dignity. Where the fuck was Frank Steen when you needed him, and where was the file on this woman? Frank had not yet completed his deep clean on her.

Julian took the offensive.

"Why do you persecute me, Anna?"

She smiled serenely.

"You know your Bible, Julian. Are you on the Road to Damascus? I do hope so. Don't make the mistake of assuming the role of Saviour."

Julian had been a smart arse since the age of ten. He couldn't bear being gainsayed.

"The Bible, Anna? I wouldn't dream of challenging you on your so valuable knowledge of that work of wisdom."

His sarcasm came with heavy breathing, revealing his simmering anger. Anna felt the spirit of release embrace her, and the wild courage of her grandfather consumed her.

"'You wanted to play games. I know a shit load of games!' Samuel L. Jackson, remake of *'Shaft'*. So important to attribute one's sources, don't you think so, Julian?"

He turned to her companions.

"May I ask who your fellow martyrs are?"

"My name is Abir Hussain. I have written to you many times concerning my husband, Faisal Hussain, who died in the church that you so bravely defended."

Only one person observed the discreet swallow made by the P.M. He stared hard at the figure of the rather tasty blonde woman. Her cultured voice said:

"My name is Fatima. I am the Chairperson of the West Yorkshire Branch of SANITAS." Her pause held the room, and then she lapsed into a broad Yorkshire accent. "Me real name is Suzie, an' I cum from Bratford! Sorry abart me appallin' accent."

A universe reeled before Julian's eyes, and it contained a desert town in the Middle East.

"This is not the way, Prime Minister!"

Anna drew him back from the rim of insanity.

"What would you know about the way, Reverend Wilbey. A comfortable cleric, with a safe salary, who can pontificate on Sunday mornings to twenty-three old fogies from the middle class who want their well-heeled consciences soothing..."

"I..."

"Permit me to finish. You know the problem with you, and with the entire Church of England? You are cowards. I've sat in congregations and heard you pontificate about perseverance, and the cost of discipleship, but you don't have the balls to do it yourself. You minister to the poor and needy. Big deal! However much they shout and bluster they always defer to authority. You've chosen the easy path. Go and proselytise in the comfortable suburban streets, and convince the young and educated that they need your God. Confront the challenges they make to you, and answer the torrent of doubt they assail you with. No! You're afraid to pay the real price of discipleship. So don't lecture me about commitment and moral behaviour. Who the hell do you think you are?"

Anna considered his question.

"I am the daughter of a beautiful mother who was struck down by a reckless man in a country lane..."

Julian knew exactly what she referred to.

"I am the granddaughter of Adam Sampson. A man broken by your callous disregard for human dignity..."

"Who the hell is Adam Sampson?"

"High Heath School. Is *'West Side Story'* still your favourite musical, Julian?"

He sagged in his chair, as memory stained his vitality. Frank Steen's report had become superfluous. The puzzled looks of his officials stiffened his spine. Pride gave him the resources to say, "A vendetta, a bloody vendetta."

Before Anna could reply a still small voice of calm soothed the ruffled tempers.

"You haven't asked me who I am."

Julian rose. He came to the front of his desk, and leaned against it.

"I'm Isa, Isa Joseph."

The vaguest of recollections caused Julian to reflect.

"Let me help you, Julian. Your nephew Hugo...High Heath School..."

It dawned on him instantly. His nephew banging on about some girl he fancied. He looked at her intently, and a compelling urge made him walk toward her.

"Yes, but who are you?"

Isa held his eyes. He did not blanch, but he felt drawn into another world.

"I am who I am."

Isa's words wheeled the universe into a kaleidoscope of infinite depths and vistas. Anna could not touch firm ground, and yet...and yet, she felt that all was decided.

The prosaic mind of Sir Ken Burke shattered the window of opportunity.

"All very well, Prime Minister, but we..."

"Yes, yes!" A tetchy Julian sprang out of his reverie. "Don't stand in my way, Reverend Wilbey. The world is not as merciful as you believe." He pointed to Fatima. "Chief Superintendent, this lady is to be detained for questioning."

Abir Hussain reacted first. "No! You invited us here to talk with you. No charges were to be levied against us."

The Chief Super' shrugged. "I have no cause to detain any of these ladies, sir."

Julian sat in his chair, his eyes lowered. Then his right hand waved them away. How the hell had the girl survived her ordeal at his hands in a desert town long ago? He didn't know, and he didn't care. There were ways to silence the incriminating evidence she could give. The women exited, and Anna stared at him, but his eyes were ensnared by the slim and smiling girl who was the last to leave.

13

"Enough words! The criminals are escaping, we the victims, we stand still."
'Oedipus at Colonus'

'T*he Once and Future King's'* fabled knightly Court metamorphosed into an overnight stop for tourists. The Camelot Castle Hotel is a cock stride from the Atlantic Ocean, washing itself clean against the cliffs of Tintagel, Cornwall. India Woake was staying at the hotel, but at present she was in the burrow-like office of her Late-Godfather. Atlantic Road swept down to the hotel, whilst Giles Wentmore's house stood separate from the highway. A dry-stone wall, a patch of turf and an access road intervened. The modern detached house was one of a select number that comprise Gavercombe Park.

India had collected the 'Will', unopened, from a nondescript solicitor's office in Bodmin. The country solicitor had no idea of its contents; the former Commander of Counter Terrorism had merely lodged the slim document with Maurice Retallack.

She reached over her shoulder for the paper knife. With a precision and deftness her Godfather would have approved of she slit the envelope open. It was intriguing, because she had already been informed of the contents of his Will by his London solicitor. Everything he once had was now hers. India's presence in Cornwall was dictated by the instruction he had given her when they last rode beside one another on the Cranborne Chase in Wiltshire. She relished the visits of Giles to the family home in Tollard Royal. For the most part, they would ride in silence fortified by the English beauty of the Chase.

The single sheet of paper made her laugh. A riddle! Good old Giles, still tormenting her with his puzzles. She put her feet up on the coffee table, but not before she had reached for her mug. A frown creased her brow. Simps! It was bloody simple. Not like Giles to be so obvious.

"The Sun cannot intrude into this den,
But still the hob is hot as hell within.
The stones of fire sweat forth sins of bodily vice,
What you find will turn your blood to ice.
Walk softly, sweetest child, eschew all risk,
Consuming flames surround the blazing disc."

India strolled through the garden. She took her time; sipping coffee, running a hand over the rim of the hot tub. A few minutes were spent examining the pond, and dead-heading flowers. A large bucket lay nearby, and she collected the dog's toys from the lawn. Khan was hers now, and he was safely quartered at Tollard Royal. In desultory fashion she wandered toward the sauna in the far corner of the garden. A bit of her sixth form *'Hamlet'* came to mind: *"By indirections find directions out…"*. She did not permit herself a smile at her own astuteness.

Giles had been a superb horseman and all-round countryman. He had taught her field craft, but he also imparted to her elements of trade craft known only to men and women who walk dangerous paths. Once within the sauna, its door firmly shut, she located the object easily. A false, and insulated, base to the heater slid open. It was apposite that a compact disc, also protected, should emerge. With the CD secreted against her tensile six-pack, she was able to linger in the garden a while longer before making her way indoors.

Tears did not come easily to India Woake. In that respect she was not unlike Deborah Marlborough. Their reticence to blub came, however, from different motives. For Debs it was a prepared defence in anticipation of the enemies she always expected to confront and face down. India could not have explained it, but for her it was an inherited mark of moral strength; a crest of honour. Somewhere along the M5 she blinked furiously to clear her eyes of saline tears. Giles' voice swirled like a rich cake mix around the interior of the vehicle. The recipe he recited, via the CD player, contained the ingredients for sickening disaster.

"Hello, my sweet. Sorry to say that if you're listening to this I am no more. My demise will have been explained away as the unfortunate accident of an old man. My money is on the cliffs where Khan and I wander daily..."

His assumption was correct. Found snagged halfway down, with Khan whining above. No one would ever know that it was the dog who prevented his body from being cast into the Ocean to set sail for America. The assassins had not wanted to use their weapons, for fear of attracting attention. Whilst their action was swift, one of them left the scene badly bitten. In their haste they failed to propel Giles as forcibly as they intended. Accidental death was the verdict...

"I'm afraid, my love, that in recent times age has got the better of me. Think the old brain box has only been getting intermittent signals. The 'Quiet Boys' may have done me a favour. Wouldn't have wanted you to see me dribbling into my porridge...."

Giles spoke softly of his love for India, and the shining months they enjoyed together when she was eighteen. It took slow deep breaths to prevent this forty-five-year-old woman from pulling on to the hard shoulder.

"Been rather indiscreet to an old friend. He assured me that the house was free from devices, and in my stupor I believed him. Shouldn't have. Always known the termites were in the attic. Told him a story. Going to tell you now. Think you're safe for the present. Know you well enough to predict that won't last long. Can't say I'm not afraid for you, but we're people who do our duty. Couple of matching legumes, you and I..."

So it was that the events leading to the military coup were described. The actions of Julian Marlborough, culminating in the slaughter of innocents in St. George's Church, Banksmore were unfolded in scarifying detail. A recitation of the evil one man can unleash upon a nation. Giles did not spare himself. His last words were, *"Mea culpa, mea culpa, mea maxima culpa."*

India listened a second time that evening, in the Manse at Tollard Royal. When it ended her mother spoke first.

"Not meaning to be intrusive, darling, but what did Giles mean about your time together when you were eighteen?"

She took a long draught from her large gin and tonic.

"A love affair, mummy, we were lovers. I initiated it, not Giles. He ended it four months later. Said I needed to be free to explore life. He was right, but I never stopped loving him. He was a wonderful man."

The fierce expression on her face dared her mother to contradict her. Mother and Father looked at each other.

"Another G & T darling?"

"Yes please, Daddy."

He stood with his back to her, as he dispensed drinks.

"You'll get no condemnation from us, my love. Isn't that right, Marion?"

Marion Woake crossed to her daughter, and embraced her.

"Not a word," she said. "Don't tell your Pa'," she announced in a stage whisper, "but there was a time when I thought Giles a bit of a dish myself!"

Archie Woake choked on his Scotch with laughter, and briefly the tension was broken. He handed the drinks around before resuming his seat.

"Got to say, Indy, we've a bit more to consider than your love life." Archie rolled the cut glass within his palms. "Bloody explosive. What do you intend to do?"

The Woake sat in confident silence. It was a confidence bred from generations who had first settled on the land during the Fifteenth Century. They were not lords and ladies, but that tier beneath. To the masses still part of the patrician class, but somehow different. Embedded in communities in every county in England. Casually, and often disparagingly, referred to as *'the county set'*. In reality people who acted, not people who chattered or shied away from difficult decisions. The bedrock of England, and its centuries of progress.

"I would destroy Julian Marlborough in an instant for what he's done to Giles. Undoubtedly, he is responsible for his death, but..."

Marion Woake held her daughter for comfort, and to stiffen her resolve.

"But what, darling?"

"I don't know how to say this..." She stood, went to the Georgian window, and pulled back the curtains. "Out there is our England...no, not just ours, but the England of all the decent people. We cannot surrender it to the vanity of this monstrous man. We...our people...our type we've stood outside the fray for too long. We've let our country down. I intend to join the battle."

Archie and Marion gazed deeply into each other's eyes, then went to their daughter.

"Wouldn't expect anything less."

"Thank you Daddy, thank you Mummy. Let me freshen your drinks. Sit yourselves down."

Marion broke the silence.

"Where will you begin? The press? TV?"

"Oh no, Mummy. He would suppress them in an instant." She withdrew the CD from the player. "I want to meet Julian Marlborough, and I think I know how that can be done. Are you still in touch with Desmond?"

Archie's eyebrows went up. "Desmond Claymore-Browne?"

"Yes."

"We foregather at lodge now and again, and we have a bit of a chinwag on the blower once a month. Poor chap, never the same since Fiona died in the church...Oh my goodness, only just realised..."

The thought of their old friend Fiona, murdered in St. George's Church, kept them sober.

"Think you could arrange for me to be billeted with him in the not-too-distant?"

"But why darling? How will that help?"

"Puts me in the vicinity of the Marlborough family seat, Mummy." Her tone was derisory.

"Oh, I see."

"Anyway, I need to spend some time in Town. There's already one person fighting that man tooth and nail, and I intend to meet her. Cheers!"

14

"It reels under a wild storm of blood, wave after wave battering Thebes."
'Oedipus Rex'

Frank thought he'd make a day of it. The order of service was the only question to settle. A firestorm was needed for the media to fan, culminating in the opportunity for the Prime Minister to address the nation in all his wisdom. Frank leant back in his chair. The small room he occupied, for his HQ, leant a certain irony. It was Julian who suggested the place, and with his usual sense of mischief had explained why to his agent. The building in West Hampstead had long since been repaired. No one would have known that it was once ripped apart, at Julian's hand. Only locals recalled greengrocer and Romanian gangster Cesar Marinescu, and his frizzled demise in the explosion. Julian also regaled Frank with his activities in the upstairs room with Charlotte cum Angela. Frank considered himself a good Roman Catholic. Whilst he would never have considered engaging a prostitute, he understood human nature and its needs. He did, however, look askance at his guvnor occasionally; always when alone. A pleasing phrase entered his mind.

"I may not be Woke, but I'm Awake!"

He glanced at his list, and speed dialled a number.

"It's your honour."

Another number.

"In precisely fifteen minutes, please."

Two further calls timed the other events.

It was five p.m. in Bradford when four masked men crashed into the office of SANITAS' West Yorkshire branch, brandishing pick axe handles. The three office workers froze.

"Where is she? Where is she?"

A young man, standing by the water cooler, was bludgeoned to the ground for effect. The two young women shrieked and shrieked until they were grasped by the hair, and forced into a back room.

"Where is she?"

One of the women jabbered, "Who, who do you want?"

"Your boss. Fatima!" he spat it out, as if he'd taken a swig of Dettol.

"She aint here..." He advanced menacingly. "I tell you she aint here!"

The younger of the two women spoke through her sobs.

"She's not been in all week. Honest, honest!"

The leader of the intruders paused, and then gestured to his men. It took two minutes to smash up the office, and they were gone.

In Broughton Street Edinburgh the explosion that ripped through the Scottish HQ of SANITAS had more serious consequences. The device had been planted via a discreet burglary the night before. Abi's assistant, Jamie, was alone and about to leave when the detonation was fired remotely. There wasn't much left of him to pick up.

Frank was in the vicinity to hear, if not see, the third incident. Anna Wilbey left the UK headquarters of SANITAS on time to collect her daughter Jenny from nursery. The watchers were under strict instruction. No-one was to be in the office, least of all the Reverend Wilbey. She was descending the High Street, and had just segued into Rosslyn Hill when she heard the blast. It was co-incidental that the SANITAS office was a few doors down from the local butcher.

The last card in the campaign was played later that night. *'Tom-from-the-Sea'* was drinking heavily these days. He lived with his sister on the outskirts of the City. Tonight he was on a pub crawl in the city centre. He was pleased when the young woman started chatting to him. They did a few pubs together, but he modified his drinking. In her company he didn't mind staying sober. At last orders she was quite upfront. Her lilting voice was as pretty as her face.

"So Tom, it's back to your place?"

Her hand rested on his thigh, and the world of horrors seemed far away.

"Aaaah, we cannie. I'm lodged wi' ma sister. She's a bit of a Wee Free, if you know what I mean. What about your place?"

"Similar. Still living with ma parents. They wouldn't exactly give us their blessing."

She laughed loudly, and they grimaced in frustration.

"Tell you what, Tom. Are you up for a bit of al fresco action?"

"Open to suggestion."

"I know a place. As long as you're no' afraid of ghosts and Ghoulies."

He never realised the ominous association of his reply.

"Lead on MacDuff!"

Tom's laugh echoed through the night air.

"Sssssh Tom!"

"The cemetery? Rosebank bloody Cemetery!"

"Come on. I know a wee spot that's covered and cosy."

The details of his torture and death add nothing to the tale. He was overpowered quickly by the waiting party. Legs and arms were broken, jaw fractured. The pathologist concluded that he had been kicked to death.

Frank and Sylvia sat beside one another in their comfortable Lymington home, the following day. Frank junior was elsewhere, focused on his homework. They didn't watch much television, but Frank wanted to hear what Julian had to say. The six o' clock news led with him.

"We are shocked to the core by events in Yorkshire, Edinburgh and London. Whilst the leaders of the SANITAS organisation do not see eye-to-eye with my government I uphold their right to protest. Our deepest sympathies to the families of the young man who lost his life in Edinburgh, and those injured in Bradford..."

"Are there any leads on the perpetrators, Prime Minister?"

"Thank you for your question, Dickie. Early indications are that this is the work of random and rogue elements in our society. None of these dreadful attacks bears the hallmarks of large-scale organised groups..."

"Prime Minister...Prime Minister..."

"Yes," he pointed, "Deborah, please."

"The attacks seem to be remarkably well-coordinated. Can they really be random?"

He flashed her his winning smile.

"Debs, there is such a thing as coincidence..."

Frank held his breath. Julian was stretching credulity.

"No Debs, you're quite right. There's every possibility that the events are linked. We do need to give the forensic boys time to do their thing. Let me reassure you all..." and he looked directly into the camera, "...we will not tolerate terrorism, and I promise you we will hunt these criminals down." Julian stepped into the waiting car, and the wrecked signage of SANITAS was held briefly on camera in Hampstead High Street.

"Small scotch, Frank?"

"Thank you, darling."

Sylvia retreated to the drinks tray. She didn't hear her husband's chuckle, nor the words he spoke under his breath.

"Clever bastard..." and as an afterthought, "...too clever by half."

He just caught the newsreader's words, "In another incident in Edinburgh a young man was found savagely beaten to death in a cemetery..."

Guy Grosvenor reported to the P.M. three days later, in Ten Downing Street.

"Saw your broadcast, sir. Have to say that forensics don't mesh with your assumption of, what was it sir, *"random and rogue"*?"

Julian sipped his coffee, whilst Fiona's hand rested on his shoulder.

"Do enlighten us Guy."

"The business in Bradford quite possibly, but the explosive devices at the other venues were top-notch professional..."

Julian cut him off abruptly.

"Quite so, Guy. Ah well, can't be right all the time."

Fiona's braying laugh interrupted his flow. Julian rose to his feet, and stood toe-to-toe with his Head of Counter Terrorism.

"Thing is, Guy, one never quite knows what extreme measures have to be put in place to ensure the security of the nation."

Guy Grosvenor held his stare, despite the smarmy smile that disgusted him. Had he but known it, the same realisation came to him as the one 'Angela' experienced as she lay beside her lover looking at a blasted building in West Hampstead on Sky News.

15

"We long to have again the vanished past..."
'Oedipus at Colonus'

The Manor House, Banksmore was resplendent in the autumnal light. It was sufficiently warm for the guests to mingle on the terrace in the early evening. Lady Deborah Marlborough was in full fig. Effusive remarks littered her path; palm leaves spread before royalty. Fulsome praise for the gardens and the house, but most of all for her. Debs sparkled, and looked ten years younger. Ladies crowded about her, demanding the secret of her new-found youthful vigour. She trotted out the names of a few high-end beauty products. After all, she couldn't reveal that the true elixir of life was a six-feet two-inch younger man bonking you senseless!

Sir Ken Burke caught her eye, and raised his glass of champers in salute. He recalled that his boss' mother was a widow woman. The thought of becoming Julian's stepfather rather tickled his fancy. He looked around the crowded terrace, to check list the great and good in his filing cabinet mind. Old goat he may be, but he was also a seasoned campaigner. Always worth lodging a few details away for a rainy day. The politicos in attendance were colleagues. He noted the Earl of Seaforth, 'Freddie' Forbes, in conclave with the P.M. and Henry Longfellow, now Lord Cockermouth. He wandered indoors, and worked the rooms. A titivation of celebrities had been invited, and his eye fell upon Felicity Bray, his *'Question Time'* inquisitor. Cracking pair of pins. Without realising he murmured, "They go all the way up to her arse!"

"What's that you say, Sir Ken?"

Debs was beside him, linking his arm.

"What! Oh yes, Lady Debs. Waitress offered me a top-up. Said I'd pass. I say, Debs, you look rather wonderful. I..."

"Why thank you Ken. Do be an angel and help me out. The couple who've just arrived, take them in hand and entertain them 'til they find their feet."

She indicated an older man in a dinner jacket that had seen better days. Ken only had eyes for his companion. A striking woman, in her forties he guessed. Flame red hair cascading onto her bare shoulders, setting off a shimmering deep green dress.

"I say Debs, who's the looker?"

Her ladyship was miffed by Ken's attention shifting elsewhere.

"Not sure. Late addition. The chap is Desmond Claymore-Browne, local farmer. Asked if he could bring his god-daughter along. Lives somewhere in Wiltshire, apparently, and made a surprise visit. Do be a poppet Ken; entertain and introduce."

Debs turned away with an explosive 'Darling," on her lips, "it's been yonks. How are you?"

Her swift backward glance at the red head did not escape Ken's attention. The old boy chuckled to himself.

He knew a nose out of joint when he saw one. He swept two glasses of champagne off the tray of a passing waitress, and set his guidance mechanism on the tasty lady, and the old agricultural.

India Woake's eyes were fixated on Sir Ken, as he regaled her and Desmond with tales of his influence. She gave the supreme impression of being captivated. A gal up from the country; wide-eyed at the adult world. Desmond Claymore-Browne looked askance at the politician. A crashing bore of the first water.

"Would you excuse me, Sir Ken? Must catch up with Derek Fisher."

"Can't say I know the name."

Chap by the fireplace, silver locks. Formerly CEO of Wassermann and Greenbaum. India, I'll leave you in Sir Ken's safe hands."

Ken clocked Derek Fisher, and tucked the name tidily away.

"So, my dear, what does one get up to in the wilds of Wiltshire?" His eyes glowed. "Are you a sporting girl?"

She laid on the far-back accent with a trowel.

"I should jolly well say so. Do you ride? They safe I have the best 'seat' in the county."

Ken edged closer. "I concur," he whispered. He leant against the wall beside her, and together they viewed the room. His serpentine arm glided slowly behind her, and his left hand settled on her buttocks. She did not look at him, but between sips she said,

"I say Sir Ken! You are a naughty boy. My nanny would have given you a spanking."

He leant against her, purring into her ear.

"Nothing wrong with a bit of slapped botty. Happens in all the best schools!"

India was a good head taller than him. The change in her demeanour shocked and thrilled him.

"Then we'd best take you in hand."

She withdrew a card from her bag.

"Call me. I'll be at my London apartment all next week."

Suddenly she reverted to the chaste girl, nodding towards the open French windows.

"Isn't that the P. M.? Gosh, you wouldn't introduce me, would you?"

Ken proffered his gallant arm.

"Prime Minister, may I introduce Miss..."

He got no further before The Earl of Seaforth exclaimed,

"Good Lord, India! Indy, darling, what on earth brings you into this august company?"

She laughed gaily, and embraced Seaforth.

"Freddie darling, what an unexpected pleasure. I've tagged along with an old friend of Pa's. That's him, the one in the rusty old DJ at the supper table."

Julian smiled benignly.

"Ah, you're with Desmond?"

"Desmond, Julian?"

"Claymore-Browne, Freddie. Rather big in local agriculture. Don't know what we'd do without him. Sound chap. So, India, have I got that right? You're Desmond's...god-daughter?"

"How clever of you, Prime Minister."

Her green eyes held him in a trance, and he was glad that his mother had insisted that Fiona should not be present at the shindig.

"Ma told me you were coming with Desmond. Said you're our mystery woman of the evening. She was charmingly correct. Do call me Julian."

Freddie Forbes nearly dropped a very dangerous brick.

"So sorry to hear about your other god-father..."

"Thank you Andrew. Awful shock. Still processing rather."

It was a trivial piece of code in their Wiltshire circle. If anyone dropped a full Christian name into the conversation the subject was verboten.

"Why India?" Julian enquired.

"Oh Ma and Pa were mad on the Mountbattens..."

"...and what does 'Pa' do?"

"Surely you remember Archie Woake, Julian. Retired Brigadier General from Intelligence."

"Bit before my time, Freddie. Think I've seen his name on some old briefing docs." He gathered himself before this gorgeous lady. "'fraid to say I must tear myself away and press the flesh." He bent over and kissed her on both cheeks. Her freshness quite took his breath away. "Are you still around at the weekend?"

"Yes."

"Then I insist you and Desmond pop over for drinks. Ma will arrange it. Just the four of us."

Julian inhaled deeply, and plastered his face with what he considered his most engaging smile.

"Into the fray! Ken, you're looking like a spare part. Help me recruit some of the chaps for a few frames of Snooker."

His eyes cast around the room, and his voice boomed over the chatter.

"Desmond, old fellow, frame of Snooker?"

His delight knew no bounds when Desmond accepted.

Sir Ken was dragged away, casting a mournful look back at India. He was cheered no end when she discreetly raised an arm to indicate the telephone.

Julian hadn't been sure about this evening, but he had promised his mother a glittering social occasion. As he exited the room he was buoyant. He looked for her. She stood in profile, framed by the open French windows. Deborah positively glowed, as she hung on every word Guy Grosvenor uttered.

"Good old Guy," Julian thought. "There's a chap who knows how to behave...and good old Ma."

It was almost like the old days. He halted mid-stride. No, better.

"Best foot forward Ken. You can keep score. After I've walloped Desmond, I'm going to give you a thrashing!"

Momentarily, Ken's eyes closed, and his nostrils flared. Nanny stood over him, and she had blazing red hair.

16

"Tell me the news, again, whatever it is...sorrow and I are hardly strangers."
'Antigone'

All the best parties take place in the kitchen. The house was located on The Mount in Hampstead, and owned by Isa Joseph's parents. Her father, also Isa, had made his fortune in timber. He and his wife Maryam had greeted their guests, and then graciously retired. The gathering of women sat, or leaned against work surfaces in silence.

"Would you introduce yourselves, please?" Isa's voice was a refreshing breeze.

"I am Anna Wilbey. Julian Marlborough killed my mother."

A blonde woman spoke.

"I used to be called Suzie. I am Muslim, and my name is Fatima." She inhaled deeply. "A long time ago, Julian Marlborough raped me!"

The silence deepened. It was broken by the trembling voice of a beautiful Asian woman.

"Abir...Abi Hussain. Julian Marlborough killed my husband."

The three women were already familiar with one another. An Italianate looking woman sheltered by the door, as if deciding whether or not to flee from this place. Welcoming eyes convinced her to stay.

"I have had many names. Now I am Samantha Baxter. Once I was a prostitute, and, God forgive me, I was Julian's girlfriend. I know what he did..."

"You are not alone, Samantha. We are sisters in misfortune, but we are sisters in love and compassion. We do not judge."

Isa's pronouncement received a murmur of approval. Then she spoke again.

"There is one more amongst us who is unfamiliar to all but Anna. Would you introduce her, please?"

Anna gestured to the athletic red-headed woman who sat beside her.

"This is India. She came to me with a story. She will tell it to you herself."

"I am India Woake. Julian Marlborough killed my godfather; the man I love."

She recited, tersely, the contents of Giles' CD, whilst looking at Sam Baxter who nodded vigorously in agreement, and gave eye witness testimony to what was related. Abi Hussain choked with tears. He was innocent, her beloved Faisal was innocent. India summarised.

"Each of us, in our own way, wants vengeance, but we have a greater task. Marlborough is taking our country down into the pit; he is spreading a fear and darkness across this land that hasn't been seen in four hundred years. I will not allow it; WE cannot allow it."

The silence of approval rested upon them. Anna rotated a biscuit slowly on her plate. India took it from her, and bit into it heartily with a loud crunch. Laughter resounded.

"India believes that you are all in danger," Isa said. "I am certain that she is right. The explosions here in Hampstead and Edinburgh; the deaths of Jamie and *'Tom-from-the-Sea'*, and our encounter in Liverpool are the raging of the beast. She has a proposal."

"Got a spread in Wiltshire. Well, Ma and Pa's actually, but they're in agreement. I'm barely known to Marlborough, but he's going to know me better," she digressed. "You're all to migrate to Wiltshire. A hideaway where we can plan..."

"I have a husband and child..." Sam began.

"Everyone. All together. Now, how many of you are...?"

"Hold on a tic, India." Anna held up a hand. "Sam, how did you find your way here?"

"Isa found me!"

She related the tale of her family holiday; the hitchhiking Isa, and their witnessing of the demonstration in Edinburgh.

"We were sitting outside a café, and Isa appeared once more. We knew that we had to share the burden we carried, especially after seeing Abi harangued."

Anna looked directly at Isa with a boldness she did not feel.

"You have a habit of just appearing Isa." She sucked in the air, and repeated the question the Prime Minister had asked the girl in Liverpool.

"Who are you?"

Isa sat across the table from her, and took her hands.

"I am who I am. Is that not enough for you Anna?"

Anna felt that she knew, but she could not accept. Isa could see it in her wondering face.

"Think of me like this, Anna, *'A voice of one calling…'"*

Puzzled minds turned inwards, pondering, "Where have I heard that before?"

Anna knew exactly where it came from. Only Isa heard her whisper,

"…In the desert prepare the way for the Lord…"

She said out loud to Isa, "So you're not…"

"I am who I am. Come, let's prepare for your departure." She addressed everyone. "For a while you must go into purdah. In safety and solitude, you can deliberate and plan. Joined as sisters; Sisters of Silence…"

"What about you!" Fatima exclaimed. "Aren't you in danger?"

Maryam and Isa the Elder came into the kitchen.

"Me? I have my mother and father to watch over me. Anyway, the temporary Master of this Land is too preoccupied to pay attention to his nephew's girlfriend." She laughed. "What possible danger can a child be to him?"

Anna kept the prophet Isaiah to herself.

"…and a little child will lead them…"

*

India's last words, as she left The Mount, were,

"I'll join you later. Got to whip up support!"

The family apartment was down the road, in Swiss Cottage. India was not given to dressing up. The last time had been for a 'Young Farmer's' do. Her only concession to the role of dominatrix was a pair of four inch stilettos. Otherwise, her outfit resembled that worn by Hattie Jacques in *'Carry on Nurse'*, as Matron.

Sir Ken Burke was secured to the metal bed head by a pair of handcuffs. He had brought his own; they were fur-lined. India looked down on him. He lay prone, glancing awkwardly over one shoulder. Her towering height thrilled him, and he burbled approval through the gag. His gelatinous body was naked, apart from a pair of shoddy Y-fronts. She got into role quickly, to stifle her rising laughter at this patent absurdity.

"Now then, my lad, I'll teach you to do as you're told. When I say wash your botty, I mean scrub it clean."

With a distaste Ken couldn't see, she rolled down his underpants.

"Disgusting!" and she meant it. "You foul, foul little urchin."

The strop whistled through the air twice, and slapped his buttocks. Ken jerked spasmodically.

"Let's have a look at those ears. Dirty, dirty, dirty!"

Each singular judgement was accompanied by a sound lash on the backside. Ken became alarmed and agitated.

"Fingernails. Uuugh! If filthy fingers were trumps you'd have a winning hand!"

She laid on with the leather strop. Captain Bligh would have promoted her instantly. Ken struggled, and muffled squeals of pain penetrated the gag. She lay down the strop within his sight.

"I'll be back!"

For a second Ken feared that she had gone to fetch Arnold Schwarzenegger to join the festivities.

When India returned she pulled up a dining chair, and sat where he could see her. She was in her day clothes.

"Now, little man, I've got something for you to listen to."

She pressed a button on the remote. Giles Wentmore's voice was quiet, but audible. Sir Ken ceased to struggle, and became deathly still.

"How about that then, Sir Kenneth?" Contempt filled her voice when she gave him his title. "Your lord and master."

India picked up the strop from the bedside cabinet, and Ken whimpered.

"Well, he isn't your lord and master anymore; I am! I won't say 'mistress', in case your seedy little mind runs away with itself. Going to remove the gag now. Should you be unpleasant toward me, it will go straight back on. Then you will receive a little more recreational scolding."

She removed the gag, and unlocked one handcuff to make him feel that he might be released, eventually.

"What do you want from me, money?" He couldn't restrain himself. "You fucking bitch!"

"Ah, ah, ah. Careful my cherub. Your botty is red enough already. I suspect one or two more slaps will draw blood."

A sullen silence reigned, and India was content.

"What do you want?"

"I've told you. I am now your lord and master."

She meandered over to the drinks cabinet, and poured two small scotches. He took the glass in his free hand.

"I don't like whiskey."

"Drink it, you little worm."

Ken threw the scotch in her face. India took a tissue from the top of the cabinet, and calmly wiped herself. Without a word she grasped the strop, and thrashed him.

"Okay, okay, okay!" he cried through the pain.

"Would you care for a drink, Ken?"

He blubbered, "Yes please, mistress..." He saw her raised eyebrow. "Master."

"You look like a G & T man Ken. Am I correct?"

"Yes...yes..."

"Here we are sweetie. Dry your tears and drink up, there's a good boy."

She crossed her legs, and smiled upon him beatifically. Ken thought he might be in the presence of Mrs. Satan.

"You know, Ken, I think it's disgusting. Oh, not this, though it is remarkably distasteful. I'm referring to the way in which the Prime Minister treats you."

"What...?"

"Hold on a tick, darling. You're so clearly a man of culture and refinement, or you wouldn't hold the post you do." Irony was thick in the air. It passed Ken by. "It's quite shameful."

"What is?"

"Oh Ken. You're Julian's court jester. He keeps you around for amusement. When you stop making him laugh he'll hang you out to dry. You heard the CD. If he can do that, he won't think twice about squashing you."

She allowed the thought to permeate his skull whilst she topped up his drink.

"Now listen to me, luvvie. From now on, you are my eyes and ears within the government." She gestured toward the sound system. "Surely, you don't approve of what he did in St. George's Church?"

Ken was appalled. "Of course I bloody don't!"

"Super! I knew you were on the side of the angels."

She was about to mention the reintroduction of public birching, but thought it inappropriate under the circumstances.

"What about these public executions he intends to grant to the nation? You're a civilised man, Ken."

Despite two large gin and tonics, he was as sober as a judge. He grumbled into his empty glass, then waggled it for a refill.

"Man's a bloody maniac."

She handed him an extra-large measure, and freed him from the other handcuff. He sat gingerly on the edge of the bed.

"*Fait accompli*, Ken..."

"Don't like the idea of being an informant..."

"This is your patriotic duty."

"What if he finds out?"

"He'll hang, draw and quarter you. So you'd best be careful." She leant forward and took his hand. "We'll take good care of you, Ken."

"Who's we?"

"You must have realised that I'm not working alone." She was about to add, "Even you're not that stupid," but thought better of it. "Apart from everything else, we have an expert in military intelligence handling our communications." She had yet to tell her father about his new role.

Ken was growing in confidence, and the alcohol gave him bravado.

"What if I were to turn you in to...you know who?"

He looked around furtively, suspecting listening devices. Quietly, India hissed.

"Good thinking, Ken. Camera as well."

In truth, the only device operating was on her mobile phone.

"Put your trousers on love."

When he was dressed he stood and faced her. Briefly, he thought about giving her a good hiding. The idea shrivelled within him; she was thirty years younger, and powerfully built.

"We'll be in touch."

She wanted to send him away with restored dignity, and a sense of hope.

"You are doing a great service to your country, Sir Kenneth. When we have succeeded in removing that abominable man from office, and your role is indispensable to the objective, I am confident that my associates will reward you handsomely. I foresee Ermine at the very least..." Once more she came close to him. "Who knows, perhaps even a Garter."

India opened the door. It was all she could do not to laugh when he shook her hand with great solemnity, and departed. She took a shower.

17

"Insolence produces the tyrant."
'Oedipus Rex'

Mr. Speaker reclined whilst the Prime Minister spoke. He retained his customary air of disdain, which he knew irritated the man who was his brother-in-law. Hilary Melton was married to Julian's older half-sister, Jessica. She was the progeny from a brief marriage between the Late-Sir Hugh Marlborough and an impressionable young deb who had worked as his researcher. Hugo Melton was their son.

"The Leader of the Opposition," he drawled languidly.

The Right Honourable Lady came to her feet with alacrity. Hilary sighed inwardly. He was a Labour M.P., but when he looked at Tamsin Starke he was unsurprised that the party had remained in Opposition for so long. She was the latest in a string of odd individuals; Miliband, who looked and sounded like a creation of Mel Blanc's; Corbyn, a cross between Catweazle and the Grinch. Now they had a young thing who played the *"I'm a no-nonsense Northern lass"* card.

"Thank you, Mr. Speaker. If I may summarise all that has been said over the last few hours, days, and weeks..."

Hilary raised an eyebrow. Summarise? Tamsin Starke took the biscuit for verbosity in the House. Considering she wasn't short on competition that was some achievement.

"Members on all sides of the House have made clear their fundamental and adamantine opposition to this bill. It brings disgrace and shame not only upon this House, but upon the nation. We will become a pariah in the Western world if the contents of this bill pass into law."

She sat down abruptly, which caught Hilary off-guard.

"The Prime Minister!"

Julian loved being in the House. From his earliest days he'd always longed for a stage to dominate. It was like being back at school, performing in the plays and musicals. He was a master of voice and timing. Every eye was on him; every ear hung on his words. The feeling was exquisite. His gaze swept the benches, fore and aft. Despite themselves, many men and women were entranced by his good looks and grooming; his absolute self-assurance. An air of excitement and danger emanated from him.

"The nation..."

He paused, as if reflecting seriously upon what his opponent had said. Then his voice rang clear and true. A supercilious sneer inhabited his very being.

"The nation will ask for the bells of Westminster to ring when this bill is enshrined in law. The nation will dance in the streets. An end to patting criminals on the head, and telling them not to be naughty boys and girls. Drug dealers, paedophiles, murderers and terrorists swept from our prisons at the end of the hangman's noose..."

"A culture of fear!"

The Leader of the Scottish Nationalists drew some sympathy from the House.

Julian was utterly still, until the House quieted down.

"I would like to thank the Right Honourable member."

It was an error to believe that Julian was little more than 'Action Man'. He possessed a good mind, and now he employed it to express what was, possibly, the nearest thing he owned to as a credo.

"For decades we have sat at the feet of psychoanalysts; we have bent the knee to the educational theorists, and listened to prison reformers. The common mantra of *"Give them a second chance,"* ringing endlessly in our ears. *'It's the fault of poverty; no father at home – that's the reason for their criminality; no education, no job, low self-esteem…'"*

He warmed to his task.

"Convenient excuses for a lack of personal responsibility. Life is tough? Yes, it can be, but not as tough as it was in the 1930's, the 1830's – the 1430's! Our country has known nothing but improvement and prosperity since 1945. Free health care, free schooling, the shops and supermarkets ever full of goods…"

A righteous indignation gripped him.

"What do you think the fucking world is – Disneyland?"

The House gasped at his obscenity. Julian recovered himself, before Hilary Melton could intervene.

"Mr. Speaker, my profound apology for using such language. I apologise to you; to the House, and to the nation."

He looked expectantly at his brother-in-law, who gestured for him to continue.

"Why did I congratulate my Right Honourable friend, the Leader of the Scottish National Party?"

The silence allowed the packed House time to reflect, but they were none the wiser after having done so. Julian took up his theme.

"Guilt – a prerequisite for acknowledging that you have done wrong. Shame – an honest feeling of remorse for inflicting harm on others.

FEAR! The sure and certain knowledge that you will not escape just punishment and retribution for your wrongdoing. FEAR! Perhaps imperfect, but, I am convinced, the best preventative we possess to avoid our nation sliding further and deeper into disorder and mayhem. A place too horrible to contemplate. Where everyone is forced to live daily in fear. Fear of being robbed, of being attacked, raped, murdered. A place where children are no longer safe from predators who want to ravage them through sex or drugs, or God alone knows what else..."

"...but why *public* executions?"

"It caught Julian by surprise, because the *Cri de Coeur* came from the Tory benches. A murmur fluttered through the spellbound House, like a flock of starlings gliding around Big Ben. The Prime Minister folded his arms, and rested his chin on one hand until a hush once more descended.

"A just question from my honourable friend. The nation has immured itself from the harsh realities and necessities of life. It needs, perhaps for a short while, to step out from the self-imprisonment of illusion and witness nature red in tooth and claw. I say *"perhaps".* There may come a time when such exhibitions are no longer necessary, nor desirable. I am, however, implacable in my resolve that Capital Punishment will be restored, and for as long as I deem it necessary it will be carried out in the public arena."

He turned his back upon the sparse Opposition benches, and faced his own M.P.'s.

"It is my will!"

The debate ended, and the Speaker called "Division!". No one was surprised when the Government won with a clear, but not overwhelming, majority. Twenty-eight Tories had voted against the Whip. Normally, such an issue would be decided on a free vote, but Julian was having none of that. The Chief Whip scrutinised the voting, and reported to his boss.

"Withdraw the Whip from them Harry. Even without twenty-eight we still retain an untouchable majority."

They sipped their Sherry in quiet companionship.

"Now for the Other Place, Julian. Anticipating bother?"

"Oh, their lordships won't rock the boat. We've created so many new peers precisely to avoid such embarrassments." He chuckled. "Lloyd George knew a thing or two."

He turned to their silent companion.

"A couple of good interventions, Ken. Can always rely on old Ken, Harry, to get under the skin of the 'Sisterhood' on the other benches. When you said you wanted to add an amendment to include the ducking stool for mother-in-laws I pissed myself. Right chaps, I'm off. Tea party at Ma's, then a weekend in the country." He paused in the doorway. "I say, Ken. Remember that red head at Ma's cocktail party, the one in the green dress? We're taking tea together, with her Godfather tagging along..."

Ken blurted, "Desmond Claymore-Browne!"

"Good God, Ken, how on earth do you know that?"

"We played Snooker together. Don't you recollect?"

"Of course, of course...well done Ken. Always a good idea to sound him out, Harry. There's very little Ken doesn't have tucked away in that processor he calls a mind. I'll give India your regards, Kenneth. I noticed you gave her your highly personal attention at the party. Wandering hands; you're a naughty boy." He opened the door, then halted with a guffaw. "Remind me, sometime, to tell you a funny story Ken. It concerns the Claymore-Brownes and the Snooker table. You'll crap yourself with hysterics."

Julian was gone. Ken made his excuses to the Chief Whip rapidly, and headed for the lavatories. He suspected that he'd already shit himself.

*

"...so there it is Desmond. There's a vacancy to fill. "Public executioner. Liberal Democrats need not apply." Julian roared in appreciation of his own wit.

India adopted a demure tone, as if expressing concern for Julian's well-being.

"Won't you face opposition in the country?"

"Smashing cake, Ma. A good old Victoria sponge. Been my favourite since I was a boy. Opposition? Yes, I suppose there will be, but it'll fizzle out. I'll make damn sure it does."

"How will you do that?" India asked sweetly.

"Oh, got my people, you know. In fact, I'll give you an exclusive. We go public after the weekend. For some time, I've had a body of lads and lasses working behind the scenes. On Monday morning there'll be a press release. The *'Defence of the Realm Force'* will be announced to the nation."

"Soldiers, Julian?"

"Mmm? Not as we know them, Desmond. More an ancillary unit. Detachments will be stationed in every city, and major town. They will deal directly with civil order. Anything from anti-social behaviour to rioting. A firm and swift hand."

He smacked the table abruptly, making the cups and saucers rattle.

Debs placed a loving hand on her son.

"Julian intends to restore the golden age of common civility, and good neighbourliness. What do you say, India?"

She chose her words circumspectly.

"Always in favour of getting on with the neighbours."

"Enough politics! I say Ma, why don't you get Desmond to have a look at 'Brexit's' paws?" He cast a friendly eye towards his guests. "Our oldest and favourite hound. Poor old soldier's been struggling lately. You're a bit of a whizz with them I'm told, Desmond."

"Be delighted, Debs..."

Julian couldn't resist it.

"As long as you don't become *'Deb's Delight'* in the process, Dezzie. You two being young, free and single, and all that!"

"Julian! You are the limit. Really!"

"Sorry Ma, sorry Des. Bit of Rugby club banter. Off you go then. I'm going to show India the daubs in the Snooker room."

Julian was a creature of habit. He closed the door, and locked it.

"Thought you might like to take a peek. You being a country girl."

He positioned himself before a small, but exquisite, Stubbs painting, studying it. When he heard the key turn in the lock he swung about face. India was beating time on her hand with a Snooker cue. Today would not be the day for a quick frame on the green baize. He studied her, and whilst he did not see through the façade she had created, he recognised a firmness of character. It excited him.

"The Stubbs is our pride and joy."

They perused paintings and prints for ten minutes, and made small talk.

"Better get back to Ma and Desmond. Not keen on the idea of a stepfather."

He laughed lightly, and she responded. A small card flashed into his hand.

"Having a bit of gathering at Chequers next month. Be marvellous if you could attend. No need to say yes right now. That's my private and personal number."

She tucked it into the pocket of her elegant trousers.

"That's very sweet of you, Julian," and she pecked him on the cheek. "Come on, I'll take charge of Desmond. No need to worry about nuptials between him and Lady Deborah. Poor soul, he'll never get over the loss of Fiona." She held his eye. "If he'd been with you, in the Church, he'd have torn her killer limb from limb and fed him to his hounds."

She broke the uncomfortable silence.

"Gosh! You were tremendously brave. I read all about it. If I come to Chequers you must promise to tell all. Deal?"

"Deal."

Rain fell heavily, as Desmond manoeuvred the Land Rover through the narrow lanes.

"Desmond."

"Yes, m'dear?"

"There's something I need to share with you. In fact, quite a lot you need to know, and it's not very pleasant. This isn't a social visit to my Godfather..."

"Figured that out an aeon ago. All the 'girlie' behaviour at that party, and again this afternoon. Not the India I know and love."

"Going to take courage and fortitude to hear what I've got to say."

"We'd best get a move on then. Been saving a Macallan Rare Cask, Batch No. 2, for a rainy day. You'll join me?"

"I'll join you."

18

"Not to be born beats all philosophy. The second best is to have seen the light."
'Oedipus at Colonus'

High dudgeon is not a hamlet in the Cumbrian fells. It coursed around the lunch table. A private room in the 'Army and Navy' Club hosted familiar faces.

"Surely you must feel the way the wind is blowing, Freddie?"

Lord Cockermouth's plaintive appeal to the Earl of Seaforth met with approval from two retired major generals, and a former Admiral of the Fleet.

Roy McKinnon purred softly at Freddie Forbes.

"Defence of the Realm Force, my arse. Private bloody army!"

The languid seafarer drawled.

"Didn't sign up for this, Freddie, when we put him in power."

"Actually, Nigel, we didn't put him in power. Bugger popped out of the bottle like the genie." Mike Montgomery, one-time commander of the Household Division, eyed the Earl. "You're closest to him, Freddie. Rein him in!"

Forbes drew imaginary doodles on the table cloth with his index finger. He was uncertain what he could say.

"Not sure I'm in a position to do that, chaps. I..."

McKinnon simmered.

"You're not in sympathy with him?"

"No, no, of course not. Fact of the matter is I have no leverage. On a personal level we rub along, but politically I'm just another pair of hands to applaud his self-awarded acumen and wisdom. He's a loose cannon..."

Nigel snorted, "Loose cannon? His ambition is big enough to have wiped out the Light Brigade..."

"Hold on there, Nigel."

A change in McKinnon's demeanour held their attention.

"Leverage Freddie. That's what we need. A pressure point. Is there not anything murky in his past we can use to persuade him of the error of his ways?"

"I've had access to his Army record."

"Yes, Mike?" Freddie looked hopeful.

"He wasn't exactly a paragon of virtue. His treatment of prisoners borders on a war crime..."

"Then we've got the bugger!"

"'fraid not, Nigel. Access to that information is highly restricted, and he has key placemen who can suppress it. Even if it were in the public domain I doubt it would amount to more than a storm in a teacup. You know how the public feels about the SAS; a cross between Superman and Jesus Christ. Throw in the fact that these prisoners were Isis fighters, and there's more likely to be a clamour to award him a testimonial match at Wembley than condemn him."

The sepulchral silence tormented Lord Cockermouth. He recalled, vividly, his late-night conversation with Giles Wentmore. What he had approved, as Home Secretary, scarified his soul. He could not reveal to present company that he sanctioned the massacre in St. George's Church. He wrung his hands.

"Something must be done. Something must be done!"

The wry McKinnon raised a sceptical eyebrow.

"Not hoping to become Prince of Wales, Henry?"

Subdued laughter broke the tension. This small group of well-educated men recognised the reference to Edward VIII's sententious pronouncement on behalf of the Welsh valleys, nearly a hundred years before. It sobered them when they realised that next to nothing had been done.

"I say Freddie, had a bit of a thought."

The Earl indicated for Nigel to continue.

"Think Roy may have inadvertently hit on the solution. You're pretty well-favoured in Court circles. Couldn't we engage His Majesty; get him to have a word with the tyke?"

A murmur of appreciation circulated. Expectant eyes rested on Freddie Forbes.

"Yes, yes, okay. Think that can be arranged. The King will have to be told far more than he knows at present?"

Nodding heads encouraged him.

"Might help. Let's give it a shot. Coffee and cognac, I think..."

"One more point, Freddie, before we bring in the dancing girls."

"Yes Rob?"

"Scotland is not as entranced by its Prime Minister, as the rest of the land. My sources tell me that the cities are already bubbling, especially after that business in Edinburgh. Unknown assailants, my arse. Had the paw prints of professionals all over it. If he pushes too far there will be resistance. We don't want to reach the point where *"Fair is foul, and foul is fair..."*

Nigel's laugh was forced. "Good Lord, Roy, don't bring the *'Scottish play'* into it! You'll jinx us all."

In separate chambers of secrecy, the Earl of Seaforth and Lord Cockermouth knew that a blasted heath was a distinct possibility.

*

Wiltshire is a beautiful county. Progress southward, and it reveals its rolls, and twists; tree-cushioned valleys appear sumptuously around bends, and hills repose in majesty as you negotiate the stark roads cutting through them. The highways and byways are, thankfully, quite unlike the unbearable roads of Cornwall. It's never long before you sweep into a welcoming village, where the solid and dependable people of old England rest their bones. You are in the heart of ancient Wessex. A process of accretion overtakes incomers. They imbibe the traditional attributes of mutual dependency and good neighbourliness. They are discreet and measured folk who take community seriously.

The Woake household, on the edge of Tollard Royal, was a much enlarged community. Nine adults and two small children were encamped. The main house and holiday lets accommodated them, with room to spare. Marion Woake was delighted with the children. Whilst the others met in the kitchen, she kept the tots occupied in India's old nursery. Jenny Wilbey and Lucy Baxter hit it off straight away.

It would not have seemed unreasonable to find the host in the 'chair'. Archie Woake, Brigadier General retired, resigned the position in favour of the Reverend Anna Wilbey.

"We know the date and location for the first executions. It's all about mobilisation. We put a spanner in his works in Liverpool, now we must do so in London."

"How do you propose we go about it, Anna?"

Anna and Abi Hussain had already been in conclave with Archie Woake. They were delighted with what he had told them. They had foreseen the obvious pitfall in spreading the news of protest like wildfire.

"The usual method, Sam. Social media."

Paul Baxter threw a worried look at his wife.

"What is it Paul?"

"Thing is, Anna, we've come to Tollard Royal for safety. If we start plastering stuff all over social media Marlborough's security boys will track us down in no time."

The deep and dependable voice of Archie Woake intervened.

"Under normal circumstances that would be the case."

He paused, and a mischievous twinkle glittered in his eye.

"It's not a secret that I was part of Intelligence. Consequently, when I retired my chaps installed the communications systems here at base. Occasionally, I'm consulted over historical matters pertaining to present operations. We have firewalls within firewalls. The beauty of it is that it's a military matter. The politicos don't know."

Anna was excited.

"Everything will go out under the heading of SANITAS. No names, no pack drill. Eh, Archie?"

The erstwhile country gentleman smiled engagingly.

"You are to the military manner born!" He continued. "Now, everyone settled in? Any problems, don't hesitate to..."

"Hold your horses, Pa. Before we get too cosy, I've got a piece of intel to share."

The assembled company looked to India expectantly.

"I've had an invitation to a weekend party."

"Oh goodie. Can we come too?"

"Think you'd prefer to stay at home, Fatima. I'm going up in the world, Pa. A weekend at Chequers with the Prime Minister!"

It was Sam Baxter who broke the astonished silence.

"You know why he's invited you, India?"

Before she could respond, Paul Baxter began to croon Al Dubin's 1934 standard:

"Cos I only have eyes for you..."

Sam and Fatima didn't laugh.

"Don't take it lightly. You're a very attractive woman, India. I can see straight away why he's taken with you."

"Oh, I know that!" India was not being boastful. "That's been my intention all along, Sam..."

"He's bloody dangerous, and he doesn't take no for an answer." Sam was pleading.

"He did after tea at Banksmore."

She related the events in the Snooker Room, and how Julian had looked wary when he saw the cue in her hands.

"Let me tell you all something. I know men like Julian Marlborough; I've known them since I was a teenager. There's been many a tussle in a Young Farmer's marquee late at night. Not to mention one or two of your old chums, Pa, when you weren't looking. Forgive me Sam, but you and Fatima were in uniquely vulnerable positions. I'm not."

Sam gave it one last plea.

"I don't like the thought of you being alone at Chequers."

A still, small voice of peace interceded.

"She won't be! I'm invited."

India was gobsmacked.

"You Isa!"

"I've succumbed to Hugo's appeals."

"Who's Hugo?" a bewildered Paul spread his arms.

"Hugo Melton. He's Julian's step-nephew. We went to school together. He'd like me to be his girlfriend."

A strange discomfort hovered in the room. No-one could quite grasp the idea of Isa being anyone's girlfriend.

"So there it is, India. We will be honoured guests. Anna, shall we get down to our plan of campaign? We need to start making use of Archie's comms."

The Brigadier was not in the least put out by the teenager's familiarity. He drew India to one side.

"Sam's right, darling, you and the girl need to tread softly."

"Don't worry, I'll keep a weather eye on Isa."

"You mistake me, darling." He glanced at the table, where the women were in conflab. "Once had a young officer like that lass. Steel all the way through. Scared the pants off me. That young lady will do just fine...when she's not watching out for you!"

19

"I have been a stranger here in my own land: All my life."
'Antigone'

Michael Barret was the last person to be hanged publicly in Britain. He was one of the Irish Republicans who set off a deadly explosion outside Clerkenwell prison in December 1867. Public execution stopped in 1868. It was seen as inhumane. Twenty-First Century Britain was about to turn back the clock.

Julian Marlborough assumed ever greater powers, and dictated his wishes to the Home Secretary for *'opening night'*. Charles Fenwick deferred to his master's instructions. The P.M., romantic that he was, proposed to locate the event at the old Tyburn gallows site, where many a soul had hanged over centuries. He dismissed the idea when the Met' Commissioner wrinkled his nose. The prospect of problematic crowd control, and traffic chaos did not appeal.

"What about Trafalgar Square? Let Nelson watch them swing from the yardarm."

Julian's enthusiasm got the better of him.

"I say, we should commission a painting. Won't have far to carry it into the National Gallery."

The Commissioner did not share the Prime Minister's mordant wit. He replied tersely.

"Excellent choice sir. The location that is, we'll leave the artistic endeavours to Sir Ken."

"Hear that Ken? Find us a body with a box of paints, and make sure the bugger can draw properly. Don't want Damien Hirst. He'd exhibit the corpses in formaldehyde. Morbid sod!"

Trafalgar Square was an ocean of bodies by 6.30 a.m. on December 13th. Julian's comedic bent had once more consumed him.

"Unlucky for some!" he'd exclaimed in Cabinet.

One of his more literate colleagues pointed out that the Church of England celebrated the life of Dr. Samuel Johnson on that date.

"Not a saint, you understand Prime Minister, but a great and notable Christian."

"That settles it! Let's send these buggers off to Purgatory, or wherever it is they're going, in honour of a great Englishman."

None present, in the Cabinet room, had the slightest realisation that Johnson would have been appalled; a man reknowned for his compassion. It was not the first time, nor would it likely be the last, when a would-be dictator co-opted and besmirched the name of a great man as a seal of approval for his heinous acts.

The gallows, with room for three, was erected at the foot of Nelson's column. The Square enabled viewing from all sides. Thousands surrounded the place of execution. It didn't prevent the food and drink sellers from circulating, and commemorative mugs and badges were selling like hot cakes. There are no flies on London street merchants.

"Protests?"

The Commissioner of the Met had raised the question before the planning committee.

Julian gnawed his lip.

"Bound to be. Bloody SANITAS all over social media."

His mind dwelt on Frank Steen. They had foregathered in Julian's Worcestershire hideaway the previous weekend.

"So what are you saying Frank?"

"Still trying, sir, but not much progress. There's clearly advanced security on their computer system. Got me beat."

"It doesn't stack up, Frank. How the hell can a tin pot group access and develop something so impenetrable?"

The P.M. returned to the present.

"You're the expert, Ronnie. *'Kettle'* them, or push 'em all off Westminster Bridge. I don't care. Keep them away from the main crowd."

"We'll do our best, sir. A few will probably get through, but we'll identify most of them from their banners and chants."

The Commissioner was surprised to be ushered into an ante-room when the planning meeting broke up. A well-spoken and modest man informed him that additional forces would be available on the day. The Defence of the Realm Corps (DRC), would make its first official appearance in London. Frank arranged a date for further consultation.

A seething and excited mass behaved beautifully. They might have been there for a rock concert. Exuberant, but controlled. The Tube had been full to capacity, as soon as it reopened at 5.00 a.m. Coaches came from as far afield as Carlisle and Newcastle; Plymouth and Bodmin; Liverpool and Hull. Julian and his entourage gazed upon the assembly from an upper room in the National Gallery.

"Let me put you doubting Thomas' straight. If the supermarkets were close to empty; if the oil ran out, people would tear each other apart in the aisles, and on the forecourts. They may have nicer teeth, and smart little starter homes, but humanity never changes. *'Old Nick'* lurks close to the surface."

"I think you may mean inhumanity, Prime Minister."

"Quite right, Ken. You should all listen to our Ken. Not as green as he's cabbage looking." He smiled benignly upon the Minister for Culture, and extended his arm. "Top me up, Ken. Black, no sugar. Great view, look at that. Good old Ronnie."

The company moved closer to the great windows to see where the P.M. was pointing.

"Smart uniforms, aren't they? Designed them myself."

They were looking straight down Northumberland Avenue, where it led out of Trafalgar Square. SANITAS protestors were visible in the distance; held well back by the DRC. It was the same for all entrance points to the Square; the Strand, the Mall, Whitehall, Charing Cross Road and all the rest. Russet-coloured uniforms stood out against the ever-burgeoning light; each man and woman wore a sidearm.

A section of the crowd, near the gallows, started to chant.

"Why are we waiting...whyyyy are we waiting..."

More and more joined in, until it reached a thunderous crescendo. Julian glanced at his Rolex, and a door opened. Every eye fell upon Guy Grosvenor.

"They're ready for you, sir."

Julian handed his coffee cup to Ken.

"Anyone care to join me?" He sniggered. "Thought not. Plenty of booze over there. Fortify yourselves gentlemen."

He swept out with the eagerness of a schoolboy about to play his first match for the school.

On the scaffold a hooded hangman waited. To the more observant, the veil could not deflect attention from the curves and outline of the woman dressed in a black leather suit. She and her boss had chosen the outfit. It had a test run during their bedroom frolics. Beside her stood another woman. Dressed in clerical robes. They did not speak. The unexpected silence caused them to look at one another. Pity and contempt flowed in opposing directions.

Seething humanity quieted to a hush. On the National Gallery steps Julian Marlborough headed the slow procession. Three handcuffed prisoners shuffled behind him, accompanied by prison officers. The P.M. paused. Why weren't they cheering? The revelation stirred his perverse pride. This was an awesome sight, unwitnessed in many lifetimes. The scene would soon change. He had supreme confidence in the work of Professor Dawkins; the *'Selfish Gene'* would howl. Grotesque spectacle to satisfy their genetic craving for fulfilment without cost. Neither they, nor Julian, believed in an immortal soul. What other price could there be? An elite detachment of the DRC lined the avenue to the gallows. Murmurs planted the seed; chatter watered the shoots, and atavistic bellowing shone brightly on the foul tree of injustice. By the time they reached the base of the platform, the very buildings shook at the noise.

Julian raised his arms in triumph before the worshipping crowd. Behind him the hangwoman placed the nooses around the prisoners' necks. He had thought to make a speech, but changed his mind. The spectacle was sufficient. If this didn't send out a message nothing would. The P.M. turned expecting to see the hooded figure of Fiona Hudson.

"You!"

The Reverend Anna Wilbey was present to bring solace and the love of Christ to those about to hang. It would be her last official duty as a priest in the Church of England.

Julian was stunned.

"How...?"

"I volunteered. The Archbishop chose me..."

He walked away, briskly. Arthur 'bloody' Cantwell, his tame Archbishop. A question flashed through his mind: *"How do you get rid of an Archbishop of Canterbury?"* He nodded at the Commissioner, who spoke to Anna.

"If you wouldn't mind, minister."

She spoke to the condemned.

"I cannot save you in this life, but you can go from this place with courage and with grace, and be received into your Father's Kingdom as forgiven people. Whatever you have done in this life will be forgiven, if you ask for forgiveness with truth in your heart. Don't confess to me; confess to our God and He will be merciful. The Grace of our Lord Jesus Christ, the love of God, and the fellowship of the Holy Spirit be with you now and evermore. Amen."

She leaned forward and kissed each captive on the forehead. The last act of love they would know in this world.

Anna stepped aside, and lifted her head. The strains of a hymn could be heard above the immediate crowd, subdued by what they had just witnessed. Fanny Crosby's words of hope reached all ears.

"To God be the glory, great things He hath done;
So loved He the world that He gave us His Son..."

A few voices closer to the scaffold took up the lyrics. The second verse was heard more clearly.

"O perfect redemption, the purchase of blood,
To every believer the promise of God;
The vilest offender who truly believes,
That moment from Jesus a pardon receives..."

Fiona Hudson recoiled, when Anna tried to lay a hand on her in prayer. Then she walked to Julian, and the words *"...vilest offender..."* thumped in her head. Her hand rested on his shoulder, and he remained immobile; their eyes searching each other. Neither wavered. The eternal battle raged.

The Met Commissioner acted. Fiona Hudson shook herself from her torpor, and despatched three human beings to their death, summarily. The enchantment that held those present was broken. The congregation of thousands gave vent to their approval. Before she knew it, Anna was alone on the platform. Hidden below her, the shells of three bodies hung limply in the chill winter.

*

The Earl of Seaforth had viewed his father being beheaded by terrorists on his son's I Pad; he was not squeamish. He sat in a secluded room in the House of Lords. Three Dukes, a Marquess, and seven Earls kept him company. They were all Scottish.

One of the Dukes switched the television off; he did not stand on ceremony.

"Barbaric and intolerable, Freddie!"

The Marquess placed his brandy balloon on a side table, with gunsight precision.

"Lord knows, we are not all in agreement concerning Capital Punishment, but surely none of us would condone turning it into a public spectacle."

None demurred.

Donald Grant spoke softly, but with a note of fierce urgency in his voice.

"Gentlemen, Scotland will not accept the imposition of these brutish practices, introduced by this...this renegade Prime Minister. We have all taken soundings, and we know that our people are in revolt against this and other draconian measures. There have been demonstrations in all the major cities, following the explosion in Edinburgh. No-one believes the nonsense about terrorists, unless you're referring to state terrorism."

Calum Forsyth chipped in.

"It is only through the good sense of an unusually united Holyrood that we have managed to limit the deployment of Marlborough's *'Defence of the Realm Corps'* to Glasgow and Edinburgh. I'm reliably informed that there is something more than mild indignation within the Scottish regiments at an alien force patrolling our streets."

It slipped out of Freddie Forbes' mouth before he could restrain himself.

"If they only knew the half of it, Forsyth."

"What do you mean by that?"

The old Duke bore down on the Earl of Seaforth.

"I...I...I've spoken out of turn. Forget you heard me say that."

The Duke was having none of it, and neither were his companions.

"Too late, Freddie...cat out of the bag. Let's hear it."

Freddie rose, and walked to the drinks trolley. He poured himself an extra-large one.

"Gentlemen, what I'm about to disclose is top secret. I only know because my *'friend'* regards me as loyal to the party; his particular brand of party. Please understand that I have not participated one scintilla in what I'm about to describe."

He outlined the bogus reasons for the evacuation of Fair Isle. The influx of illegal immigrants into camps on the island, and the method of their eventual disposal in Icelandic waters.

"Good God! You mean the Navy is playing a part in this, and the Admiralty condones their actions?"

"Not the entire service, Donald. You used the apposite term a moment ago...*'renegade'*. Regrettably, a number of the miscreants hold high position, and they collude with our more secret brethren. They, naturally, take their instructions from the highest office of government."

The most senior member of the august company spoke firmly. Paradoxically, he was also the youngest man in the room.

"My father taught me never to pitch an issue too high, but I think we are on a course that will leave our people in misery and oppression. Our nation will be a pariah in the civilised world. The problem Scotland faces...no, I correct myself. The fracture of the tenets and values of civilised life that have been forged in these islands can only be healed through the removal of the hand that wields the hammer of destruction."

An ominous silence fell. Not because any were doubters, or fearful, but because they knew their young companion had spoken the truth. The issue was how it could be done. The Earl of Seaforth ventured forth.

“There is someone...I must be circumspect...someone well-placed who is as appalled as we are by the direction of this foul wind. Perhaps...” he hesitated, but resolve gripped him. “Would you all care to join me for a shoot in Wiltshire? Shall we say the second weekend in January?”

Mutterings of assent gratified Freddie.

“If our potential *‘ally’* is amenable I will invite him to join the party.”

The young Duke once more held their attention.

“There is another factor to take into account. Since my elevation I have devoted some energy to the cultivation of the clan chiefs...”

“To what purpose, sir?”

“Oh, our admirable friends in Holyrood continue to grind away at the Independence issue like bad dentists. I wanted another conduit for understanding the temperature of the nation. However, recent events have focused their minds elsewhere. It seems the chiefs have agreed to celebrate Burns’ Night together. Should be a jolly and innocent gathering, in the full gaze of the public eye. Other matters will, no doubt be discussed.” He became serious. “They are in deadly earnest, gentlemen, and their fuse is short. Either we act quickly, or they will.”

*

The Bible provides a truism; none of us knows the time when we will die. It is probable that many reflect, periodically, about the imponderables surrounding death. What season will it be? What time of day? Who will be present? More serious questions might occupy our concerns. Will it be a lingering death in hospital, or at home? Might I be taken suddenly and unexpectedly at work or play; in the car or on the street? We soon tuck the troublesome speculations away, and get on with living; so we should.

Thousands had witnessed the deaths of three convicted criminals, then they dispersed. Visitors from afar enjoyed a full day in the capital city. With Christmas less than a fortnight away shops and restaurants were doing a roaring trade. For London's indigenous population it was business as usual. When the working day ended the Underground was not its customary sardine self. A holiday air kept many in Town.

Anna Wilbey was the only one of the Wiltshire hideaways to attend the hangings. Her presence had been discussed heatedly. The other women tried everything they could to dissuade her from going. She was not to be convinced. Believing her profile to be too public for the P.M. to threaten her safety, she insisted on doing this one last service for the condemned. Once the executions had taken place she spent the day in the company of a band of ministers.

It was seven p.m. and dark, but the Christmas lights of Covent Garden illuminated the famous landmark, supplementing the merriment that fluttered in the air. Anna and her companions sat in a café, warming their hands around mugs of hot chocolate. They had earned a break. Throughout the day they appropriated landmarks: Speaker's Corner, outside Westminster Abbey, on Oxford

Street...so many places. The Word of Christ was preached to the passing public; brief and to the point in each location. Despite not always speaking, Anna was recognised by many. Abuse was flung at her by some, but many approached her with words of encouragement. She and the other ministers comforted those who wept. A mixture of curiosity, questions and hostility came their way, as it does to all who speak in the marketplace. Each short address ended with the words:

"Love the Lord your God with all your heart and with all your soul and with all your mind and with all your strength. The second is this: Love your neighbour as yourself. There is no commandment greater than these."

Anna drained her mug of its delicious contents.

"Time to gather folks. One last push."

The seven stepped into the cold night air, and they sang:

"One more step along the world I go,
One more step along the world I go;
From the old things to the new
Keep me travelling along with you
And it's from the old I travel to the new;
Keep me travelling along with you..."

The first verse carried them to their destination. They took position outside the 'Oakley' store on King Street. St. Paul's Church Covent Garden lay adjacent in Bedford Street; testimony to Inigo Jones' genius. The Noel Coward

Theatre resided nearby. Mischievously, Anna opened her address with a quotation from the 'Master'.

"An Englishman is the highest example of a human being who is a free man."

She didn't believe in the inherent inequality of Coward's hubristic statement for one moment, but it certainly grabbed attention. Before she could expatiate further, on the merits and imperfections of all mankind, a scream rent the festive air. A young woman dressed like a Gypsy ran into the middle of King street. She was pursued and surrounded by a group of shaven-headed young men. They corralled her in seconds. She sank to her knees, and they showered her in shredded copies of the *'Big Issue'* that she had been attempting to sell. To the horror of the watching people they started to urinate on her. Anna flew across the street.

"Stop that! Stop! In the name of God, stop!"

She knelt beside the young woman and embraced her. The dreadful stench was nothing to Anna.

"How could you?"

Not one of the young men was abashed. They stared at her with calculation in their eyes.

"She could be your mother, your daughter, your sister..."

A Northern Irish accent spat the words, "She's no sister of mine, I tell you..."

"We are all brothers and sisters, friend."

Contemptuous looks fell upon the young minister who had spoken. A sarcastic voice, speaking mangled *'Estuary English'*, intervened.

"Well fuck me, what 'ave we 'ere? 'avin' a night on the town are we, padre? You wanna get down King's Cross, get yerself a girl. Might make a man of you."

"'ere Dazzer, look! They're all friggin' padres."

"I can see that, dickhead. A *'Puff of Padres'* out on the razzle." His tone changed. "Keep your nose out of other people's business, and..." He paused, peering intently at Anna. "I know you; I've sin you before...fuck me! You were on the platform when dem wankers was hung. She's dat vicar who's all over the news."

Dazzer's mate interrupted again.

"She kissed 'em, Daz. I remember. Last thing she did, she kissed 'em."

"That's right, my son. I sin it too." Dazzer grabbed Anna by her lapels, and pulled her to her feet. "You kissed 'em, you bitch. You kissed a woman who killed her husband; you kissed a Paki paedo', an' a bloke wot's killed a copper. You bitch, you bitch, you're a fuckin' bitch!"

Londoners are born with the ability to walk on by, but not on this occasion. The first to come to Anna's aid were her fellow ministers, but they were easily manhandled. Men and women flew from all sides of the Garden. King Street was a battlefield. As if by osmosis, two forces opposed each other. Shopfronts disintegrated, and blood flew everywhere. Somewhere in the crush, Anna and her companions were trapped. The sound of sirens wailed, and people started to walk away hurriedly.

Two women lay on the ground, their blood mingling in an ever-growing pool. It emitted an opalescent hue under the Christmas lights. The thinning crowd kept its distance. The curiosity of rubberneckers held them. Anna's head was cradled in the lap of a teenage girl; the Albanian woman was already dead.

"Anna...Anna. Open your eyes."

"Isa! How?"

"Sssssh. There is only a little time left to you..."

Anna's body arched, and a great cry rent the night sky.

"Jenny, my child!"

"Hush, my sweet. Jenny will be cared for; she will be safe, and she will lead a wonderful life; remembering her mother and her grandfather always."

"Adam. I'm going to meet him..."

"...and everyone else. Peter, who gave you joy, and joined with you in creating life. You have done your duty, Anna. Like your grandfather, you acted with honour, and now you have paid the price. The cost of discipleship is always expensive. Your Saviour waits for you, and he is well-pleased..."

Anna struggled for breath. Intently, she locked onto Isa's eyes.

"...but I have already met Him."

"No, not yet. Despite what you think, I am not He."

"Then who are you? Please, I need to know."

"I am *'a voice of one calling: In the desert prepare the way for the Lord'*." She moved the lock of hair from Anna's face. "The world is foolish. Prophets of doom fill our screens each day, but they do not want to hear or believe in a prophet of joy. We persevere, Anna, we do our duty. That is all we can do; that is what you were called to do, and you have accomplished your task. Go in peace now. We will meet again."

Before the paramedics took her away they stood in awe. Anna's face outshone the luminous Christmas scene around her.

20

"Grief teaches the steadiest minds to waver."
'Antigone'

Chequers is 16th Century in origin. Before it was bequeathed to Prime Ministers, as their country retreat, a line of middle-ranking nobs occupied the premises. The house passed through several families, with descent along the female line. In 1715, the owner married a grandson of Oliver Cromwell. Of the weekend party, going about its pleasures, only Sir Ken Burke was aware of the fact.

At dinner he hummed like an over-used telephone line. Being at table with two 'masters' shredded his nerves. He relaxed when he saw that Julian was engrossed in India. An exceedingly fine Bordeaux slipped down easily. Ken's capacity was the stuff of legend, and his mind sharpened with every sip. He was the servant of two masters. Ha! Title of a play; Goldoni, that was the chap. His companions either side were occupied in conversation with their neighbours. Ken took the opportunity to study his guvnors.

Initially, he considered the idea preposterous, but warmed to it quickly. The Prime Minister was outwardly a Cavalier, but Ken recognised his more dominant trait. The man was a bloody Puritan at heart. His single-minded and obsessive drive to restore a mythical England was utterly devoid of recognised religion, but it sat on the same throne as Cromwell's totalitarian self-righteousness. He took a gulp from his glass. It gave him time to recover from the startling revelation.

My God! That woman was a beauty. Ken took great pleasure from all things beautiful. That was why he'd been appointed to Culture. He smiled in admiration. She gave rapt attention to her table companion, but was by no means silent. He glanced at the second hand on his watch, and timed how long she spoke for before Julian could interject. Impressive! The P.M. was not one for listening to others. Julian looked over his shoulder, and responded to his companion on the other side. India's head turned sharply, and her searchlight eyes transfixed Ken. The sheen of highly-polished steel flashed in them before she resumed her conversation with Julian. Dear Lord in Heaven. Ken was in no doubt; he had just seen honourable and immoveable resolution. He knew who his true master was in that dining room.

"Ken...Ken..."

"Mmm?"

"What on earth are you looking at? My dear, you appear to have entered a state of rapture."

Other diners overheard the remark, and laughed.

"Forgive me Debs. Was studying the tapestries – 16th Century – when I should only have eyes for you."

Lady Deborah was in high spirits. It wasn't often that she was invited to Chequers.

"...and so you should, darling."

Her dirty laugh drew glances from around the table.

"Will you be shooting in the morning, Kenneth?"

"Not much of a shot, I'm afraid, but I'd be honoured to handle your accoutrements."

His soapy old eyes were awash with booze, and he licked his lips. Debs whispered in his ear.

"I'm sure you would, my honey. You may carry my cartridge bag."

For a second he thought she'd employed a euphemism. Disappointment overcame him. On the bright side, there'd been a rising in the south. Ken had a discreet feel of the front of his trousers. Not bad for a fellow in his seventies, and chock full of a 2000 Margaux.

The gay young things jived away in a distant part of the house. Julian and India were not quite alone. His mother and old Ken occupied a Chesterfield in a far corner of the comfortable room. Together they perused the Racing Post, and Debs marked the paper with their choices.

"What next, Jules?"

She had entered his inner sanctum, and was the inheritor of many privileges.

He swirled the Armagnac around the glass. Julian was in good humour, and had allowed himself more drink than he was capable of holding. He was eager to impress this woman, because he knew that she wasn't easily impressed. For the first time in his life he wanted the approval of someone other than his mother. That was partially why he had dismissed Fiona Hudson.

"You shrank from her!" he exclaimed in his office, after the executions. "You showed fear. No use to me at all. See Guy Grosvenor, he'll fix you up with something."

Fiona's humiliation was complete, because someone else was in the room.

"I'm sorry, Julian..."

"Prime Minister! I say Ken, you can have Fiona. In the non-biblical sense, you understand. She can be your personal bodyguard."

His mouth was like a steel trap.

"What about it Ms. Hudson, prepared to take on Ken?"

"Yes...Prime Minister."

"Off you trot."

"Next Indy?"

"Well, you've rattled a few cages with the reintroduction of corporal and capital punishment. My goodness, when you announced that you'd already executed those under lock and key I thought the Woke were going to have an attack of the vapours."

"The Woke!" he laughed. "Nice pun. Always like a girl with a sense of humour." His middle finger stroked the back of her hand.

"Different spelling, love."

He thrilled at her term of affection.

"Where does it originate?"

"Oh, I suppose it's the same as 'Woakes' without the 's'. Medieval Germany, I believe. Something to do with collecting money from the peasants on behalf of the lord."

Her face was stone, and she looked at him fiercely.

"We always make sure people pay their dues. We always get our man."

Julian was befuddled, until she laughed uproariously.

"Got you!"

He threw his head back, and laughed until he cried.

"Tell you what's next. Prisons; punishment not luxury, and no remission for good behaviour. The unemployed; work gangs on minimum wage. Schools; any kid playing 'wag', or constantly arsing around, into state run re-education establishments, and they won't be holiday camps. Best of all, my DRC..."

"DRC?"

"Defence of the Realm Corps."

"The guys in brown uniforms?"

"Right. They're going to be everywhere. Drop a piece of litter and they'll give you what for; swear in public, and you'll get a good hiding on the spot. Putting right all those petty nuisances that annoy the shit out of ordinary everyday folk. Zero tolerance. I'll put common decency back into this nation, and I aint asking, I'm telling."

India was aghast, but hid her feelings. It wasn't that she approved of people who eschewed common civility, but she understood history. Ultimately, civilisation advanced through consent, not force.

"There's a rumour doing the rounds that your DRC had a hand in the death of the lady vicar in London. Lads off-duty."

It took a great deal of self-control on her part to fly this kite. Inside she wept at the loss of a friend she'd only just become acquainted with.

Julian threw a leg over one arm of his armchair.

"Guy Grosvenor's looking into it. Got the hallmarks of yobbos on the lash. Just the type I intend to sort out."

His blasé response infuriated. She masked her disgust by placing a hand over her mouth and yawning.

"Long day, Julian. Awful drive from Wilshire. If you'd excuse me, I'll hit the hay."

Before he could say anything, she pecked him on the cheek and strode from the room.

Within an hour the great house had settled into the lassitude that eventually overcomes weary revellers. Bedroom doors closed. The delight of peaceful slumber beckoned the carefree privileged. India leapt like a cat when her door handle rattled. She stood against the panel.

"Yes?"

"It's me, Julian."

A smile creased her face, and she was tempted to exclaim, "I'm ahead of you." Instead she unlocked the door, and retreated a few steps.

Julian wore a rather splendid dressing gown. A bottle of champagne and two glasses were thrust forth.

"Nightcap?"

"Lovely."

"Yes, you are..."

"Awfully sorry, Jules."

"About what?"

"I'm *hors de combat*."

A gormless look crossed his drunken features.

"Time of the month, love!"

"Ah...oh...yes..."

So, he wasn't that different from most men. Didn't know where to put himself.

"Lovely champers. Gosh! Want to look my best for you in the morning. So looking forward to the shoot. Sleep well. Sweet dreams."

She made sure that the lingering kiss on his cheek just caught the edge of his mouth.

"Night."

He was ushered out. She locked the door, and listened for thirty seconds until his footsteps faded.

"Out you come, Ken."

A puffing and trembling Ken Burke emerged from under the bed. His legs were so wobbly that he collapsed onto a stool.

"Bloody close shave!"

"Don't you worry yourself, my precious. All in hand. Carry on with what you were saying."

"Got rid of his woman, Fiona. Thick as thieves those two. She isn't a happy bunny, and she's big trouble. Some queer stories doing the rounds about her. Could put you off women."

"Like what?"

"Chap I know in security reckons she positively relishes hurting folk...and I mean badly. That bugger," he gestured toward the door, "has bequeathed her to me."

"You might come to like her, Ken."

"Not on your nelly."

"Thanks for the intel. Might come in useful. Disgruntled employee, and all that."

"Employee! Rogering each other senseless those two. Been at it for years."

"Oooh nice, pissed off lover. Suspect there'll be a few tales worth hearing. Stick close to her, my dearest. Now off you trot."

He hesitated.

"I say, couldn't give me a billet for the night, could you?"

India let her robe fall to the ground, and the old boy gulped as he glimpsed Nirvana through her diaphanous night dress.

"Ken, get a grip on yourself."

Power is sought in multiple shapes and sizes. That night more than one male sought to exercise his primitive wants. Hugo Melton, the *'Junior Minister for Lustful Enterprises'*, shook whilst he walked softly in the direction of Isa's bedroom. He'd been stunned when she accepted the weekend invitation.

His opening gambit had been,

"You'll get to meet the rich and powerful."

She was decidedly unimpressed, and his head drooped in anticipation of rejection.

"I'd love to come, Hugo. Thank you. It will be a wonderful opportunity for us to get to know each other better."

He wanted to drive her down from London, but she arrived by taxi on Friday afternoon. Hugo introduced her to his uncle. Julian recognised her immediately from the farce in Liverpool.

"You never told me it was her!"

Hugo shrank before Julian's fierce gaze.

"Sorry...sorry sir...didn't think..."

He eyed his nephew, and then relaxed. Frank had the girl on his list to check out. She wasn't a threat. He waved a hand.

"No sweat, son. I'm looking forward to a weekend of delights, why shouldn't you?"

Hugo was chock full of pride. Isa mingled with important guests during afternoon tea, and was a wonderful dinner companion. When the men took port, in the absence of the ladies, he got a ribbing.

"You're a sly old dog, Hugo." Sir Ken gave him a dig. "Got yourself a cracker there."

The gentlemen remarked upon her charming manners. Charles Fenwick's comment drew a chorus of "Hear, hear."

"Damn good listener. Could do with a few like her in the House."

When the dancing ended, Hugo sought out his Step-Uncle.

"Wanted to say thank you, sir."

Julian was organising his hands around a bottle of champagne and two glasses.

"Pleasure Hugo. Off to bed?"

"Yes sir."

The leering Prime Minister thrust his saturnine face into his nephew's and chuckled.

"Give her the high hard one for me!"

To his tremulous surprise her door was ajar.

"Come in Hugo."

He almost disgraced himself in the corridor.

She was staring out of the window.

"Come and look at the night sky, Hugo."

Speech would not come, so he stood beside her. Isa took his hand. He became lost in the myriad stars. Infinity lay before him, and for the first time in his life he felt humble.

"You're right, Hugo. We are insignificant in this vast universe. We come and we go. That..." she pointed to the heavens, "that lives on. Each of us has our purpose. A choice lies before us, like cards on a table. Will I choose to do good or evil with my life. The first is the narrow way of honour and duty; the second is dishonour and abandonment to selfish desires. See! The Moon."

They stood hand-in-hand staring at eternity. She looked at him, and he averted his eyes.

"Hugo, choose."

He lifted his head, a quizzical look on his features.

"Will you live in darkness, under the pale light of the Moon, or will you decide to come out into the day and be enriched by the living light of the Sun? I hope that we can be friends, Hugo – brother and sister."

Tears trickled down his cheeks, and she brushed them away with a finger. A memory surfaced. He saw his Mother leaning over his cot.

"Good night, and God bless you my darling."

When he woke, the next morning, he could not recall if he had said the words out loud.

Ken Burke padded stealthily along the corridor. It wasn't merely his head that drooped. Suddenly he heard familiar noises. They quite perked him up. The sounds emanated from two doors down. A lady, clearly in the throes of ecstasy, was having the time of her life. He looked up and down the corridor, furtively, and sank to his knees in front of the keyhole. My word! It was Lady Debs, naked as a Jaybird, bouncing up and down on some lucky chap's chopper.

"Not bad for her age," he muttered.

A great cry emerged from the man below, and she fell to one side.

"Well, well, well," he whispered under his breath. "Naughty mummy. Your boy won't like that."

He considered returning to India with the revelation, but decided it would keep until the morning. When he finally clambered into bed he followed India's advice. Ken took a firm grip upon himself.

It was fortunate that he decided not to retrace his steps. India also stood before her window. Her empty gaze did not disclose the turmoil of her feelings. Anna Wilbey was dead, and she mourned her grievously. Rare and fine human beings enter our lives infrequently. To have such a noble person as a friend, and then to lose her so suddenly was nigh unbearable. She sat before the dressing table mirror and studied herself. The image of that abominable man manifested itself over her shoulder. For a moment she shrank, thinking that he had somehow re-entered her room. The apparition faded. Fury boiled within her; first at herself, and then at Julian Marlborough. Now was not the time to waver. She would see this through to the bitter end. No matter the cost.

21

"The weak can defeat the strong in a case as just as mine."
'Oedipus at Colonus'

Arthur Cantwell opened the envelope. He had received it unopened. Anna Wilbey did not spare him. The massacre at St. George's Church, Banksmore was described in scarifying detail. The Prime Minister's subsequent assault upon the British people was something he knew about already. The paper hung limply in his hands, and as he wept he repeated over and over,

"Lord, have mercy, Christ, mercy, Lord, Have mercy."

The supplication was not for Anna. He knew with certainty that she had been welcomed by her Father in honour, joy and love. The Archbishop of Canterbury was pleading for forgiveness.

Arthur picked up his copy of The Guardian newspaper. He read again the conjecture that Anna, and her Albanian companion, had been murdered by off-duty members of the DRC. Even that rag, the Daily Mail, had expressed its unease. The Sun, as usual, came up with a corking headline:

"Dead Righteous & Christian

Julian Marlborough was castigated in the article. His denial that the auxiliary force had any part in Anna's death drew the comment,

"Pull the other one, it's got bells on!"

The Archbishop acted decisively.

"David, would you get the Dean of Westminster on the line, please?"

Whilst he waited he flapped the explosive letter up and down. He would need to secrete it somewhere. No-one else must know of its contents. Well, not just yet.

"Good morning Ingrid. Forgive me if I get down to business."

He outlined the proposal to his Archdeacon of yesteryear, and was relieved to receive her enthusiastic support.

"David, would you join me, please?"

The young man entered his superior's office.

"We have some planning to undertake, and we're short on time."

David made notes furiously.

"I think that will be all. Liaise with the Dean's office. I trust your judgement. Oh, one last thing. Please inform Canon Mortimer that I shall preach at Choral Evensong today. My apologies to whoever was rostered."

*

"He's done what?"

The Cabinet Secretary, Sir Robert Bruce, maintained his urbane demeanour.

"Funeral service and interment at Westminster Abbey, for both women."

Julian gnawed the end of his pen.

"Can I put a stop to this...legally?"

"Not a snowball's, sir."

"What?"

"Chance in Hell, sir."

Bob Bruce was rather enjoying himself. Good to see the arrogant bugger discomfited. He had dug into his boss' background. The chaps at the club were in concord when he remarked,

"*Parvenu!* No bottom."

His musings returned to the present.

"Right Bob, right. Press release. I will attend to honour the 'fallen'."

Sir Robert winced. The remark was tasteless, and dishonourable.

"Is that wise, sir?"

"Why shouldn't it be? The people will expect to see their Prime Minister in attendance. Look bloody odd if I wasn't there."

"You may wish to see this, sir."

A folded newspaper was handed across the table.

"The 'Canterbury Star', sir."

Julian studied the marked article. It was headed: *"Archbishop on Song."*

His face became thunderous as he read. Arthur Cantwell had preached with unaccustomed boldness and fervour, the reporter noted.

He praised immigrants for their contribution to the country; lauded social schemes to aid the poor and unemployed, and gave his "...unfettered support for SANITAS..." Arthur's closing remarks were for Christ's servant the Reverend Anna Wilbey, and her companion in death, the Albanian woman. He likened the loss of Anna to that of the Reverend Peter Standish in Banksmore; speaking of them as the victims of dark and unknown forces. When Julian read the Archbishop's closing injunction a shadow fell upon him.

"Be self-controlled and alert. Your enemy the devil prowls around like a roaring lion looking for someone to devour. Resist him, standing firm in the faith, because you know that your brothers throughout the world are undergoing the same kind of sufferings."

Brilliant winter sunlight streamed through the window. He heard Peter Standish intoning those very words. In the dust motes Julian saw the blade flashing in his hand. Machine gun fire deafened him. Above the noise he heard the voice of Giles Wentmore, in a country pub.

"...it could haunt you for the rest of your days."

"Are you alright, sir?"

"Yes, yes. Do you find it chilly in here?"

Bob Bruce cast a non-committal look. Julian tossed the newspaper back to him. He rested his elbows on the desk; hands propping up his chin. Malicious barbs about Arthur Cantwell were kept to himself.

"That decides it, Bob. I will be attending. On parade; bags of swagger."

*

SANITAS issued one post on social media, relating to Anna's funeral. No words, just a short video. It worked a treat. Thousands would imitate the solemn figure onscreen, after it went viral on Facebook and Twitter.

The car turned right out of Downing Street. The Cenotaph, that monument to the fallen in battle, loomed quickly. It is a short journey to Westminster Abbey. Julian cast a disinterested eye out of the window, then stiffened in his seat. The movement of the vast crowd resembled a Mexican wave. When the car came abreast of people they turned their backs on him. It rippled all the way down Parliament Street. Thousands turned from him in defiant rejection. He opened the car window a fraction, and was unnerved by the absolute silence.

The Dean of Westminster overcame her distaste, and managed not to forgo all the courtesies. She gave his hand a perfunctory shake, and indicated that he should follow a verger. Julian was glad to do so. He felt the power of hostility from thousands of eyes watching him. With haste he hurried after the official, entering the Abbey through the West Door. He skirted the tomb of the Unknown Warrior, and processed down the Nave. Surly looks didn't bother him. Julian was more alert to the fact that so many powerful people were ignoring his presence. He took his seat, and wished his Mother were with him. When he invited her she made excuses. Never in her life had Debs Marlborough declined so rich an offer.

Two simple coffins rested side by side. It took an effort of will to tear his eyes from them. They oppressed him with silent admonitions. A single trumpeter blew a short and solemn fanfare. The congregation rose. Julian stumbled after them. What the hell was going on? He faced resolutely forward. It was only when the person came into his peripheral vision that he was aghast. The Prince of Wales! Why hadn't he been told? He turned this way and that in search of a friendly face. Suddenly, he was distracted by four robed figures, high in gallery. Monks? What were they doing there? Perhaps it was something to do with the Albanian woman. He strained his eyes. No, they weren't monks. He could see wisps of long hair emerging from their hoods. The Dean's voice drew his attention, and he dismissed them from his mind. Probably some oddball group of bloody feminists.

The obsequies for the dead don't vary that much. It wasn't until the Archbishop of Canterbury took to the pulpit that the Prime Minister gave his full attention to proceedings.

"Woe to you Pharisees, because you give God a tenth of your mint, rue and all other kinds of garden herbs, but you neglect justice and the love of God. You should have practised the latter without leaving the former undone."

Arthur Cantwell was unrecognisable. Few recalled that his biography revealed an upbringing as a Methodist. His words thundered throughout the ancient Collegiate Church of St. Peter. With his beard, he resembled a grizzled old fisherman and patriarch.

"We must have law..."

An aroused congregation murmured.

"We must have law, but we must also have humanity. Our humanity is rooted in knowing that there is something greater than ourselves. If we obstinately refuse to acknowledge that truth, then we are consumed and tormented by the demon of Self. When we see ourselves as unaccountable to anyone we become Pharisees. The law becomes the law for its own sake, and it is inevitable that those in whose hands it resides will use it perversely; the end a justification for the means. The law becomes a weapon to impose self-will. It divides, instead of unifying."

The hot eyes of the recently disinterested fell upon Julian.

"Anna Wilbey was not one of those people. She was a Christian woman who embodied Christian values. No doubt she had her failings; in that she is no different than you and I. May God forgive me, there were times when I failed her. When she ran to the aid of Antigona Kreshnik, in that Christmas-decorated street, she did not know what the price would be. Only that there would be a reckoning. Anna founded the SANITAS movement. She, and her co-workers, created a garden of hope for those oppressed by poverty and injustice. It is fitting that her closest companions in mercy are present today to honour her."

Arthur raised an outstretched arm, and pointed to a gallery. Heads looked upwards. Three women pulled back their hoods. Julian seethed when the features of Abi Hussain, Fatima, and Isa were revealed. He muttered under his breath.

"That bloody child again. Turns up like a bad penny."

He would get Frank to hurry his enquiries along. Julian was so distracted that he forgot about the fourth figure, who remained hooded. Arthur continued his peroration.

"Anna Wilbey was, as we all should be, a servant of Christ in the pursuit of unity."

He paused, and his stern gaze looked down on the Prime Minister, and quoted Mark's Gospel.

"If a house is divided against itself, that house cannot stand. And if Satan opposes himself and is divided, he cannot stand; his end is come."

Arthur's composure forsook him, and he wiped a tear on his stole. He descended from the pulpit, to stand between the coffins. A hand was placed on each casket.

"We honour Anna and Antigona by remembering their sacrifice."

His hands rose heavenward to reveal the sprigs he was holding.

"Rue, for remembrance!" He placed a sprig on each coffin.

Julian stood with everyone else. The pall bearers carried the coffins down the aisle. A man wearing the uniform of a Chief Constable walked behind Anna. David Wilbey bore himself with dignity, but could not resist the impulse to cast a look of disdain upon the Prime Minister. There was the man who had destroyed the lives of his wife and daughter, and distorted the life of his Late-Father-in-Law.

The Prime Minister joined the procession. It was slow-moving, and he craved a drink. His eyes looked up to the gallery for the women. Only one remained. Slowly she peeled back her hood, and Julian's face was ashen. It couldn't possibly be. He shook his head, then looked again. Gone, she was gone. He had no time for ghosts and ghouls. How, how?

The Prince of Wales stood close by the Unknown Warrior, in conversation with David Wilbey. He shook his hand, as Julian drew closer.

"Suppose I'll have to speak to the boy," he thought, and stretched out his hand.

The heir to the throne wheeled about face and walked away. The snub did not go unnoticed.

"Prime Minister! Sir...sir."

"What is it Guy?"

Guy Grosvenor handed him a piece of paper.

"Take me to the Palace, Guy."

*

A curt, "Prime Minister," issued from the Monarch's lips. Julian was not invited to sit.

"Your Majesty. It is not customary to summon the Prime Minister in such a peremptory manner."

No point in arsing around. They disliked each other intensely.

"I would say that your manner of speech surprises me, Prime Minister, but it does not. Neither is it *de rigeur* to address your Sovereign in so peremptory a fashion."

Julian admired him for a moment. The gloves had come off *tout suite*.

"May I remind you, sir, that yours is the position of Constitutional Monarch. I am the elected representative of the people, and my authority comes from their voice. Affairs of state are always pressing. Power brings with it responsibility, and..."

"Quite so, Prime Minister. That is my purpose in granting you an audience. I watched the funeral service on the television and observed the reaction to you as your motorcade progressed. Your reception inside was hardly warmer. Perhaps you may like to reflect that the *'voice of the people'* can remove that power as swiftly as it grants it."

The King's next words threw him off-balance.

"I recognised the three ladies in the gallery from your debacle in Liverpool. Who was the fourth?"

"I...I've no idea, sir. Presumably, another friend within the rather troublesome SANITAS body..."

"You think them troublesome, Prime Minister?"

Julian became agitated.

"What is it you want from me, sir?"

The King rose from his seat, and strolled to a window, keeping his back to the P.M.

"We are deeply troubled, Prime Minister, by the direction in which the country is being taken – I won't say led, because I think that it is a catastrophic failure of leadership."

Disdain dribbled from Julian.

"You are entitled to your viewpoint, sir, as is the meanest citizen. I am charged with the redemption of this country from the social disaster it has become throughout your reign."

"You see yourself as a redeemer. Do you bring salvation? You certainly exhibit Messianic zeal."

Julian ignored the sarcasm.

"Thank you, your Majesty."

"It was not a compliment, sir! This Defence Corp you have created. Disband it, man. My advisers tell me that they are little more than thugs, terrorising the public. The Scots are already on the verge of revolt, thanks to their reprehensible behaviour in Glasgow and Edinburgh."

"The responsibility for order and civil behaviour in the nation rests on my shoulders. The police are overstretched, and hindered by laws which I intend to change. I assume you do not wish me to employ the military on our streets, again! The Defence of the Realm Corps is a well-regulated body which, in due course, may no longer be required. For now, they are essential to the re-establishment of good citizenship. Is there anything else I can help you with, sir?"

The King examined him intently.

"I'm told you're a man of the theatre, Prime Minister."

"A passion since childhood, sir..."

"...civil blood makes civil hands unclean..."

"*Romeo and Juliet*, your Majesty. Fond memories. I portrayed the eponymous chap at school."

"Not to be taken lightly, then. Good day, Prime Minister."

When Julian gave a nod of the head he had an afterthought.

"Oh sir! It is customary for my office to be informed when a Royal personage will be in attendance..."

"You refer to the Prince of Wales' presence at the Abbey?"

"Indeed sir. Your family has been adroit at avoiding the tainted ground of politics. It would be unwise to consider involvement now..."

He waved aside the footman who had entered discreetly, and held the door for him.

"...and sir. The young man's public snub. How can I put this? It was most uncivil!"

Shuttered in his car, Julian made a short telephone call on his decidedly unofficial mobile.

"Frank. Sunday morning, please."

22

"Time, which sees all things, has found you out."
'Oedipus Rex'

Edith Wharton wrote wisely about life in the country.

"...but these backwaters of existence sometimes breed, in their sluggish depths, strange acuities of emotion..."

Frank stood mesmerised before the Prime Minister.

Since childhood he had been blessed with an eye for beauty. The previous evening, he and Sylvia had taken their son, Frank Jr., to his first performance at the Royal Shakespeare Theatre, Stratford-Upon-Avon. It was Sunday morning, and Frank rode his motorcycle a shorter distance than usual to Saintbury in Gloucestershire. He reflected upon the dismal performance of *'Twelfth Night'*. The RSC up to its usual trick. Theatrical gewgaws for the tourists, and the secular luvvies who *'just adore a likkle bit of theatre'*; no discrimination. Shakespeare's wonders torpedoed by glitzy tech and inexperienced young actors. Frank acknowledged inwardly his lifelong problem. When beauty was absent he saw, with equal clarity, ugliness and danger.

"What would you say, Frank, if I gave the UK back to Rome?"

"I'm sorry..."

"You're a left-footer, aren't you? Let his Holiness rule the roost. It's in my gift."

Frank was rooted to the spot. With perfect vision he recognised the madman sitting in front of him.

"For God's sake man, sit down and have a bacon buttie and another cuppa."

Cautiously, Frank lowered himself onto a chair, and refilled his mug from the pot on the kitchen table.

"Time for the gloves to come off. We've been tinkering so far..."

"...but how could you..."

"History, Frank, read your history. Nothing is immutable. I don't give a fart who runs the religious show. Faith is nothing to me; not one jot of belief for the Tooth Fairy. Take that farce at the Abbey the other day. The Church of England out in force, with a cast big enough for a West End musical, all dolled up in gorgeous finery. Salvation by haberdashery! About as much use as a pork pie at a Jewish wedding. Much prefer your gang who enforce discipline. Now listen, Frank, you're my man body and soul. Listen."

Julian unfurled his inglorious and dishonourable past, without omission. Fatima and Abir Hussain, Billy Conway and Charlotte cum Angela – even Cesar Marinescu got a mention. His peroration ended on Christmas Eve in St. George's Church, Banksmore.

Frank was motionless. His face did not betray the putrid emotions he felt.

"Three women, dangerous to the well-being of the State. Find them, Frank, and deal with them. Time you accessed their computer system as well. Getting a bit irritated by the lack of progress."

His eyes burned into Frank. Soul mate or no, he expected results.

"I want *'Operation Round-Up'* brought forward to next week. Knock some sense into these layabouts. Get them ready for your priests, eh Frank?"

Julian rose, and walked around the table. He gripped Frank's shoulders.

"Don't let me down, Frank. Let's keep our eyes on the prize...brother!"

Frank rode the Vincent Black Shadow as sedately as ever. It had been towed on a trailer behind their motorhome, from Lymington to Stratford. Road signs for Evesham caught his attention. He needed time to compose himself before re-joining his family.

The 'bike growled to a halt on the outdoor top storey of the car park, behind the Riverside Shopping Centre. Frank removed his helmet and examined the sky. Winter clouds scudded, and he thought that they truly *"...lour'd upon* our *house."* Glancing to his left, he half-expected to see Richard 'Crookback' scuttling across the sloping lawns. The view revealed a magnificent war memorial, its curved shape resembled the Royal Crescent in Bath.

He meandered down a tarmacked slope, and turned right. The Bell Tower of Evesham Abbey rose colossus-like before him. The edifice was all that remained from Henry VIII's desecration of the Abbey during that period known as *'The Dissolution of the Monasteries'*. Another tyrant imposing his will.

His attention was captured by a low-lying monument to his left. Frank walked gingerly across the wet lawn. The altar-like memorial was to Simon de Montfort, 6th Earl of Leicester. Despite what Julian may have thought, Frank knew his history. The 13th Century aristocrat was regarded as one of the progenitors of modern parliamentary democracy. His track record also included anti-Semitism, and Frank recalled the part the Earl played in vicious pogroms.

When he looked down the slope he saw the River Avon, burbling and full-bellied from the winter rains. Shame and guilt overcame him like a flood tide. A flash of lightning rent the sky, and distant thunder shook his composure. Without warning, lashing rain tore the heavens open. Frank shivered uncontrollably. The River Avon seemed to be a torrent. The apparition of endless bodies spewing forth on to the drowning banks assaulted his bloodless face. Widespread arms were raised to the morbid sky. Only he could hear his voice shouting above the storm.

"What have I done? What have I done?"

It was the cry of the penitent, seeking forgiveness and redemption. Bodies tumbled from the sky upon his head, as he sank to his knees in supplication.

"Are you alright, lovey?"

The elderly lady was protected against the elements in heavy oilskins. He saw that she had multiple layers beneath. Over her shoulder he caught sight of a sleeping bag, and half-a-dozen bulging plastic bags lying on the war memorial. She was homeless.

"Come on, lovey, let's get you on your feet. You'll catch your death down there. Are you lost?"

Gall twisted Frank's features; indeed, he was.

"Is there a church nearby?"

"You've a couple to choose from behind the Bell Tower."

"Are they Roman Catholic?"

"Oh, you want St. Mary's and St. Egwin's, over there my love in the High Street. Go and get yourself warm."

Tears pricked his eyes at the unsolicited love and compassion being showered upon him, by one whose life was immeasurably harder than his. He fumbled for his wallet, and thrust a twenty-pound note into her hand. Then he fled. Frank sprinted as if the Devil himself were behind him, and his boots threw divots into the air.

*

"Guy."

"Mmm?"

"Is it alright to say I love you?"

Guy Grosvenor's powerful arm pulled her to him. She found it difficult to meet his eyes. There it was, she'd gone and said it, and she felt foolish. How could this man, in the prime of life, love a seventy-year old woman?

"Hey, look at me."

Deborah Marlborough had never been shy in her life, but now her face was beset with vulnerability.

"This," he patted the bed they were lying in, "this is wonderful, but it's not everything. I love you Debs. There's something that makes it even bigger and better, I like you."

"Then...then our age difference..."

"Doesn't matter. You're smart, you're funny, and beneath the armour you're kind."

Tears wet her cheeks, and Guy reached for a tissue. He wiped them from her face one by one. Then he kissed the tissue.

She laughed.

"You big softie. How can the Head of Counter Terrorism be such a softie?"

He looked at her sternly.

"I'm no softie, have a feel."

Debs hand went under the duvet.

"Oooh!"

He rolled her over, and they melded in companionship.

Guy went for his usual run, and arranged to meet Debs at the Church. She was on flower arranging duty. He was eager to visit the infamous St. George's so he upped his pace.

The four rows of graves startled him. They resembled a military cemetery, and their newness shone. In the bright sunshine of a matchless January morning an elderly man was kneeling before a grave; oblivious to the hardened and frosted ground. Tenderly, he eased the sparse weeds from the mass of snowdrops. Guy opened the gate quietly, and padded stealthily down the path. He was moved by the sight of the old boy, and didn't want to disturb his communion.

"Good morning!"

The gentleman stood upright, a garden fork in his hand.

"Lovely morning. Been out for a jog?"

Guy's running gear made that self-evident. The man had a lugubrious smile. His features were sad, but welcoming. He clearly wanted someone to chat with, so Guy strolled toward him.

"Yes indeed. Try to keep in trim."

They looked at the gravestone.

"My late wife, Wendy. I am sorry, Derek, Derek Fisher." He extended his hand.

"Guy."

"She was murdered in there, along with the rest of them. Are you another sightseer? No bloody end to them. More people in that place at weekends than there ever was at Sunday service."

"No, no. I'm visiting a friend."

Derek did not appear to hear the reply. He was on his knees, tracing his hand across his wife's name; carved into cold and unyielding stone.

"Bloody funny business," he muttered.

"What is?"

"Help me up, would you Guy. Thank you."

"Forgive me asking, but weren't you with," he looked at the inscription on the grave, "Wendy when it happened?"

Derek eyed him, as if he were soft in the head.

"Not likely is it, when there weren't any survivors. Mind you, I'm not convinced of that."

"Really?"

Guy was alert, and in professional mode.

"Forgive *me*, Guy. Used to be ratarsed most nights, not now. Probably seeing things."

"Shadows?" Guy prompted and prodded.

"Exactly old son. Shadows flitting." Derek became excited. "Wendy wasn't best pleased with me. She stomped off to Midnight Communion alone – last time I saw her. Lord knows what the time was, but I came out of my stupor and went to close the curtains. I live just there, right opposite the Church. Could swear I saw three or four people running like bats out of hell just over there. That's where the West door is; leads from the Vestry. Well, had another sharpener and fell asleep again. Next thing I know is bells and sirens going off everywhere."

The old man paused, deep in his memories.

"Odd, bloody odd I'm telling you."

"What was?"

"Got me coat on, and stumbled outside. Cold night. Rozzers had it all taped off, nobody could get near the place."

Derek tapped the side of his nose, adopting a crafty expression.

"Except me! Know the lie of the land, and sidled into the Rectory garden. Hid in the trees, and watched."

Guy contained his emotions. This was fascinating, and he wanted to hear more.

"Smart move, sir."

The old fellow basked in the praise.

"First thing I see is well-dressed man in civvies drive up. Takes command, and the police retreat. Left them with crowd control. Had a bit of team with him, this feller. From then on, only him and his blokes entered the church. Big chap, not dissimilar to you."

Guy was fairly certain that he knew the man identified by Derek.

"That was the end of it then?"

"Not on your Nelly! They start demolishing the wall – just there – then an ambulance arrives and reverses through the opening. Almost up to the porch, but not quite. Odd, bloody odd..."

Guy held his breath.

"Why would you be taking bodies *into* the church?"

He couldn't help himself; he was so startled.

"What!"

"The bloody paramedics were taking bodies from the ambulance into the building. Mind you, suppose I could be mistaken. Was three sheets to the wind, and worried about Wendy."

Silence dwelt upon them. From the distance there came the squeal of an animal in its death throes. When it stopped, a fox barked.

"Dark night and alcohol combined. Not always conducive to clarity."

"Humph! One thing crystal clear was that bugger, sitting on the Whitlock family tomb."

Guy raised a quizzical eyebrow.

"Marlborough, Julian bloody Marlborough. Now he's Prime Minister, and we're going to hell in a handcart. Wouldn't trust him as far as I can spit."

Derek became animated.

"Tell me this, Guy. How does one disarm machine gun toting terrorists, and save yourself and mummy, when they've already blasted sixty people to Hell? God in Heaven, we all know he was SA bloody S, but Superman he aint."

The chill of the winter's morning bit into Guy's flimsy running apparel. It became colder at the mention of Debs.

"His mother was with him?"

"When isn't she?" he laughed. "Been wet nursing the bugger all his life. I'll tell you this for nothing, Guy. Once upon a time I was the CEO of...", and he mentioned a name which impressed his listener. "Faced down some hard men in my time, but none like Debs Marlborough at PCC meetings."

"PCC?"

"Parochial Church Council. That woman could have your trousers down, and whip your nuts off before you'd time to shout 'Geronimo'. Nice to meet you Guy, hope you enjoy your weekend. Forgive an old man blethering on. Cheerio."

Guy watched him walk to his cottage. When Derek disappeared, he moved pensively towards the porch. He paused to examine the Whitlock tomb, which Derek had indicated. Nothing to see. Stiffening his shoulders, and subduing his troubled thoughts, he entered the porch. He paused, to look back at the smoke rising from Derek's chimney. Pity about the demise of Giles Wentmore. He would have liked to chew the fat with him.

Half an hour later Derek stood at the window, his one beer of the day in hand. The glass froze in mid-air. That chap, Guy, was coming down the path beside Debs Marlborough. He took a glug, and reflected that they'd probably got chatting to each other in the church. Derek had exchanged a brief word with her before she'd gone in, her arms full of flowers. When he saw Guy get into the driving seat of her Range Rover he changed his mind. Derek recollected an old saying his first boss had taught him, over half a century ago.

"Be careful who you vent to. A listening ear is also a running mouth."

The remainder of his beer went down in one. He positively sprinted to the 'fridge' for a second.

*

It would have been more sensible to make the journey by car. Frank would have none of it, and Sylvia knew better than to argue. Lymington into South-West Wiltshire is a short commute, but the snows made it a more arduous trek than usual on the Black Shadow.

The noble spire of Salisbury Cathedral hove into view. Frank fought to keep disturbing thoughts at bay; now they crowded his mind. He had unburdened himself to the priest, leaving nothing unsaid. The old man remained silent for a long time, in his half of the Confession Box. Then he spoke with shocking intensity.

"If I were not a priest I would not believe the enormity of what you have confessed. I believe you. In due course I will give you your penance. I do not know what power you possess, but you must move heaven and earth to put a stop to these crimes. Personal penance goes hand-in-hand with personal action. You know that you have imperilled your immortal soul, but God does not reject you; He loves you and seeks your repentance. Go from this place, and exchange evil for good...pay the price."

Frank chewed over the problem, and decided to follow his hunch. The Prime Minister's aggravation, at not uncovering the source of SANITAS' computer system, gave grim satisfaction. Frank's people had narrowed down the location to the Dorset/Wiltshire border; then he took over. His background was military intelligence, and he adopted lateral thinking. A voluntary outfit, like SANITAS, could never access, let alone afford, the sophisticated equipment and expertise to make them untraceable. Somebody with connections was helping them. He scrolled his way around Google Earth. Wiltshire, yes Wiltshire. A county almost given over to the Army, and lots of big-wigs had their retirement homes close to former glories. Oddly, it was an incident with Frank Jr. that set him on his cold motorbike ride. He heard the boy scream in the middle of the night, and rushed to his room.

"Hush my boy, hush. Everything is alright."

He stroked his son's hair, and held him in a tight embrace.

"Just a bad dream, son. All gone."

When the boy spoke Frank's mind was elsewhere. He was thinking of the impending *'Operation Round-Up'*. In his imagination Frank Jr. was taken from him. Without warning he was transported to the entrance hall of Chequers. Whilst waiting to be ushered into Julian's office, he surreptitiously examined mail lying open on a salver. It was all social stuff; invitations and thank you notes.

"What did you say?"

"I said, 'I'm glad I woke up.'"

"Say it again."

"I'm glad I woke, Daddy, it was an awful dream."

Frank kissed his son.

"Everything better now. I'll stay a while. Off to sleep."

He tucked the boy in, and went to the window. Peering through a crack in the curtains, he could see that dawn was near. Then he was at Chequers once more. On the salver a short note.

"Dearest Jules, thank you for a wonderful weekend. Keep in touch. Hope to see you soon, India."

Falling snowflakes coalesced into a sheet of pristine white paper, marked with India's elegant hand. Frank went to the bedside, intent on promising his boy that they would build a snowman. Frank Jr. was fast asleep. He kissed the lad, and hurried to his office.

The census glowed brightly on the computer screen. He risked a mirthless laugh. Of course, of course, she'd been a teenager when their paths had crossed. You don't meet many gals named 'India'. The rest of the census page confirmed his supposition. It might be a red herring, but too many threads were weaving in close proximity to one another. Frank Jr.'s snowman would have to wait. Dad must make a speculative journey.

The door was opened by a beautiful Asian lady. Frank knew his expedition was not in vain.

"Awfully sorry to trouble you. My motorcycle is running short on fuel. Is there a petrol station nearby?"

A grey head poked itself over Abi Hussain's shoulder. The trace of a Scouse accent steamed on the freezing air.

"Nearest one's six miles away."

"Heck! Don't think I'll make it that far."

"No sweat, mate. We keep fuel on the farm."

"I'll pay..."

"Yeh, yeh. Come in a minute, and let's get this door shut."

Frank was ushered into the kitchen. The other two women were sitting at the large table peeling vegetables. An older woman was at the Aga, with her back to him. Paul Baxter addressed the unexpected guest.

"Come far, mate?"

"Southampton."

"Fancy a brew? Marion, we can spare a brew for...what's your name, mate?"

"Frank."

"I'm Paul, and that's my wife Sam. These two gals are..."

Shrieking childish laughter drowned Paul, and two little girls burst into the room, pursued by two older men. Lucy Baxter buried herself in her mother, and Jenny Wilbey was swept off her feet exclaiming, "Grandad!"

"Sugar's on the table, Frank."

"Thank you...Mrs. Woake."

The women presented a still life, and stared at their visitor. Marion and Paul looked puzzled.

"Good morning, Brigadier. The boys maintained their usual high standards. It's been the Devil's-own-job to locate your computer system."

Archie Woake wasn't often lost for words.

"My word! J..."

"Frank Steen, sir. Major Frank Steen."

A trip switch flicked, and Archie's brain was illuminated. He strode across the flagstones, hand extended.

"Good Lord! Frank Steen. You remember him Marion. Always cadging drinks from us in Cyprus."

He pumped his hand furiously. Paul Baxter interrupted the love-fest.

"Why have you been trying to track us down?"

Archie was all eagerness.

"Indeed, indeed. Still working for the 'firm', Frank?"

Warm tea always gave Frank the sense that he was in the right place. It was home, the place he loved best.

"Oh no, Paul. I've orders to kill these three ladies!"

Marion let a mug slip from her hand. It hit the flagstones like the crack of doom, echoing in a mountain pass.

"That would be unwise!"

The voice seemed to come from the same emptiness. Its owner took form, as she emerged from the large pantry. A double-barrelled shotgun proceeded her.

"Hello India. Haven't seen you since you were fifteen. Do you still ride?"

India's face was granite, and her hand was steady.

"We have...we all have...a mutual friend."

Sam Baxter filled the silence.

"Julian Marlborough."

"Just so, Sam, or is it Charlotte or Angela?"

Paul Baxter took a threatening step towards him.

"Steady on Paul, or perhaps you'd prefer Billy. He briefed me on you, but we weren't sure you'd made it out of the church."

Agitation rose in the room, so Frank stifled it with his confession.

"I said I'd been ordered to erase you, not that I intend to carry out the command." He sank onto a chair, and all the vim and vigour went out of him. "I work...I worked for him, but I was never on his side. God forgive me, I've only just realised that. Now I am against him. I oppose him with all of my will, and all of my strength." Frank trembled.

"Marion darling. Would you occupy the children elsewhere, please? India, put that bloody thing down. There's a bottle of scotch in that cupboard, David. Frank and I will have a large one each, do help yourself."

In a trice they became aware of their shared knowledge. When Frank told them something they didn't know they were chastened and horrified.

"The Defence of the Realm Corp has its own command structure, like any other military or paramilitary organisation. I am its Civilian Head, but that is not common knowledge. I can't put a stop to what's about to happen, but with your help we might be able to lessen its impact. *Operation Round-Up'* will start at six a.m. a week on Monday. We must put our heads together, and use social media to place the public on stand-by. The main point to impress upon them is that passive resistance is the only course. If they try to fight, there will be a bloodbath."

Jenny Wilbey's grandpa refilled the glasses.

"May I make a contribution, Frank?"

Chief Constable David Wilbey proceeded to outline his thoughts.

23

"There was the girl, screaming like an angry bird,
When it finds its nest empty and little ones gone."
'Antigone'

"You aint takin' 'er!"

The angry bellowing was repeated across the United Kingdom. Notices were issued on doorsteps, and immediate compliance was required. Armed DRC snatch squads stood by, ready to intervene at the first refusal. The police force was tasked with confronting the parents.

*

Facebook had been ablaze with the revelation. *'Operation Round-Up'* would take into custody all children under the age of eighteen, who were troublemakers in their communities and beyond. Education and social service records were trawled under the guise of statistical analysis. Lists were compiled throughout the previous year. Julian created a perverse 'Doomsday Book'. Court jester, Ken Burke, came up with the soubriquet, adding,

"All you've done, Julian, is exchange a pair of vowels."

The guvnor gave vent to howling laughter.

"Priceless Ken, priceless. I've told you all before, listen to Ken. Mind like a steel trap."

Members of the Cabinet hee-hawed in sycophantic appreciation.

The disquiet and outrage generated on social media prompted the P.M. to listen to his advisors, for once. So it was that on the previous Thursday evening he found himself in the BBC studios in Salford. To his delight they had dredged out of retirement a once ferocious interviewer, famed for his put-downs and sarcasm. Julian silenced him at the first interruption.

"That's just the sort of incivility I intend to crack down on, Mr. Paxton. It ill- behoves a public servant, and may I remind you that you are working for a public broadcaster, to address a guest in so rude and ill-mannered a fashion..."

"I..."

"No you may not, sir. I am elected by the people, and answerable to them. You are part of, what many see as, a self-serving clique. This interview will proceed in a civil manner, or it will not proceed at all."

The old man's best days were long past. He acquiesced, and settled for being a *'national treasure'*.

"We are set upon this course, Mr. Paxton, because of the multi-generational failure of parents, teachers, social services, and the judicial system to reform anti-social elements effectively."

Julian became animated.

"It's well-known, Andrew, that I am a devotee of theatre and the arts. I recall a line from a play I performed in at school. Gosh, they were golden years, when I didn't have to bear responsibilities."

The studio audience laughed in appreciation, and returned his winning smile.

"Liverpool playwright, I think it was. A piece about disadvantaged children on a school trip."

He sat on the edge of his seat.

"A big lad, nothing but trouble all day, until one teacher could put up with it no longer. His colleague says, *"Why don't you just have a werd with him?"* Problem I intend to solve, in a nutshell."

Audience and Presenter sat in mystified silence. Julian smiled.

"Let me explain. Having a *'werd'* does no good with some people. You can talk to them until you're blue in the face. Action, that's what's required."

Andrew Paxton cleared his throat.

"May I ask, Prime Minister, what form this action will take?"

"Certainly Andrew. In the last twelve months we have built detention centres in remote country environments. These disadvantaged and troubled children will be removed from their homes, and rehoused in splendid accommodation. There they will follow a regime which will transform them into model citizens."

"Boot camps!"

"My goodness, Andrew, you do lead with your chin. Not at all. Full educational facilities will be provided, good food, nice rooms, and the opportunity to engage in a host of activities."

Some of the feisty old Andrew surfaced, and his voice had an edge.

"I fail to see, Prime Minister, how that alone is going to transform the lives of the volatile and intransigent youths you intend to detain."

"Discipline Andrew..."

"Yes, but that's been tried..."

"Bear with me. On arrival at their new homes our guests will be assembled. Each will receive a set of rules in plain English. For those whose literacy is challenged, they will be read out. That's it!"

"What's it?"

"You've been told the rules. If you break them you do so wilfully, and you will be punished. No second chances; no third-rate teachers saying, *"If you do that again I'll have to do something about it."* On your own head be it."

"Short, sharp shock?"

"Andrew, Andrew, nothing short about it at all. Hammered home until they learn."

"What happens with those who won't learn?"

"Indefinite detention."

Julian addressed the audience directly, his eyes afire with certainty.

"Just think. No more mayhem in the classroom holding back the good kids. An end to foul-mouthed aggression on our streets, fuelled by drink and drugs. Bad neighbours making your life a misery? A thing of the past. Children reformed, so that they don't enter adult life as feckless and idle good-for-nothings; a lifelong drain on your taxes. Civility! A return to the *'Golden Age of Civility'* and civic duty."

Studio and television audiences alike were mesmerised by his passion and eloquence. Then the spell broke. To a man and woman, the studio rose, applauding and cheering Julian's vision. The scene was repeated in homes across the nation.

Andrew Paxton's education included Cambridge University. He sat still, and reflected upon the words of H. L. Mencken:

"The demagogue is one who preaches doctrines he knows to be untrue to men he knows to be idiots."

Had Julian been party to his musings he would not have been displeased. After all, the American polymath had been an opponent of representative democracy. Mencken viewed it as a system in which inferior men dominated their superiors.

*

Six hours passed before all the coaches had deposited the children at the new Bodmin Moor facility in Cornwall. Four hundred inmates were bedded into their new quarters. Now they assembled in the Refectory. Julian insisted that name be used in all centres. It reminded him of schooldays, and anyway it was more appropriate than dining room. Before evening meal was served the children underwent their first course of instruction. A severe lady demonstrated to all four hundred the correct way to use their knife, fork and spoon.

"You will apply what you have learnt at all meals. Take your trays, and line up for your food."

Forty children at a time took their trays to the serving hatches, watched by a dozen DRC men lining the walls.

Jermaine Wilson had imbibed a combination of indulgence and neglect from the moment he could crawl. At seventeen-years of age he was a large and muscular lump of violent and abusive trouble. He was in the fourth batch to collect their food. A wholesome meal of beef stew, mashed potatoes and vegetables filled each plate.

"What's this shit? I aint eatin' this fuckin' crap. Why can't we 'ave chips 'n' a burger?"

Jermaine was too busy eyeballing the serving lady to see it coming. A baton fell across his wrists, and food flew everywhere. He screamed in pain.

"My wrist, you've broken my wrist, cunt. I'm gonna report you!"

The fist struck his face, and dropped him to the floor. The burly DRC man towered over him.

"Who? Who are you going to report me to, sonny? Get up!"

The seething Jermaine came to his feet painfully.

"Now, pick up the tray, the broken plate, and the food..."

"Fuck off!"

The blow to his stomach cut him in half. Hands grabbed him, twisting his arms behind his back while he screamed in pain from his fractured wrist. The two paramilitaries ran him at the swing doors, using his head to part them.

Behind them, their colleagues stood with batons drawn shouting at the assembly.

"Outside! Outside, by table number. One, two, three...Go, go!"

More than one child under the age of ten left a puddle on the floor.

When they were lined up in trembling ranks they saw Jermaine dragged forward. The parade ground had a flagstaff, with the cross of St. George flying. Beneath it stood a piece of World War One artillery. The Commandant emerged from the administrative building with his adjutant.

"No. 1 Field Punishment, sergeant."

Jermaine was handcuffed to a gun wheel, in the crucifix position.

"Carry on, sergeant. Twelve strokes."

A knife shredded Jermaine's trousers. His bare backside was exposed to the winter elements. The cane thrashed him at a steady rhythm. When he was released he faced the ranks, undecided whether to cover his genitals, or smear away the tears from his cheeks. Without warning a hose blasted freezing water, and drove him to his knees. It poured upon him for ten minutes.

"That's enough."

Commandant Christopher Iverson's look menaced the other three hundred and ninety-nine children.

"For self-inflicted damage to his uniform the miscreant will lose fifty per-cent of his weekly allowance until paid for. Mr. Ganson, get them back inside. All food to be eaten, no waste."

It would have been small comfort to Jermaine to know that not dissimilar scenes had occurred nationwide. Spot the biggest troublemaker, and make an example of him.

*

A greater surprise shattered the serene demeanour of Lady Deborah Marlborough. Assistant Chief Constable Simon Reynolds of the Buckinghamshire Constabulary stood in her reception room.

"Lady Marlborough, you are to be detained for questioning relating to enquiries into acts of terrorism in St. George's Church, Banksmore on December 24th..."

Her outrage cut him off, but did not perturb him one bit. Chief Constable David Wilbey had taken Simon into his confidence. The man who had come through so much with the Khans, and who had stood in that sacred space with butchery all around him, was content to do his duty.

"We keep her away from her 'brief' as long as possible, Simon."

Deborah Marlborough was processed and held in a cell for an hour, before being taken to an interview room. The only officers present were Wilbey and Reynolds.

"You do know that you're both finished. When my son hears about..."

"We will make sure that he hears, madam."

David Wilbey's eyes never left the face of the woman who had given birth to the killer of his family, and countless others.

Simon Reynolds smiled, and spoke disarmingly.

"Would you describe for us the death of your husband, please?"

Debs was taken aback. She had expected to be asked about Julian, or the blameless young men he had cut down, along with the congregation.

"Let me help you. Was Sir Hugh the first to die?"

"Yes, yes he was."

She felt herself to be on safe ground, because it was true. That son had shot father she would never reveal. The next question puzzled her.

"Marjorie Whitlock. You recall Marjorie, your Ladyship? How did she die?"

Debs had steel in her blood. She was collecting herself now, and she was smart enough to blend truth and fiction.

"Like the others, they shot her down. In fact, they killed my dear husband first, and Marjorie was the last. You know, they made her play the organ throughout their massacre of the congregation." She withdrew a pretty handkerchief from her sleeve, and dabbed her eyes. "So many dear, dear friends lost."

Reynolds was a picture of sympathy.

"Take your time Deborah. It must be very distressing for you to relive those dreadful events."

She overlooked his impertinence at using her Christian name.

"It is, it is," she gulped. "I can't conceive how I can be of any use to you. Wasn't this all cut and dried? We know who the culprits were."

“One more question, Deborah, and then we can drive you home. What sort of weapon was used to shoot Miss Whitlock and your husband?”

She adopted a surprised and innocent look.

“Why, the same as with all the others. Some sort of machine gun, so my son informed me in the aftermath. He’s a decorated soldier you know, as well as being our current Prime Minister.”

David Wilbey permitted himself a razor sharp smile, but remained silent. Simon Reynolds shook his head, as if bewildered.

“What is it Mr. Reynolds? Something seems to puzzle you. I assure you, this was dealt with most efficiently at the time by gentlemen from the security services.” For good measure, she name-dropped again. “Or so the Prime Minister told me.”

“You see, Deborah...there’s a discrepancy.”

She was alarmed. How could two provincial police officers, however high-ranking, know any different to what was stage-managed way back when?

“We have been able to ascertain that Sir Hugh and Marjorie were shot using the same pistol. Forensic evidence showed it to be of a type issued to British military personnel of...how shall we say...a distinct regimental hue.”

David Wilbey chuckled. He thought it a most delightful pun on her Late-husband’s name. It was not intentional on his assistant’s part. David spoke.

“Thank you Lady Marlborough. We need detain you no longer. My profound apologies for the inconvenience.”

She took his proffered hand, and he ushered her through the door to the waiting policewoman.

"Why aren't we blowing this entire affair apart, David? Go public with the lot."

"Simon, he has the whole apparatus of the State at his fingertips. Not to mention that his popularity is sky high in the country..."

"A great deal of the population is dead set against him."

"You're right Simon, you're right, but they're largely the educated; the polite middle class. I'm going to tell you something, strictly *entre nous*. This country has a fissure running through it, and the mob is on his side, not ours. There is a small, and discreet, body of Chief Constables which maintains communication. We monitor the temper of the country; all points of the compass. I say a small group, because not every colleague shares our view. There's a big enough powder keg already. If we move against Marlborough too precipitously it could blow up in everyone's faces. No, softly, softly catchee monkee."

"He'll be furious when he hears that we hauled mummy over the coals."

David Wilbey laughed heartily.

"Oh, I do hope so...I do hope so. No doubt our *'eyes and ears'* will inform us, in due course."

*

"Frank is my Cromwell, Ken. He stalks the land setting right the wrongs inflicted upon my person."

Julian's orotund assertion witnessed to his spiralling hubris. Both men recognised the sign.

"Oliver or Thomas, Prime Minister?"

"Most definitely the latter, Kenneth. You mustn't mind old Ken." He addressed Frank Steen. "He's as discreet as a clam, and keeps me sane. Big day this. Early reports say *'...Round-Up'* is going swimmingly. A few protestors carted away, but nothing violent." A rap on the door interrupted his flow. "Come! Home Secretary?"

A protestor outside Parliament once called Charles Fenwick, *"A long streak of paralysed piss!"* When he entered the room he looked as though he wanted to shrivel, and hide under a table.

"My apology for interrupting, Prime Minister. If it's inconvenient I'll..."

"Not at all Charles. Only shooting the shit with old Ken."

Frank Steen studied the portrait of Sir Robert Walpole, above the fireplace. He was uneasy about answering Julian's summons to Ten Downing Street, but the die was cast. Still, better that as few people as possible saw his face.

"What news from the front, Charles?"

"Ahem, reports of some difficulties have been received. Rather fewer detentions than we'd hoped for in Buckinghamshire..."

"Why?"

“It appears that, with the beans being spilt last week, a number of children went into hiding. Possibly given shelter in middle class homes, with church ministers the catalyst for this, erm, manoeuvre.”

Julian shrugged.

“So a few escaped the net. They can’t stay hidden for ever. Well Charles, is there something else?”

“I’m sorry to report, Prime Minister, that the Buckinghamshire Constabulary refused to co-operate with the DRC...”

“On whose authority?”

“Ahem, the Chief Constable’s, a chap called Wilbey...”

“I know who he is, damn you. Why didn’t the DRC snatch squads go in?”

“They met with resistance.” Before Julian could interrupt he explained. “Passive resistance. Whole neighbourhoods turned out. They blocked roads with sit-downs, even individual houses. The commanders didn’t think it appropriate to employ force against peaceful protestors...”

“Damn and blast it, my home county. I’ll look a complete fool. Alright Charles, appreciate your honesty. Somebody had to play *‘Messenger’*. Keep me informed of developments.”

Charles Fenwick hopped from foot to foot.

“For God’s sake, Charles, not more bad news. Spit it out!”

“I regret to inform you, Prime Minister, that your mother, Lady Marlborough that is, has been arrested by the Buckinghamshire Police.”

"What!"

"It's alright sir, I understand that she has been released..."

"It bloody well isn't alright," he raged. "How dare they, how fucking well dare they! Why?"

"Why what, sir?"

"Why was my Mother taken into custody, you long streak of paralysed piss!"

Ken Burke was a quivering jelly, on the verge of hysterics. It was he who had told Julian of the mildly obscene soubriquet labelling Charles Fenwick. The latter swallowed hard. He liked to pretend that he was from the patrician class. The insult was in poor taste, and beneath the dignity of a Prime Minister. He adopted the pose of a Grenadier Guardsman.

"I am reliably informed that her Ladyship was questioned, briefly, about an historical murder case."

"Get to the fucking point, Charles. You're not running a fucking filibuster through Parliament. What murder?"

"Actually, Prime Minister, 'murders'. The events in St. George's Church Banksmore, which you are more cognisant of than I."

Julian took his seat in the Cabinet Room.

"Charles, please find Commander Grosvenor, and ask him to present himself immediately."

Fenwick half-bowed and exited.

Ken thought he should say something to dispel the unease that lay like broken wind upon the room, and its occupants.

"Disgraceful sir. Absolute travesty. Poor Lady Deborah. Will you go to her, sir?"

Julian's mind was elsewhere. What in God's name was going on? Why should Banksmore resurface? Yesterday's fish and chips were wrapped in that old news. Was it her? He said nothing. The tick of a clock jangled the nerves. Frank continued his study of Walpole. *"Time and tide wait for no man,"* he reflected.

Julian leapt from his seat. "Come!"

Guy Grosvenor presented himself.

"Have you heard, Guy?"

"The bare bones, sir. What would you like me to do?"

"Go to her, Guy. You two seem to get along well. I feel sure that she'll be pleased to see you. I'll telephone tonight...and Guy. Start digging. I want to know on whose authority Mother was arrested, how long she was held, and who interviewed her..."

Charles Fenwick burst into the room.

"Prime Minister! We have trouble, big trouble."

"Yes?"

Scotland, sir, is up in arms."

Julian gave a grim smile.

"When aren't the buggers complaining about something?"

Only Ken laughed.

"No, Prime Minister. I mean literally in arms. At 03:00 hours this morning the City of Edinburgh Garrison marched out of barracks in full battle order, with their colonels at the head. Some were despatched by truck to

Glasgow. They have disarmed and detained the entire Defence of the Realm Corps in both cities."

"Mutiny?"

"No sir. The Scottish Parliament held an emergency sitting at midnight. It took them barely half-an-hour to back the uprising."

Julian stood beside Frank, in front of the fireplace. He barely noticed his presence.

"There is one more matter to report, Prime Minister."

Julian held his hands behind his back, fists clenched. He nodded for Fenwick to continue.

"The Prince of Wales, in his capacity as Prince and Great Steward of Scotland, supported by the Earl of Seaforth and all the Chiefs, has..."

Fenwick hesitated, before his voice boomed.

"He has raised the clans!"

In disbelief, Julian trudged to a far window. Frank Steen revealed his face to Guy Grosvenor, and they smiled. Ken Burke studied them keenly.

"My, oh me!"

He failed to hide his glee when they looked at him.

24

"The hunter has been hunted down..."
'Oedipus at Colonus'

'Heilan Laddie' was played by massed pipers, as they led the procession the length of Princes Street, Edinburgh. The dense crowds, heaving on the pavements, alternately cheered and booed. One thousand bedraggled members of the Defence of the Realm Force were jeered and insulted, whilst their heavily armed escort was hailed. *'Filthy Sassenach'* was a popular insult. Few in the crowd knew that two-thirds of the DRC men and women were Lowland Scots. The more educated were aware that at the 'Battle of Culloden', in 1746, Scotland had not just been defeated by English soldiers. The Duke of Cumberland had four Scottish units in his ranks.

It took all afternoon to entrain the enemy at Waverley Station, and for the trains to depart southward. The determined crowds waited in snow and biting wind for the return of their heroes. Soon they came into view. For the return to barracks the pipers played the traditional and magnificent *'Black Bear'*. Pubs and clubs did a roaring trade that night.

The Scottish Parliament sat late. In a packed Chamber the Presiding Officer chastised some of the more vainglorious members, and the result of the vote was announced; seventy-eight per cent in favour. Everyone had the grace to rise when the Great Steward of Scotland entered the Chamber, at their invitation. He offered his hand to the President, who shook it and walked him to the microphone.

"My humble thanks to you for the privilege of entering this Chamber. I have not come to tell you what to do."

He searched their faces, and drew breath.

"Today Scotland has taken a bold step. You have cast out of our land those intent on great harm to the lifeblood of the nation. I am aware that, for some of you, it may be seen as the first step to independence."

Excited chatter fluttered round the room.

"Whilst I am Prince and Great Steward of Scotland, I retain loyalties to other parts of this island and to *all* its peoples – Welsh, Irish...English! The peril you have disarmed in Scotland still looms in those countries. It is an honourable thing you, and our servicemen, have done for Scotland. Now you are left with the onerous and complex task of deciding where your duty lies, and how widely it may be rendered."

Once more the stern young man scanned the eyes upon him.

"I am ever your servant, and each may speak with me at any time, if you think I can be of service. I bid you goodnight, and God's wisdom and compassion in your deliberations."

The Clan Chiefs met elsewhere in the great city. They foregathered in Regency rooms, and men in uniform were present.

"Irrespective of what Holyrood decides we must prepare our strategy."

Andrew 'Freddie' Forbes, Earl of Seaforth, opened the proceedings.

"Duncan, would you fetch us up to speed on clan recruitment, please?"

The giant, bearded, figure hauled himself to his feet. His kilt strained a little at the waist.

"Social media makes it so much easier these days." With a wry eyebrow cocked he added. "I'm no inclined to think that the clans have been raised by such device before." A subdued chuckle rumbled through the room. "The response on each clan website and Facebook page has been magnificent. Volunteers are ready to bear arms. Roy will tell you more."

Retired Major General Roy McKinnon did not bother to stand.

"We are inundated with men and women dusting off their claymores!"

Another quiet laugh interrupted.

"In order to put some structure into it we have responded to those with prior military experience. They will arrive in Edinburgh and Glasgow by noon today. We will house them in the now derelict DRC barracks. Our Finance Minister has assured me that funds will be made available for all associated contingencies. They will come under Army command..."

Freddie Forbes butted in.

"Yes. In case you don't already know the present Scottish command has come over to us in its entirety. Every man, in every regiment, has been told what is happening, and has been given the opportunity to stay or be honourably discharged. Few have taken the latter option. Roy..."

"Thank you, Freddie. Gradually, but with urgency, we will vet the thousands of others who wish to defend Scotland. They will be organised according to their clan groups, and stationed in border towns. The Regulars will see to their ongoing training."

Freddie took the floor once more.

"So gentlemen, we await our Parliament's decision at this late hour. May I just reiterate? Whether regular army, or irregular clansmen we remain subject to the will of the Scottish Parliament. Ah sir, good of you to join us."

The gentlemen rose as one to greet the entry of their Prince.

It is an ancient axiom, adhered to by military commanders and wise grandmothers, that the darkest hour comes before the dawn. January in Edinburgh was drawing to a close, but the chiefs could not expect to see daylight for a couple more hours. Breakfast had been wheeled into their conclave, and they set about it with a will. The young Prince was the exception to the rule, and they joshed their lord respectfully.

"Keeping your figure in trim, sir?"

Calum Forsyth's enquiry amused the Prince.

"Need to keep fighting fit, Forsyth."

A leaden silence fell upon them at the thought of fighting. Donald Grant would have none it, and he gripped Forsyth in a bear hug.

"Dropped a brick, Forsyth, dropped a brick. You'll pay a penance. Is that no' right, boys?"

A chorus of "Ayes" lifted the mood.

"What shall it be, sir?" Grant asked the Prince.

He chewed his toast with delicacy.

"I'd say a song. Wouldn't you like a song, my laddies?"

Forsyth remained in Donald Grant's mighty grip.

"A song it is then, sir. Right Forsyth, sing us all a cheery tune. I'm no' letting go until you sing. Sing!"

The boisterous yelps of the company were smothered when Forsyth began. If they had anticipated a rousing call to arms or a jocular ditty they were disappointed. The gentle strains of *"Will Ye Go Lassie Go,"* pulsed lightly on the air. It spoke of the promise of summer; of the heather and the wild mountain thyme; of loving companionship and fellowship. A mesmerised Grant released his hold. Forsyth mounted a chair, and stepped onto the middle of the grand dining table. As he began the second verse the company stood, and their voices joined him, *"And we'll all go together..."* These great men sang as doves, cooing their affection to one another and for their nation. When the song concluded there was stillness. Forsyth stepped down, and they resumed their breakfast.

An aide de camp stole into the room, almost unnoticed, and spoke discreetly in the Prince's ear.

"Would you excuse me, gentlemen?"

He was gone but a few minutes. When he walked back into the room the murmuring ceased. The Prince stood with his head bowed, his young face pale and wan. Papers hung loosely in his right hand. The only sound was a scraping of chairs. With a resolve, visible to all, the Prince squared his shoulders and his resolute eyes challenged them. He lifted his arm, and without preamble read out the missive he had received.

"It is the decision of the Scottish Parliament, by a majority of one-hundred and sixteen votes to thirteen, that until such time as there is a change of Prime Minister in the Westminster Parliament, the business of Scotland will be conducted as that of an independent nation. Whenever such an alteration in circumstances occurs, subject to a new incumbent at Westminster restoring the full democratic rights of all citizens of the United Kingdom, and repealing certain laws listed herein, the Scottish Parliament will resume normal relationships with the Westminster Parliament, subject to the immediate granting of a Scottish referendum to determine whether or not the people of Scotland wish to live as an independent nation."

The Prince and Great Steward of Scotland walked with measured tread to the head of the table.

"Be seated gentlemen."

An uncomfortable air fell upon them, and their looks became increasingly puzzled. The Prince just stood behind his chair. A look of disbelief marred his features, as he stared at a second piece of paper. The Earl of Seaforth spoke.

"Sir...sir! We have much to discuss. The disposition of our armed forces in all this; what to do about the clan volunteers. Not least, Westminster's reaction..."

"They have reacted already!"

He lay the piece of paper on the table, and gestured towards it with anger and contempt.

"I take your point, Andrew, but there is something else. A personal reaction has been applied against my family."

He drew breath, then announced in a stentorian voice.

"My father, His Majesty the King, has been taken prisoner. He is being held incommunicado in Windsor Castle."

Song stole upon the dislocated hush that had descended. Andrew Forbes, Earl of Seaforth, began the refrain. Scotland was in the very marrow of each man there, but they were visionary men, and so they joined with him. Initially, it was sung with solemn respect, by its conclusion they roared it with the terrifying ferocity of a warrior class.

"...Send him victorious,
Happy and glorious,
Long to reign over us,
God save the King."

25

"The city mourns for this girl; they think she is dying most wrongly and undeservedly of all womenkind, for the most glorious acts..."
'Antigone'

Paul Baxter pleaded with, cajoled and even threatened his wife Samantha. The row was heard throughout the house. She ended it with her plaintive question.

"Paul, you were a soldier. Would you have me shirk my duty?"

He turned his face to the wall, and she saw his shoulders heaving. Sam wrapped her arms about him.

"Sssssh, I'll be okay. Isa will be my bodyguard."

He did not respond to her whimsy.

"You've read the reports we've received, Paul. We can't abandon the children to their suffering."

He clasped her to him in a fierce embrace.

"I know...I know. I just can't bear the thought of losing you. You're walking into the lion's den."

"We'll never be lost to one another. I'll be home once a month. It won't be long before we will have garnered all the evidence we need."

A tapping on the door interrupted them. Isa appeared.

"It's time Sam."

She kissed her husband with the passion of absolute love, and swept out of the room.

The Nadder Valley stretches from Wilton, on the outskirts of Salisbury, to Shaftesbury in Dorset. A detention centre for girls had been built on compulsory-purchased land from the Fonthill Estate. There was considerable outrage at the despoiling of this breath-taking scenic area, but it cut no ice with the relevant government department. The DRC had to employ some local people, and frightened rumours spread throughout the Valley of the abuse within the austere compound. Sam and Isa got themselves taken on as kitchen assistants. They were residential posts; one month on, and a week off.

Within a fortnight they had accumulated enough evidence to blow the whole child detention programme apart. It was helped when Isa was moved from kitchen to household duties. She and Sam were able to see what was going on from two perspectives. Aside from the everyday brutality and punishments, darker sins were inflicted upon the children. Barely a night passed when girls, as young as thirteen, were not roused from their beds to be taken into DRC quarters to be raped and tormented by men and women alike.

Surreptitiously, Sam and Isa photographed and recorded material on their mobile phones. In the spirit of the great British cock-up, incoming staff were not deprived of their phones and tablets. The DRC as a whole comprised the dregs of society, and the standard of education amongst even the higher ranks was unimpressive.

Isa became a legend in the Centre within a short space of time. She listened, smiled shyly, and was cheerfully helpful to children and guards alike. The Commandment referred to her as *"Our little treasure."* Unlike Sam, she was never pestered. For a striking and mature woman, it was a different matter. Sam was the butt of endless sexual innuendo, and a target for the Commandant especially.

He was surprisingly old, around seventy years of age. Adrian Midgard was a ludicrous little man. His physique resembled a beach ball. He like to purse his lips and affect a superior smile. It made his face look like a well-smacked arse. What he loved most of all, apart from himself, was the uniform; especially the highly-polished boots. Adrian's life had passed in underwhelming mediocrity. His saving grace was his attention to detail. From an unremarkable career in a provincial grammar school, he had risen to the dizzy heights of assistant manager in a local estate agent's office.

What nobody had ever discovered was his drooling lecherous behaviour. The advent of the mobile phone was a boon to him. The memory capacity of his device was almost overwhelmed by girls and ladies in various stages of undress. His favourite haunts were parks in hot summers, and around hotel swimming pools whilst on annual holiday.

Adrian was bored in retirement, and chanced his arm when whispers of a new force circulated around the Rugger club. He breezed through the interview, and was assigned to admin. His assiduous application to the task saw him rise through the ranks.

When he met Samantha, at interview, he virtually waived the formalities. Within two days she was instructed to take him his elevenses and afternoon tea. So far, she had deflected his sly and insidious innuendo with a toss of the head, and a gay laugh. It served to inflame Adrian.

Her last encounter led to a more overt statement of his lust. She was bending low over the coffee table, collecting up the remnants of his tea. Adrian entered the room stealthily from his private bathroom. She reacted with a jump when she felt his groin pressed against her buttocks.

"You'd look wonderful in a blue basque and stockings!"

Samantha wheeled round, forcing him to take a step backwards, as the tea tray became a barrier between them.

"My husband says just the same thing. Excuse me, sir, we're rather pressed for time in the kitchens."

She exited without a smile, or a laugh. Not that Adrian was bothered.

The following day lunch was over, and Sam was alone in the kitchen, clattering plates and cutlery around. She wasn't aware of his presence until she felt his hands on her breasts. He had her pressed up against the sink. Slowly, he rotated his groin against her buttocks.

"You like that don't you?"

Her instinct was to smash a plate over his head. Instead she held herself upright. The years she had spent as a prostitute could not, however, prevent her from keeping the revulsion she felt for this man to herself.

"From my husband, yes. He's a real man, and he used to be a real soldier, not a jailer."

Adrian boiled at her demeaning remark. He was ready to slap and punch her until she begged him to stop, but he was interrupted.

"Sir, sir..."

"In here," he barked.

"Sir, we have a visitor. A VIP." The young woman whispered into his ear.

"My God! Inform my adjutant immediately. Full parade; civilian staff included."

Adrian paused in the exit.

"You! You're finished here – fired. See out the day, and then get off the premises."

Sam couldn't care less. They had the goods on the whole operation. She gave him a parting shot.

"Your VIP is waiting. Go and change your trousers."

Adrian Midgard almost creamed his pants again.

"Sir, a great honour sir."

He bowed like a waiter, in expectation of a large tip. Julian Marlborough looked through him.

"Just passing nearby, Commandant. Supervising manoeuvres on Salisbury Plain. Thought we'd have a look at how you're getting on."

Julian stepped past him, and strolled down the lines of rigid children. Adrian scuttled along behind him.

"Over here we have our civilian employees, Prime Minister."

Julian cast a disinterested eye over the cooks and bottle washers, exchanging a word or two. Samantha had emerged from the kitchen at the last minute, and saw him getting out of his car. She managed to secrete herself in the rear rank, and as he stood three rows away from her she blew her nose, masking her face in a handkerchief.

"All looks very smart, Commandant. May I use your bathroom?"

Everyone remained on parade. Julian and Adrian re-appeared ten minutes later. The former stood in front of the limousine's passenger door. His parade ground voice dominated the square.

"Do what you're told; learn from your mistakes, and you'll soon be out of here. Fail to see the error of your ways, and you'll be here a long time."

His unwavering gaze intimidated them, and his all-seeing eye seemed to penetrate the soul of each person present. The Prime Minister's car drew away, and the parade was dismissed. One person watched him disappear into the distance. The diminutive Isa peered through an upstairs window. Her attention went from the receding vehicle, and followed her friend drifting back towards the Refectory.

Evening meal was done and dusted, and the ladies were finishing the washing up. The young woman who had informed Adrian of the P.M.'s arrival spoke to Sam politely.

"The Commandant would like to speak with you in his office, before you leave the premises. Straight away, please."

When the door slammed shut behind her she was gripped by two DRC officers. Adrian sat with his boots up on his desk.

"Good evening, Mrs. Baxter, or should I say Samantha...or perhaps Charlotte or Angela? You need to buy a bigger handkerchief. My apartment with her, now. You two can have her first, but leave her clean and tidy...and restrain her."

Adrian Midgard was not one for putting pleasure before business. It was 21:30 hours before he entered his bedroom. Sam lay naked, bound and gagged. It excited him to see bruises on her body, where his men had been at work. He did not deign to speak to her. First he undressed, and then straddled her. Sam couldn't take her eyes off him, until he punched her in the face. She lost consciousness, as blows rained down on her.

The night was long. At his leisure he raped her. Soon, it became unnecessary to batter her into unconsciousness; she just lapsed into periods of oblivion. When it suited him he roused her with fire; burning her breasts with lighted cigarettes. Dawn was breaking when she gave up the ghost. He thrust the bottle deep into her vagina. Even through the gag, her cry echoed. She gave a great sigh, and life passed from her.

Paul Baxter had not been allowed to see her. An official explanation was given. A workplace accident, attributable to the victim's own carelessness. Her casket was already sealed when she was returned to him, in Salisbury. The funeral directors convinced him that it would be too distressing to view her body. Paul received her ashes a few days after cremation. Reverently, he placed them in his car. Isa had already spoken to him, and related Julian's visit to the centre. Neither was in doubt about the cause of Sam's death. He held little Lucy tightly, and kissed her.

"Daddy will be back soon. Isa will take care of you."

He stood in the small orchard, that was a part of their garden in Cartmel, and scattered her ashes in the cold Cumbrian wind.

He had made the decision whilst mulling over the sports pages in an M6 service station. Paul Baxter went into his garden shed. He unlocked a metal box and removed its contents. When he emerged he was Sergeant Billy Conway, Liverpudlian and hard nut.

*

The Calcutta Cup was first competed for in 1879. It is awarded to the winner of the Rugby Union international match between England and Scotland. Given the political temperature, it was uncertain that the game would go ahead. The freemasonry of the sport put a stop to any such conjecture. After all, chaps are chaps wherever they come from. Differences are always set aside, and the fellows could be relied upon to act honourably.

Twickenham had a capacity crowd for the occasion. The support for both sides was more rabid than usual. Twickers, the home of hooray Henries and grammar school boys pursuing social mobility. Writer Philip Toynbee got it spot on, sometime in the 1930's.

"A bomb in the West Car Park at Twickenham on an international day would end fascism in England for a generation."

Rugby was Julian's passion, second only to theatre. When he was presented to the teams the overwhelmingly English crowd chanted his name. The Scottish players took his hand respectfully, but with stony faces. From the first whistle it was war. A French referee is not best placed to arbitrate in such circumstances. Matters came to a head when he brandished a red card from his pocket to dismiss a player from each side. For the first time in fifty-five minutes the two captains were in accord. Kenton McCallum spoke for Scotland.

"Respectfully, sir, if he goes we all go."

"Absolutely sir. My guys too. It's like the old days, before they put the bloody cameras in situ'. You just ref the technical bits, sir, and leave the rest to us."

The Frenchman collaborated.

Aubrey Benson ascended the steps to collect the Calcutta Cup from the Prime Minister; an English victory. Hysteria gripped the crowd, and two stadium security guards deflected arms and backslapping hands, whilst they rose higher and higher in the towering stadium. Benson cleared the last two steps alone. He shook the P. M.'s hand vigorously, and held the trophy aloft. The roar subsided, and a Scouse voice called out,

"Hello Skipper!"

The real Captain of England looked down at the man in the high-visibility jacket. Marlborough knew who it was before he saw him. The pistol was levelled at him, but the shot flew upwards into the roof of the stand. Nearby hands had reacted swiftly, and they hauled the assailant into the crowd. The Prime Minister placed a restraining hand on Guy Grosvenor, and let the *'Rugger Buggers'* beat Billy Conway to death.

26

"For time alone shows a man's honesty, but in one day you may discern his guilt."
'Oedipus Rex'

"Prime Minister, this is indefensible."

The studio audience hammered its approval. The noise of stamping feet and handclapping went on and on. Julian's obvious insouciance towards them only sustained the barrage.

Humphrey Bickerstaffe was the doyen of TV interrogators. Young, but with an old school demeanour. He listened to his interviewees long enough to let them hang themselves. What followed was always polite, but forensic in its dissection of the living cadaver in front of him.

"My dear Humphrey, I couldn't agree with you more. The shocking scenes we have all witnessed on social media, and reproduced in some of the more...how shall I say it...lurid newspapers are unacceptable."

It was the perfect word, because it remained open to interpretation. The lack of acceptability, in Julian's view, was the absolute incompetence of Adrian Midgard. He said so, whilst railing at Home Secretary Charles Fenwick.

“I met the little turd. Didn’t strike me as the brightest foreskin on the scrotum pole.”

Charles winced at the obscene metaphor, but inwardly gave marks for linguistic invention.

“Where’s the fucking report, Charles? I want to know who made those videos. How, in God’s non-existent name did they manage to interview girls?”

Fenwick was no longer to be intimidated. This man offended him to his core. On the right wing of the Party he may be, but unlike Julian he was not to the right of Attila the Hun.

“Early indications suggest that it was probably carried out by a civilian employee, or employees. Our erstwhile Commandant...er...” He perused his notes. “Mr. Midgard, did not impose either vetting or restrictions on mobile devices for civilian staff.”

“Cunt!”

Charles resigned himself to a morning given over to the exploration of the entire lexicon of obscenity.

“Midgard! Well, he’ll fucking need one when I kick him in the balls. He’s headed for that bourne from which no traveller returns. Cunt!”

Inexplicably, Julian lapsed into reverie.

“Always wanted to play Hamlet. Suggested it to my Drama teacher, bitch wouldn’t listen.”

For the first time in years, Holly Browne’s image rose before him, like the Ghost of Hamlet’s father. He made an odd noise, and shrugged it off. Staring into space, he mused further.

"God, I miss my acting. Should have been an actor, Charles. You should have seen me in the Sixth Form, I was fucking brilliant. Too old for Hamlet. Wonder what else I could play. Wouldn't that be something, Charles, the Prime Minister treading the boards in triumph?"

Charles was agog. He peered intently at the man before him, whose mind was a whirligig of fantasy. He permitted himself an obscenity to express his thought, inwardly.

"Cunt! You are on the stage, and the applause is turning to catcalls. Let's hope we can avoid a riot."

"What did you say, Charles?"

A flustered Home Secretary buried himself in his papers. Surely the bugger wasn't a mind-reader.

"Frank Steen is of the opinion..."

"We don't speak that name aloud!"

"My profuse apology, Prime Minister. Our investigative agent believes the material may have left the compound with the corpse of the deceased lady. Her belongings would, naturally, have been returned to her next of kin."

Julian was puzzled. He had last seen her in her incarnation as Samantha Baxter. The *'inadequate foreskin'* had revealed that to him from her employment record. Paul Baxter was named as next of kin. What he didn't know was that Baxter and Billy Conway were one and the same person.

"Sir...sir..."

"Proceed Charles."

"It appears that when the lady was employed she was in companionship with a young girl. They were separated shortly after arrival. The latter was moved from kitchen to household duties."

"Name?"

"Er..." He turned a page. "Oh yes, unusual name. Isa Joseph."

"What?"

"Isa..."

"I heard you the first time."

Julian paced back and forth, muttering to himself.

"One hounds me from beyond the grave, and the other...who, in the name of the Holy Ghost is she? Hugo, fucking Hugo. I must have a word with that little wank stain."

"I beg your pardon, Prime Minister?"

"Nothing...nothing. Not talking to you."

Charles was rather pleased to hear so. There were some things one simply couldn't endure. Besides, masturbation was a mortal sin.

"So, you've received a preliminary report from Fra...our associate."

"He's in Wiltshire as we speak, Prime Minister. On the premises, grilling Mr. Midgard."

"Good. That will be all."

The Home Secretary reached the door, and wasn't sure he heard correctly.

"Oh Charles, clear your desk."

"I beg your pardon?"

"Someone's got to carry the can. I'll be announcing your resignation during that fucking interview I've got to give on the box."

His mind was distracted again, whilst he wondered if his mother would record the programme. It returned to the present.

"Well I'm not taking the blame. Don't worry yourself. We'll put it about that you took your eye off the ball. Occupied with serious personal difficulties. How's your marriage?"

Charles drew himself up to his most imposing height.

"As safe as the Bank of England."

"As bad as that!"

Julian snorted at his own witticism.

"Okay, we'll say something like, oh I don't know...that you play too much pocket billiards. No-one will think you're a nonce! Out of the building by noon."

Charles Fenwick closed the door behind him, and stood with his nose against the wood panelling. He whispered another line from *'Hamlet'*. It was an assurance to his former master that the public would, *"By indirections find directions out..."* His long stride ate up the corridor. Before he turned the corner, he looked back and took another stab at Middle Low German, mixed with Old Norse.

"Cunt!"

"Let me assure you, and the British public, that this is an aberration, Humphrey. Nonetheless, it is a grave dereliction of duty towards our children."

"Dereliction of duty by whom, sir?"

"This morning I received the Home Secretary's resignation. It was the honourable thing to do."

"You accepted his resignation?"

"I did."

"So, you're saying that Charles Fenwick is culpable?"

"You're putting words into my mouth, Humphrey. An investigation will be undertaken by the Metropolitan Police. The Commissioner himself will direct proceedings. Charges will be laid."

"Will that include the former Home Secretary?"

Charles Fenwick was hung out to dry.

"My colleague, and dear friend, will be interviewed at some stage. I feel sure that he will be exonerated."

"Prime Minister, you are famous, if not infamous, for your hands on approach to government. One former colleague described you as, and I quote, *"An octopus, whose tentacles grip the minutiae of government and never let go."* How is it possible that these heinous acts escaped your attention? Are you losing your grip, Prime Minister?"

Julian clutched for words, but they would not come. He was saved by the bell. Humphrey Bickerstaffe was touching his earpiece, and a flush of excitement came to his features.

"Forgive me, Prime Minister, but I'm receiving some important and startling news."

Humphrey's producer drip-fed it into his ear, while he recited it to the studio and the watching nation.

"The detention centre for children six miles south of Carlisle has been attacked. The children have been freed, and bused into Carlisle where they will be housed, temporarily…as soon as it is practical, they will be returned to their families."

He held one palm against his free ear to block out the excited audience.

"What? Say again please."

Humphrey was on the edge of his seat.

"The DRC contingent is held under armed guard in Carlisle Cathedral. What?"

The volume at which he shrieked the word silenced the audience.

"Yes, yes, fifty-eight miles within England!"

Julian leaned forward, straining to hear what was being transmitted to his interviewer.

"Right, right."

Humphrey sat back, and eyeballed the Prime Minister.

"Four Rifle Companies of the 43rd Lowland Reservists have undertaken this mission, sir. That is battalion strength. The operation was led by full-time officers from other Scottish regiments. Volunteers!"

Julian held his head high, but his face was stony white.

"Prime Minister, British Army troops have penetrated nearly sixty miles into England, presumably without Parliamentary approval."

The figure before him might have been a statue.

"Sir, sir, England has been invaded. What do you intend to do?"

Julian unclipped his microphone, and signalled to a wing of the studio set. Two hulking gentlemen, in well-cut suits, hove into view. They escorted him to his waiting vehicle.

Deborah Marlborough was numb. She sat transfixed before the bedroom TV, and shivered. Goose bumps appeared on her bare breasts. Guy Grosvenor wrapped his redundant pyjama jacket around her. She clung to him for dear life.

27

"There is no happiness where there is no wisdom"
'Antigone'

"Thomas Didymus hard of belief, bit a cat's arse and swore it was beef."

When Eddie Jackson surveyed the packed congregation, from the pulpit, he did not actually give voice to one of his mother's favourite phrases. She used to recite it when he was being sceptical about something she said.

His opening remark struck a sardonic note.

"The great professors of philosophy tell us that the world is determined by the laws of nature. Not just part of it; not the portion which it suits you to believe, but everything, including human beings. Consequently, they say our actions are predetermined and beyond our control. We do not have a choice; we do not possess Free Will."

He permitted the thought to percolate amongst the worshippers at St. Thomas' Church, in St. Helens Merseyside.

"Still, I suppose these intellectual giants need something to occupy their minds during school holidays."

Even the BBC producer, and her radio crew gave a chuckle. They had done right to choose this provincial northern town to broadcast Sunday service from. The tip-off they'd received, from Radio Merseyside, about this lay preacher looked like being gold dust.

"So, my friends, you are not responsible for your actions. Anything you do, and I mean anything, is excusable because you have no choice. Moral responsibility? Strictly for the birds. Compassion, kindness and love? Whims of nature. If we follow this doctrine, then we're going to save ourselves an awful lot of money. Why? Well, we can empty the prisons."

An uncomfortable buzz grew in the pews below him.

"How can it be just to punish people for actions they were compelled to commit by the laws of nature?"

The disquiet grew louder. He quelled the disturbance.

"Nonsense! Arrant nonsense. Such ideas are nihilistic – a complete denial and rejection of all values, and of a world founded on civil exchange between peoples. Those who promulgate it are men and women of knowledge, but without wisdom. It is the abandonment of those Christian values which form the bedrock of this nation. We have hidden below the parapets for too long. It is time to speak the Word of God boldly, and to enact in our daily lives the values and virtues of our Saviour, Jesus Christ."

Eddie gripped the rim of the pulpit, and appealed with fervour.

"Do we take a day off work to see a man hang from a gibbet for our entertainment? Is it a day's holiday to watch young men and women beaten for trivial crimes? Do we, as Christian people, stand idly by whilst our children – however fractious and disruptive they may be – are imprisoned and abused? Lost and alone in the world with no-one to turn to. I beseech you, in the name of Christ, we cannot permit such evil to flourish. We have a choice. Each one of us can exercise his or her free will, and say, *'I will not turn away from my neighbour'*."

His words reached beyond the confines of this parish church. Radio carried them to those who listened, and they would set a fire in the land when they were shared widely.

"I do not know the secrets of your heart. You may be full of doubt, as St. Thomas was when he stood before the Risen Christ. Doubt is good. It prompts us to go on seeking. We need not go far to seek one truth."

Eddie inhaled slowly. He was coming to the revelation.

"The truth we face, as individuals and as a nation, is that we have elevated a man to power based upon a fabrication; upon a fairy story."

No one present doubted that the preacher referred to Julian Marlborough, but all were mightily puzzled.

"I have lived among you, my friends, for a short time. You know me as Eddie Jackson. My real name is Jack Preston. I was formerly a Licensed Lay Minister at the Church of St. George, Banksmore in Buckinghamshire. On a Christmas night I witnessed our Prime Minister, Julian Marlborough, behead the Reverend Peter Standish. He, and his companions, then slaughtered the entire congregation, including the two Muslim men present."

Tears flowed down his face for the first time since that dreadful night. He wiped them on his surplice.

"God be with you in the free choices you now face."

Once more he had to flee from a church, in search of sanctuary. He disrobed, and exposed his day clothes, as the car sped towards the M62. The getaway driver was a smart man. It was the Baxters who had hinted at, and then been persuaded to reveal, the existence of Caroline Allsop and Jack Preston. They needed to put distance between themselves and St. Helens. Wisely, Frank Steen stuck to the speed limit.

In the distant South West, a woman dwelt on her past. She had lived beside him without knowing. Civilian life gave him the freedom to grow a heavy beard and longer hair, the colour of snow. Fatima had broken bread with him. One of the men who had raped her in the abandoned building of a desert town. She recalled how humble and respectful he had been towards her, eager to help. Now, with his death, she knew that Billy Conway had been present with her every day in the Woake household.

"No!" she exclaimed quietly, within the confines of her bedroom. "Paul Baxter was the man I knew here."

Fatima stood before an eastern window, and knelt to the leaden February sky. Her words were heard throughout the house. The language was alien to the listeners, but they would have shared the sentiment and belief.

"Let them forgive and overlook, do you not wish that Allah should forgive you? For Allah is oft-forgiving, most merciful..."

She heard a voice saying,

"Have mercy on those on earth, and the One in heaven will have mercy on you."

Her breath was visible upon the icy winter air. She eschewed heating, one day each week; an act of penance.

"I forgive you, Paul. Rest in Paradise with your beloved Samantha."

The kitchen below reflected a familiar scene. They would eat late that day. Their visitors had a long journey, and would not be with them before sunset.

Marion Woake and Abi Hussain were warmed by the Aga, as they fiddled and fettled around the room preparing the Sunday roast. Archie Woake was in his operations room studying the traffic concerning events in Carlisle, and beyond. India popped her head around the door.

"Hi Pa. Okay to uncork a 2000 St. Estephe?"

He didn't look up.

"Certainly, push the boat out. Open a brace."

"A couple of the ladies don't drink alcohol."

He beamed a cheery smile at her.

"Two bottles, I think."

The smile changed to a frown.

"Sit with me, India."

She rolled a chair over on its casters.

"What is it Pa?"

"Funny doings, my love. Picking up some rather disturbing comms. You know that the Catterick Garrison, in North Yorkshire, is used for infantry training? It seems that equipment is being shipped in for a field operation."

Archie placed the tip of a finger on the screen. India's eyebrows shot northward. A hefty contingent of AS-90 Self-Propelled Guns was en route to join the garrison. This piece of kit had served as the backbone of British self-propelled artillery regiments for some years.

"What can it mean?"

"Doesn't have the smell of an exercise. Perhaps the whiff of something less savoury."

India had not seen her father look so solemn in years. He brightened, unexpectedly.

"Come on, let's give that wine time to breathe. While it's gasping we can knock off a few G & T's, and see what the teetotallers would like. Like to hear your plans."

Frank decided they would drive to their destination without stopping. M6 – M5 to Bristol, then eastwards towards London on the M4. They would exit at junction 17, and fiddle their way down to Tollard Royal via Chippenham. Both of their bladders needed relieving, so they pulled in to Leigh Delamere service station, just before they were due to leave the motorway. Jack Preston cajoled Frank into taking a cup of coffee. He added a sandwich to his own order, but his driver declined food.

Conversation was sparse on the journey, and confined to trivial matters. Frank had asked his companion how he'd liked living in the North-West of England, him being a southerner originally.

"They need to cheer up a bit, Frank, but they're good people. Where do you live?"

A vague reference was given to the South Coast, and Frank lapsed into silence. Now he eyed the younger man over the rim of his coffee cup.

"How did you get into preaching, Eddie?"

Frank insisted that his companion retain his assumed name in public.

"We'd be here for hours, Frank. Suffice to say that one day closed doors opened, and I saw the light of Christ. What about you, are you Christian, Frank?"

The coffee wasn't bad, and Frank took a long draught.

"Roman Catholic," he murmured.

"Practising?"

"Practising – and not getting any better."

When it came it was spontaneous. Frank had recited his crimes to the Woake household, but this was different. He could not accept Jack Preston as a priest in the apostolic line, but he discerned his priestly nature. There might not be another opportunity, and Frank wished to be shriven before it was too late.

Marion Woake did a cracking, late, Sunday lunch. Her husband took the lead, over apple crumble.

"Now that Anna is no longer with us, we feel the need for a spiritual voice. Not only to minister to us, but to provide you with a social media platform to reach out to the nation."

Jack Preston was no longer the impetuous young man who had discombobulated the wealthy residents of Banksmore. His gaze fell upon Abir Hussain and Fatima.

"I'd like to know what these two ladies think of your proposition."

Fatima smiled the smile of the tolerant.

"We are all the children of Abraham. Details may differ, but you are a godly man. You may speak for me, Jack. I will tell you when I disagree."

Abi Hussain felt embarrassed.

"It was my husband, Faisal, who attended Mosque. I did not go with him. To be truthful, I don't know where I am with Allah, God – the name is unimportant. If you speak of friendship; if you help to make good neighbours...if you create the bonds of love, you may speak for me, also."

Jack raised his head, and his shining tears were shed unashamedly. He was so overcome that he could only nod his assent. Isa remained silent and watchful throughout the meal. Now she addressed practical issues.

"Your broadcasts will need a title."

The assembled company stretched in their chairs, searching mentally for an idea. India burst out laughing.

"Got it,", and she started to hum *'Jerusalem'*. Before they knew it they were all singing William Blake's words in a raucous uproar. India shushed them.

"How about *'Green and Pleasant Land?'*"

Excited chatter discussed the proposal. It was Frank Steen who voiced the reality of England's present condition.

"Might help to demolish the *"...dark satanic mills*."

Marion was having none of the gloom and doom.

"Men's turn to clear the table and load the dishwasher. Coffee and cognac to follow."

Isa's piping treble drew Frank's attention.

"We need more logs, Archie, I'll get them. Frank, would you help me, please?"

Together they marched toward the utility room for their coats and boots. Frank turned sharply.

"I'd like to say thank you..."

"Not necessary, dear boy..."

"No Archie, it is. I'm grateful to you all for accepting me into your company. I have done great evil in this world, and am undeserving. There is only one more service I can give you. Jack and I will prepare that this evening. Tomorrow I will say goodbye."

Sympathetic voices protested, but to no avail. Isa silenced them.

"Frank is right. His time has passed. We must let him go. Come Frank."

When they reached the barn they set to, loading a pair of wheelbarrows with logs. The night sky was ablaze with stars, in the depths of the Wiltshire countryside. Frank looked upwards in wonderment.

"So clean, the air is so clean. My God and Saviour, I need clean air."

Isa sat on a bale, just inside the barn.

"You have it Frank. God knows your repentance is sincere. Remember the words, *'...the vilest offender who truly believes...'*. He knows you John Candon."

Frank's face was a portrait of shock.

"You know my real name. How?"

"I may wander in the desert, so to speak, but I am computer literate. Archie found me rooting around, and he let me into the secret."

He ran to her, and collapsed at her feet. Isa's hand rested on his bowed head.

"Sssssh. Sylvia and young Frank will be fine. We've already taken steps to bring them into the community. They will be safe."

"Then you already knew that I would be leaving?"

"Not that you would, but that it was likely. I have no eye into the secrets of the future, but I observe. Perhaps the gift I possess is to make maps from those observations. I see the highways and byways where people may travel next. You have brought Jack to us, and now you feel redundant. Far greater is the fact that, despite your confessions and repentance, your burdens still weigh heavily upon you."

Her fingers lifted his chin, so that she could look into his eyes.

"There is something else, John. You have a plan, don't you?"

He nodded.

"If I tell you that you have already done sufficient penance you won't believe me, will you?"

His head sank to his chest once more.

"Whatever you intend to do, John, in your eyes it will be a penitent act. I will not judge you; I will not tell you that what you do is good or evil. It is your journey and you must travel your chosen path. Promise me one thing.

Before the final act you will kneel humbly before your God, as John Candon."

At her words, the weight of ages was shed. He had spent his life defying the goodness of his nature. John Candon had thought that he was serving his country, and his family. He knew now that he had mimicked Sisyphus, King of Corinth. It amounted to nothing more than the perpetual struggle to push the stone of evil to the top of the heap. It was the futile illusion that once you stood on the Olympian heights you were safe.

Archie acted as producer, whilst Frank and Jack worked long into the night. After numerous revisions, they completed their work by three in the morning. Frank detailed the murder of thousands of immigrants on sunken cruise liners, and the unlawful execution of convicted criminals on the Isle of Wight. He recorded for the nation the doings of his master, Julian Marlborough. Jack Preston's short homily followed. It did not sermonise, or mention God. Speaking simply, he gave thought to how England became a green and pleasant land, and the significant part that Christian values had played in the realisation of that desirable state. The stirring hymn *'Jerusalem'*, known even to many an unbeliever, played the broadcast in and out.

When the household filtered downstairs at eight Frank had gone.

Adrian Midgard was surprised. He was under the impression that their business had been concluded at the last visit.

"One or two minor details that the Prime Minister would like to clarify."

"Of course Mr. Steen, only too happy to be of assistance."

God, this man was verbose. The word *'help'* would have sufficed. Frank gritted his teeth.

"No need to stand on ceremony. Frank will do. May I call you Adrian? Thing is Adrian, we read the autopsy report on the young woman. You weren't entirely honest with me, were you?"

The Commandant of defenceless children blustered.

"I...I didn't think the details were important."

"My dear Adrian, details are always important. The Devil is in the detail."

Frank leant forwards.

"Permit me to alleviate your concerns, Adrian."

He decided to adopt the pompous tone of his host.

"Your conduct in the administration of this centre is highly regarded. You have been most judicious in all of your dealings. Nobody is going to chastise you for taking...how shall we say...the perks of the job."

Frank's conscience turned to ice when he saw the reptilian grin spread across his host's face.

"Waited all my life for that. You should have heard her squeal. She was a whore you know."

Frank had read the report of Samantha Baxter's injuries. His stomach churned at having to share the same air as this abominable beast.

"Tell you what, Adrian. Why don't you tell me about it over dinner? The boss wants to know everything that happened. To say he had a grievance against the woman is putting it mildly. I saw a rather nice pub restaurant a couple of miles away."

"The Oddfellows Arms. They have a rather good wine list."

"I believe you're right. Let me treat you. I'll drive, so you can make inroads into that wine. The P.M. is paying."

Adrian was a good trencherman. He ate massively, and with a will. Frank ate sparingly. The detail of Sam Baxter's torment was not conducive to good digestion.

A drunken Midgard did not pay attention to their direction of travel on the return journey. Nor did he demur when Frank stopped the car, ostensibly to take a leak. The Wiltshire night was stygian black, as they crossed fields which Frank had previously reconnoitred. His handgun never left the small of his captive's back. They climbed a long hillside. The trek seemed interminable.

Archie Woake did not spare his family and guests, as he recited the report in terse military style. News travels fast in the country, and his source was reliable.

"It was Jeff Potter who found them, in one of his fields. Naturally, he saw Frank first, given the elevation. When he got close, though, it was Mr. Midgard who attracted his attention. He was dead, slumped against the tree trunk."

He drew breath.

"Apparently, parts of him had been redistributed. His mouth contained a certain appendage, and..."

Marion prompted him.

"Don't be coy, darling. We're all grown-ups."

"Jerry Masters tells me that the gentleman was sporting a most original pair of earrings. John Candon was not a man for idle boasting."

"What about Frank, sorry, John?"

"I'm afraid, India, that he hanged himself."

Isa and Jack Preston exchanged a grim smile. They did not voice their mutual thought. John had chosen to die in a Potter's field. The lay preacher would not accept John's opinion of himself. He was not a Judas.

Isa's sweet voice said, "We shall pray for the real man; for John Candon."

28

"A State for one man is no State at all."
'Antigone'

Google maps calculates that it takes one hour and twenty-nine minutes to journey from Catterick to Carlisle by road. The planned operation allowed for a more leisurely drive. A substantial convoy of troop carriers and AS-90 Self-Propelled Guns moves at a slower pace than the average family car.

The expeditionary force left camp at midnight. Traffic diversions secured the roads for the Army alone. They took the conventional route along the A66 to Penrith, and then northwards on the M6. Around 03:30 hours they left the motorway at Junction 43, and headed East along the A69 towards Warwick Bridge. Somewhere between Carlisle Golf Club and Warwick-On-Eden they pulled off the road, heading across country, northward, for one mile.

Scouts moved on foot to reconnoitre. Within forty minutes they returned, and informed the Colonel that the now defunct detention centre was showing few lights. Satellite had confirmed that three companies of the 43rd Lowland Reservists were still billeted in the centre. The other company was guarding the defeated DRC troops in Carlisle Cathedral. The logistics of despatching them to Birmingham by train was taking time. The scouts reported sentries on duty, but they were few in number.

When dawn broke the detention centre was surrounded. Infantry waited behind the artillery. It was the Colonel who broke the bewitchment that ensnared them all on that cold and miasmic February morn.

The tannoy fractured the northern landscape, but it drew the men together. Hardly a one of the attacking force had not expressed an opinion during the waiting hours. British troops engaging with British troops. Unheard of in hundreds of years. The Colonel's voice implanted reality, and bonded them to the rule of obedience.

"On the orders of His Majesty's government I am commanded to ask for your unconditional surrender. You have committed the unlawful act of mutiny, and you are to be taken into custody. All customary rights will be afforded to you as prisoners. The centre you occupy is surrounded. You have one hour in which to prepare, then you may march out with dignity. All weapons must be left in the compound."

A doleful stillness embraced the land, only to be broken by the skirl of bagpipes rousing the Scottish troops. Hustle and bustle could be observed through the binoculars of the offensive force. Before long the Lowlanders were drawn up on parade. The officer commanding stood on a hastily-erected podium, and addressed his men. There was a pause, before hundreds of kilted men let out a roar.

The English colonel turned to his second-in-command.

"I fear this will not turn out well, Johnny. Prepare the men."

The colonel peered at his watch. Five minutes to go. The seconds ticked past like a tortoise out for a stroll.

"Switch it on corporal."

Once more he spoke to the beleaguered Scotsmen.

"Gentlemen, in good faith, I ask you once more for your surrender. Do not set yourself on a disastrous course. Ten minutes."

He looked through his binoculars. They were immobile on parade, not a man amongst them twitched a muscle. Six hundred seconds of unbearable tension.

"Right Johnny, warning shots."

The AS-90's opened up with a barrage that fell just short of the perimeter; three rounds.

"My God Johnny, I've known some *sang-froid* in my time. You'd think they were out for inspection. Give me the mike, corporal... I beg you, for the sake of your country; for the sake of this island, march out now.!"

Still they held their ranks.

"Buildings Johnny, but have a care."

The artillery opened up once more, and buildings within the compound took hits.

Thick dust clouded the air, obscuring the scene. The officers trained their binoculars on the compound.

"Hold your horses, Johnny. Yes...yes, the gates are opening...they're on the move. Thank God!"

Three pipers led the way; noisy wraiths emerging through a mixture of brick dust and the dawn mist. The sound of *"Blue Bonnets over the Border,"* imposed itself upon the attacking troops. They grinned at one another, and relaxed. No fighting today was the welcome thought. On they came, with their lads swinging along behind in perfect formation.

Quite suddenly, a gauche 2nd Lieutenant let his binoculars fall to his chest, and exclaimed,

"My God, they're still bearing arms!"

He had no sooner said it than a great cry went up from the advancing Scotsmen. Their ranks broke and they charged, firing as they went.

"Artillery Johnny," the Colonel barked over the noise.

They stood no chance. The brass hat who had planned the short campaign had insisted upon creating an overwhelming force. Shells from AS-90's hit them from three sides. It resembled the carnage of the First World War; men scythed down as they advanced bravely. The English infantry waded in briefly to deal with those who, by chance or good fortune, escaped shell blasts. It was little more than mopping up.

Men's hearing gradually returned to normal, as the sound of battle dwindled to nothing. Now the cries of wounded men played on the nerves.

"Dear Lord in Heaven, Johnny, what have we done?"

"Our duty sir."

"I fear, Johnny, I fear that we have just set the land ablaze."

Major John Welbourne did not agree.

"Mutiny sir, we can't countenance that. It would lead to the breakdown of all order."

"...but to fire on our own troops; to kill our fellow citizens. This will mean civil war."

Welbourne kept his thoughts to himself. So be it. He rather liked the Prime Minister, and approved of his policies. He knew that many officers and men were in agreement with him. It would divide the armed services; of that he was sure. Nonetheless, he was confident of ultimate victory. There was a job to be done.

*

The House was mesmerised. Who would have guessed that Tamsin Starke had it in her?

"Mr. Speaker, the Prime Minister's announcement, concerning events just outside Carlisle, has shocked honourable members. We, on the Opposition benches, are equally dismayed by his apparent indifference to the murder of fellow British citizens on British soil. The wholesale slaughter of servicemen who wore the uniform of this once united island. This presses hard on the heels of the social media broadcast made by a former government agent – or perhaps he was the personal agent of the Prime Minister's – revealing genocide and mass unlawful executions. Even as we speak, the Scottish Parliament is in session, deciding upon its response to the unspeakable atrocity inflicted upon its citizens.

Mr. Speaker, the nations of this Island are holding their collective breath. None wishes to utter the two most terrible words signifying peoples divided, and in conflict with one another."

She looked across the Chamber, a fierce glare lighting upon the Prime Minister.

"In the name of all that is merciful and compassionate, I appeal to the Prime Minister to draw back from the abyss into which he is leading the British people. Sir, you have besmirched and dishonoured the history of these islands; you cast the toils and struggles of the past into a fire of destruction. Step back, I say, step back! If you will not, I call upon honourable members on the Government benches to assert the democratic freedoms of these islands, and remove you from office. The State is more than one man."

Opposition members, of all parties, cheered as one. It took three minutes for the Speaker to restore order. Throughout the hullabaloo Tory M.P.s fidgeted and shifted uncomfortably, not daring to speak out against their master.

"The Prime Minister."

The crack about dishonour had visibly upset Julian; it outraged the view he had of himself. His growing sense of delusion convinced him that he was the scion of a noble house. How could a chap with his background be anything but honourable?

Sarcasm dripped heavily.

"I congratulate the Right Honourable lady. Even tommy rot can be spoken eloquently."

He cast a look behind to his own benches.

"Night school classes, perhaps."

Ken Burke did not permit himself the slightest smirk, and no-one else responded. Now that Ken was Home

Secretary he sat beside the P.M. on the front bench, and was far more visible. Who knew which way the wind would carry events? He was smart enough to realise that, one way or another, there would be a day of reckoning. Best not to show too much partisanship, just yet.

Whilst Julian was showboating a note made its way down the Opposition front bench, until it resided safely in Tamsin Starke's hands.

"Point of order, Mr. Speaker!"

Hilary Melton waved a hand for her to proceed.

"Would it be appropriate for the contents of this press release to be read to the House?"

She gave it to a clerk, who passed it on to the Speaker.

Hilary was genuine old school, and his face remained impassive as he read. The paper flopped in his lap, and he reclined into the depths of the Speaker's Chair. He and Julian engaged in a staring contest, causing an eerie silence to fall upon the House. Julian thought he could perceive an expression of sardonic amusement on his brother-in-law's face, mingled with barely suppressed excitement.

"The lady is most correct in drawing this matter to the attention of the House. She will understand that its contents transcend party politics. As such, and with her permission, I will read this statement to honourable members."

Tamsin Starke acquiesced.

Hilary Melton came to his feet before commencing. He examined members' faces on all sides of the House. In his mind, he was gauging potential reactions to the forthcoming announcement.

"The International Criminal Court, in The Hague, has issued the following statement. Julian Hugh Marlborough, British citizen, and Prime Minister of the United Kingdom, is hereby indicted on charges of genocide and crimes against humanity. An arrest warrant will be issued. The Court calls upon the British government to surrender the said Julian Hugh Marlborough into the custody of its appointed officers."

The atmosphere was reminiscent of the opening of Clement Clarke Moore's *'Twas the Night Before Christmas'*...

"...when all through the house

Not a creature was stirring, not even a mouse..."

Julian's self-possession was shaken, but not stirred. He raised his eyes to the packed Visitor's Gallery. The signal was barely perceptible, and no-one paid much attention to the attractive, if blousy, woman who exited. Fiona Hudson did not have far to go. In Westminster Hall she stood on the precise spot where King Charles I had sat, whilst his trial took place. She looked down at the assembled men, and said, "Go!"

Hilary Melton had lost control of the House. Fury and rage commanded the Chamber. So loud was it that no-one heard them approaching. For a second time, in a handful of years, a detachment of British soldiers entered the Commons. There were no officers this time. Thirty non-commissioned officers, heavily armed, hustled and bustled M.P.s back onto the benches.

Julian stood at the Despatch Box.

"This House has shown itself unfit to conduct the affairs of the nation. Yet again it falls to these men to speak for the people."

A sarcastic leer swept the Chamber.

"Don't worry, it's not Martial Law, not just yet. They will speak through me, and express their wish to cleanse this nation, once and for all, of the undesirable elements who drag us down into mediocrity. You are dismissed."

The men of The Rifles, formerly the Royal Oxsters and Julian's old regiment, drove the M.P.s out into Parliament Square where the array of tanks and infantry was as chill as the late-winter air.

Two people remained inside the Chamber of the House of Commons. One was busy trying the Speaker's Chair for size.

"It might have been made for you, Julian."

"Thank you, Ken."

29

"He came to know the god intimately, and the strange mad flower of his mind dripped in the dark."
'Antigone'

"Mother, do you have any idea how busy I am?"

"For God's sake, Julian. You're only at Chequers. I need twenty minutes of your time."

Lady Deborah was a keenly observant woman, and she knew how to handle men.

"By the way, that lady at the *soiree.* She's at her godfather's."

"Lady! What lady? What on earth are you on about?"

"Desmond Claymore-Browne..."

"Oh..."

She detected the slight pause, and knew that she had guessed correctly. Throughout that magical evening she had watched her son drooling over the woman. Apart from when exquisite dew drops of love cascaded from her, in the presence of her adorable Guy.

"Yes, yes Mother, I recall her. Unusual name. Something like...India?"

Deborah could scarcely suppress her mirth.

"I do believe you're right. You are clever darling."

She had massaged his ego since he was able to toddle. Her late, and very distant, husband Sir Hugh controlled

Julian through the cold efficiency of corporal punishment. Her son responded more fondly to her flattering and encouraging ministrations. It explained, entirely, how he had come to inhabit the world of self. His mother's clam-like attentions, sustained him throughout his childhood and adolescence. They created a certified sociopath. That was not a casual opinion. Following the suicide of his Drama teacher, and his insidious involvement in driving her to despair, Sir Hugh had insisted he be examined. Deborah protested vigorously, but for once her husband had his way over the boy. She filed the damning report in the old priest hole. Only she knew of its existence.

"Tell you what, Ma, I can be over around two. Be delighted to see you. Oh, may I beg a small favour? Give Desmond a bell. Say I'll call on him around threeish. Always been rather concerned about the old boy. He's not been the same since Fiona passed on to glory."

"Of course darling, popping in to bring good cheer. You are so kind, and you with all these dreadful responsibilities. Oh, and darling, you know I do so hate being addressed as 'Ma'. Makes me sound like a 1920's brothel keeper."

"You would have been a splendid one."

They laughed in the old complicity.

"Two then. Bye...mater!"

Each chuckled at the formality, before telephones were replaced in receivers.

"This Cremant is rather good, my love."

"Glad you like it darling."

"He's coming then? How do you think he'll react?"

Debs flung her legs over the arm of the sofa, and sipped her drink. She had to think very hard about the question. It was a surprising revelation that came over her.

"You know, Guy, I don't care."

To begin with the realisation was scary. Within a minute she felt an extraordinary sense of freedom. She was no longer bound to the past. The man in front of her had freed her from the sterility of filtered emotion. Her love for Guy Grosvenor was like a waterfall in a sylvan glade; pure and unadulterated.

A thrill of delight made her shudder, as he undressed her with his eyes.

"Nice legs. What time do they open?"

Siren-like, she drew her pleated skirt up around her waist to reveal her nakedness.

"You are a naughty girl."

Her filthy laugh rocked the drawing room. Then she purred with delight, as he took her on the sofa.

Julian was punctual, and goggle-eyed to discover Guy Grosvenor sitting beside his mother, holding hands.

"I beg your pardon?"

"Your mother has kindly accepted my proposal of marriage."

He was at a loss for words.

"...but your...she's..."

"You mean I'm an old woman, and Guy's in his prime. Would you like me to take up crochet, d...?"

She was going to call him 'darling', but a sudden insight made her reserve that word for Guy.

"May I pour you a drink, sir?"

Debs was relishing every moment.

"Better get used to calling him Julian, darling. After all, you're going to be his stepfather."

Given national events, Julian was deep in madness already. This was just surreal. He walloped down the Armagnac that Guy had proffered to him, and held out the glass for a refill. The second went down just as swiftly. He didn't begin to understand how their relationship had developed, nor how it had reached this point. The cut glass ceased to rotate in his hand. It was unimportant; the matter was entirely unimportant to him. If that's what Ma wanted – fine. Guy was a good chap, and...

"I must be on my way. Congratulations, yes congratulations."

Julian shook Guy's hand, then kissed his Mother.

"Tell you what, Guy. Give it a week, and we'll appoint a replacement for you. Don't like the idea of you being at the sharp end any more. I've always considered you irreplaceable, and you are. To Mother, not me! Gosh, look at the time. Desmond will be wondering where I am. Cheerio."

He lolled in the back of the Bentley, whilst it manoeuvred through the tight lanes. Within half a mile, the oddest sensation gripped him.

"I'm free," he thought. "I'm free, and I'm going to see India."

Desmond Claymore-Browne was underwhelmed by the Prime Minister's visit, but ensured that he did not reveal his true feelings. His god-daughter had informed him of the purpose of her visit. Julian's decision to pop in had been unexpected; it merely advanced her programme.

"Drink, Prime Minister?"

"What? Oh yes Desmond. Coffee please. Just had a couple of sharpeners with mother. Need a clear head; busy evening beckoning."

India's arrival distracted him. Through the window he watched her lead the horse to the stable. When she bent over to pick up the bucket of water, the tightness of her jodhpurs made him salivate.

"While you're brewing up I'll pop outside. See if India needs a hand with the stallion."

Desmond smiled at the retreating back. In his opinion, it was the *'stallion'* who would need to hold hard on India's reins.

Julian saw her disappear inside the stable. He wondered if there might be a haystack nearby. The idea of tumbling with her in it inflamed him. Yet it wasn't merely lust. She was older than the women who usually attracted his attention. Mid to late forties maybe? A little older than him. In some things he was perceptive, and he saw the same resolve and fortitude in her that possessed the woman who'd nurtured him. A fatal flower bloomed, and he knew that he must have India for his wife.

"Julian! My goodness, what a wonderful surprise."

She gambolled over to him like a new-born lamb, and his heart thumped. Her arms chained him in a tight embrace, and he felt the weight of her breasts against his chest. India took a step backwards.

"You look tired, darling, and not very happy."

Julian had noticed his mother's reluctance to call him darling. Coming from India's lips it was bliss, but he experienced a sense of loss and a tear stained his cheek.

She held him tightly.

"Come on now. I'll tell you what, let's go into the stable. Get away from prying eyes."

There wasn't a haystack, but they were able to sit side-by-side on a bench.

"You don't have to say anything, darling, but I'm a good listener."

Nobody had ever heard Julian speak so softly.

"You must be aware of everything that's going on."

"More aware than you think," she thought. Her mind flipped momentarily to a communications room in a Wiltshire manse.

"We're on the brink of civil war, and I'm labelled a warmonger and a criminal."

He looked down at his feet.

"Nobody likes me!"

India didn't know whether to laugh, or pour scorn upon him. She was dealing with *'Peter Pan'*; the boy refused to become an adult. A line from Oscar Wilde gave her food for thought. She couldn't recall the play, but some Lady Bracknell figure had exclaimed:

"Never give in to the passions of the young. It makes them selfish when they grow up!"

India was perfectly clear about one thing. She knew who must shoulder the blame for creating this monster. In her time, she'd known more than a few Lady Marlboroughs. Women thwarted in their married lives, pouring devotion into their children; indulging them to such a degree that it crippled their lives. A disabling force leading them in turn to inflict harm on others. Julian was doing it on a monumental scale.

Her hand rested on his neck.

"You're a poor old sausage, you need someone to look after you. I like you."

His eagerness was pathetic.

"Come back to Chequers with me; stay with me India, don't leave me alone."

She timed her hesitation to perfection. Then she took his face into the palms of her hands, and she kissed him.

"Give me an hour. I need to shower and pack."

He was reluctant to say so, but he had to return to Chequers post-haste.

"I've got to leave now. All hell is breaking loose. Can I send a car for you?"

"I quite understand, darling. Thanks awfully, but I'll drive over in mine. Be with you in an hour-and-a-half."

When they got indoors Desmond was full of bonhomie, and coffee was on the table. For the sake of courtesy, Julian took a gulp then made his excuses. They smiled and waved, as his car receded into the distance.

"I'll be leaving, Desmond. Invitation to Chequers."

“Is that wise, my dear?”

“To paraphrase Mr. Shakespeare, if it’s to be done, ‘twere best it be done now. Where is immaterial.”

She clung to her godfather in a true and loving embrace.

“I love you Desmond. You are the very best of England. I need to shower; oh boy, do I need to shower.”

India rather enjoyed her free afternoon. The staff at Chequers were gracious and helpful. Afternoon tea was scrumptious. Julian popped a hasty head around the door, then pirouetted away in buoyant mood to attend to his duties.

It was eight-thirty before they sat down to dinner. A sumptuous repast, with the finest wines to accompany the meal. He made a gallant attempt to show interest in India’s life, but like all men he soon relapsed into talking about himself. Over coffee and liqueurs, sinking deeper and deeper into the seductive armchairs, he revealed his true passion.

“Acting Julian! Gosh, that’s terrific.”

He related his triumphs at school.

“Wish I had time to tread the boards now. God, it would be a relief to get away from it all into another world, just for a little while.”

A tiny motor cranked itself into life in India’s mind. What was it he’d just said? It reminded her of a piece of Shakespeare, but she couldn’t quite locate the verse.

“Idle dreaming. Even if I had the time, where would I perform?”

"Definitely on a big scale, darling. You were born to be centre stage."

He had the shining face and eyes of a schoolboy, who'd just received the Latin prize. She was clearly devoted to him. The unspoken longing for love, that had consumed his subconscious for years, vanished like a will-o-the-wisp. It did not diminish his desire for power one iota. The famous 1 Corinthians 13 was remote from his consciousness. If it surfaced, he would have been unable to grasp that *"Love does not delight in evil."* Julian was a clanging cymbal. The shattered nation could not care less how, why, or who had brought him to this pass. He did not eschew charity towards his fellow men and women.

The quotation flashed into her mind, and inwardly she was amused.

"I have just the part for you. Shakespeare might have written it with you in mind."

He replenished their coffee, and sat on the arm of her chair.

"Do tell."

"Coriolanus!"

"I know of it, but the detail escapes me for a moment."

"A great man, a tragic hero, whose only desire is to serve Rome."

Julian's demeanour assumed the 'Robe of Thespis'. He stood and peered into the future. A physical transformation occurred, as he adopted a pose of noble *mien*. India deconstructed it, and found no truth in him.

"I've got to do it. All this business will be settled soon, and then...then. Where would I perform?"

The wickedest of thoughts grasped her.

"Why not the RSC?"

"London, or Stratford?"

"Stratford-Upon-Avon, of course. I understand that they celebrate the great man's birthday. That's it, Julian."

"What is?"

"Gala performance of 'Coriolanus' on April 23rd. St. George's Day. A greater man paying homage to a great man, for a nation he has saved from perdition, and returned to peace and prosperity."

He fell at her feet.

"May I come to your room tonight?"

"You better jolly well had."

She kissed him.

"Half an hour!"

She wore the same diaphanous gown that once sent Ken Burke into paroxysms of delight. Julian entered her room, and took her into his arms. The flimsy was peeled to her waist, and he lay her on the bed. His mouth sought her nipples, and he settled on to her left breast sucking fiercely like a baby in the pangs of hunger.

"Gently darling, gently."

She took him into her hand, and manipulated him in long, slow strokes. Without warning, he straddled her, and tore the nightdress in half. On the point of entry there was a hammering on the bedroom door.

"Sir, sir! It's of the utmost urgency, sir."

He swept up a pillow and buried his face. Every muscle in his body was taut, as his seed spilt onto her.

The banging on the door resumed.

"Yes, yes. Give me a minute, for God's sake."

She helped him into his dressing gown, and he stepped into the corridor. Julian's raised voice diminished rapidly in volume. With her ear to the door panel she strained to pick up what was said. Odd words came to her, like "The King" and "battle." She hurtled back to the bed when she heard Julian say loudly,

"Downstairs in twenty minutes!"

He closed the door, and looked down at her in profound disappointment.

"I'm so sorry India. There's a major flap on."

"Don't worry, darling, there'll be another time; lots of them."

She noted the deep concern on his face, and could see that his mind was already elsewhere.

"You sleep well. We'll meet over breakfast."

He was gone, and she flopped on to her pillow in relief. She cast aside the tattered remnants of her night attire, and slipped into the shower. When she was dry she put on a pair of old pyjamas.

The bedside lamp glowed on a low wattage. India's hand reached under the bed. The fearsome blade she held up to the light had been her father's. She got out of bed and wrapped the deadly weapon in a towel. Soon it was secreted in the depths of her overnight bag. Perhaps there would be another day. She wasn't sure. The bedside lamp was extinguished. In the darkness she announced to no-one,

"My God, the things I do for England!"

30

"Alas! How terrible it is to know, when no good comes of knowing!"
'Oedipus Rex'

Ten Wildcat Mk 1's, of the Army Air Corps transported the Royal Marine contingent. Twenty Apache Attack helicopters escorted them on their mission. The Apache can detect, classify and prioritise up to two hundred and fifty-six targets in a matter of seconds. Its M230 Chain Gun is the least of your worries; watch out for the Hellfire missiles and CRV7 rockets, they make for a wonderful laxative.

Approaching the target at low level, the Wildcats were soon on the ground. Disgorging the Marines into the Upper and Lower Wards, they declined the *'Precincts Tour'*. Each man knew perfectly well where he was headed. The Apaches circled; birds of prey, waiting to obliterate any resistance. A few shots were fired but the garrison was so small that its soldiers gave up the ghost quickly.

His Majesty was located, and swiftly ensconced in the command helicopter without ceremony. An argument ensued.

"We have orders to fly you to Scotland, sir. The Prince of Wales awaits you."

"Absolutely not, Brigadier. You will convey me to London. Buckingham Palace, if you please."

"I beg you, sir, for the sake of your own safety..."

"Brigadier! In due course I shall be delighted to visit my Scottish people, but I am also King of England. *'Here I stand; I can do no other!'*"

The meaning of Martin Luther's words did not go over the Brigadier's head, but he had no inkling of their origin.

"London it is, Your Majesty. You will permit my men to remain with you?"

"Of course, but I am confident that they will be surplus to requirement. Sources have been able to inform me that most, if not all, of the Household Division is loyal. The Scots Guards we can rely upon utterly. I believe that the Life Guards and The Blues and Royals are, as they say, as solid as the Bank of England. As to the other four regiments of Foot Guards, we shall discover their allegiance in due course."

The fleet of helicopters soared away, in the direction of the Capital. Windsor Castle receded, and the King looked back. The oldest and largest occupied castle in the world tugged at his heart strings, but he shoved sentiment aside. If he and his family were ever to return, a war must be waged. A civil war.

*

"Like shelling peas!"

Julian was incandescent.

"They just walk in, and take him from us. Off to Scotland I suppose to join the Prince of Whelps."

The *'Brass Hats'* numbered five. They had gone over to Julian without a second thought. Britain has always flown with rumour about this or that military conspiracy and coup, but apart from the recent Martial Law none had been realised in centuries.

"Actually, Prime Minister, His Majesty has returned to Buckingham Palace."

Julian slammed his fists into the desk.

"Then we've got him. Twenty-four hours to plan your operation. When it's over you can stick him in the *'Bloody Tower'*. He can rot there, for all I care."

The Generals caught each other's eyes, and shifted uncomfortably. It was not out of concern for the King of England. They had cast their lot, and they knew that there would be no going back. The Chief of General Staff had remained loyal to the Crown, but Julian had appointed his own from the renegades.

General Roland Vaughan spoke for them.

"That won't be possible in the immediate term, sir."

Julian sat behind his capacious desk, the contours of insanity visible.

"The Palace is well-defended, sir, by troops loyal to the King. Intelligence tells us that more flock to his side, as we speak."

Julian gnawed his knuckles.

"Right...right...only one thing for it then. We'll use the RAF; blow the whole bloody place to smithereens, with everyone in it."

A collective shudder possessed the listeners, and one of them muttered audibly,

"My God, regicide!"

Vaughan spoke again.

"I regret to inform you, sir, that the Air Chief Marshal spoke with me half an hour ago. Under no circumstances will the RAF participate, on either side."

For good measure he threw the other bit of bad news into the cauldron.

"The Admiral of the Fleet has placed the Royal Navy on the same footing."

"No Navy? No Airforce?"

"It's not quite as simple as that, Prime Minister. There are elements in both of those Services who support your stance. However, it appears that, at this stage, none wish to engage in internecine warfare. The thought of blowing each other out of the air, or water, has concentrated their minds. I do believe, sir, that they are adopting the *'Lord Stanley'* gambit."

"What?"

"Battle of Bosworth, 1485. Stanley sat on a hilltop and watched the battle, until he could decide who it would be most advantageous to support."

"We're buggered then."

"Not entirely, sir. I wouldn't say that the Army is split fifty-fifty, but significant numbers have come over to our side. The outcome is a long way from decided."

"Right, yes. Okay, let's hear your ideas; let's plan how..."

"Prime Minister, we have concerns for your safety. We would advise that you set up your headquarters farther away from London. Chequers is too well-known, and it makes you vulnerable. I would suggest..."

"I have a bolt-hole ready-made. Come, we'll go together."

The group followed him, decisively, towards the door. They halted when he did.

"Oh, who has control of our tactical nuclear capability?"

A permafrost descended upon the company. General Dyer answered, in a whisper.

"We do!"

"Good."

*

Civil war tends to luxuriate in symmetry. The clan chiefs continued to urge and encourage their people to answer the call. Already five thousand men and women were in training.

The expedition, to avenge the massacre of the Lowland Reservists, was sanctioned by the Scottish Parliament, and manned with Scottish Regulars. Two Highland regiments, at full strength, accompanied by a fleet of twenty-seven Challenger 2 Tanks, arrived at Richmond, N. Yorkshire. Four thousand men, plus armour. Catterick Camp still billeted the troops and light artillery that had done such devastating work outside Carlisle. They were not caught unawares. That section of military intelligence loyal to the Prime Minister was able to give them twelve hours' notice.

General Robertson, commanding Scottish forces, enjoyed a most agreeable parley with his opposite number. Regrettably, the unstoppable force met the immovable object.

The Catterick Garrison made a surprise attack on the Scots at seven p.m. Colonel Laurence Merrill had been talked into it by his second-in-command, Johnny Welbourne. Against an overwhelming force it might be their only chance for some success, before the inevitable retreat.

Robertson was an old hand, and he left nothing to chance. He had distributed his forces around the outskirts of Richmond; three groups, each supported by nine battle tanks.

When the English opened up with the AS-90's the tanks in the centre plunged immediately into battle. Self-propelled guns are no match for full armour, and ninety per cent of them were out of action in short order. Six hundred infantry followed the tanks. Before long they were engaged in hand-to-hand fighting with the enemy. Fixed bayonets, and bludgeoning rifle butts were as effective as bullets in close combat. They might have been in No man's land on the Somme, over a century before.

The infantry battle was in the balance, as one thousand Englishmen outnumbered the Scots in front of them. It wasn't their front they needed to worry about. The landscape South of Richmond is fairly open, but to the

South-West there is some cover. Seven hundred Scots emerged from Sand Beck, and took the English from the rear. The remaining Scottish force came from the South-East, from where Sand Beck extends on its West-East axis. A dense screen of trees had hidden them. Now they fell upon the enemy. The air was a cacophony of gunfire, screams and oaths, and ancient battle cries.

One hundred and thirteen English soldiers survived unhurt. They were marched back to Catterick Camp, along with seventy-eight wounded. Three hundred Scots were left to guard the prisoner-of-war camp.

On the way to York the victorious force passed Marston Moor. In 1644 Oliver Cromwell, and his parliamentary forces, had defeated the Army of the King, led by Prince Rupert of the Rhine. The result was now reversed. Pipes and drums led them into York, where they were welcomed with open arms. Within the confines of the Minster Yard, the troops crowded below the West door of York Minster. They knelt as the Archbishop of York blessed their endeavours. She spoke the language of peace, but recognised the necessity to struggle for the resumption of national harmony. The grave statue of the Roman Emperor Constantine looked down upon them; approving her sagacity, and their courage.

31

"...for I owe a longer allegiance to the dead than to the living."
'Antigone'

She came to know the land intimately. It was somewhat ironic that she bore the rifle in Nomansland. The L115A3 Long Range Rifle is the primary weapon of the British military sniper. It is chambered in 338 Lapua Magnum (8.59mm), with an effective range out to 1.2km.

Custom dictates that snipers operate in two-man teams. The mate is the 'Spotter'. The latter is usually the more experienced of the two, and in command. His job is to plan routes, and select targets. The spotter also gauges shooting parameters such as windage, range to target, angle of shot etc.

When she approached the powers-that-be they almost dismissed her out of hand. The Adjutant to the General Officer Commanding South-West, loyal to the Crown, only agreed to meet her on his chaplain's recommendation. He had already been apprised of her former rank and reputation, gained when she had been a member of the Army's top sniper team. Her opening statement convinced him that she was stark staring mad, and had *'gone off the reservation.'*

"Thank you for agreeing to see me, sir. I intend to assassinate the Prime Minister, and put an end to this bloody mess."

The Reverend Michael Normandy was in attendance, and it was he who convinced the Adjutant to hear her out.

She unfolded her story twice. The second telling was for the benefit of the GOC. When she had finished he turned to his Adjutant.

"Sanctioned! Every possible assistance to be given."

To everyone's surprise, the General came to attention and saluted the lady, as if she were the senior officer present. He strode briskly from the office, not wanting the tears welling in his eyes to be seen. She was quite the bravest soldier he had ever met.

Now she moved cautiously through the wooded area. She had avoided the village of Nomansland, on the Wiltshire/Hampshire border, and parked her nondescript car to the west of it, adjacent to St. Peter's Church, Bramshaw on the B3081. It wasn't serendipity that brought her to this place; St. Peter was her saint and guardian angel. When she researched the 12th Century church, a distressing newspaper report from 2019 grabbed her attention. Apparently, vandals had sprayed phallic symbols and the Devil's number '666' on doors and signs. Other factors apart, that confirmed her in her choice. The journey would commence from this ancient place of worship, and at its end she would remove Julian Marlborough's diabolic presence from the earth. In the chill confines of the Chancel she sought a blessing.

The pack she carried was larger than necessary for someone out for a day's walking, but she had to risk the possibility of curious eyes. As chance would have it, she was able to slip into the woods unseen. The March air retained its winter bite, and kept folk indoors. She decided against the full camouflage kit. Floppy hat and jacket sufficed, set off against ordinary denim jeans, plus hiking boots. Thermal underwear kept her warm under the outer garb, and gloves with similar properties covered the slender, and close-fitting, pair beneath them.

Eventually, she found what she was looking for; a clear line of fire, through the trees, for a distance of two-hundred and fifty metres. She was glad to unpack the muscular bulge of four Galia melons that weighted her pack. Soon they were targets; spiked on branches. She chose a satisfactory position to practice from, and assembled the rifle. The map, studied in advance, reminded her that habitation was in earshot, on all sides. It was of no consequence; the suppressor (silencer), would maintain her secrecy.

Rusty, yes, but not as bad as she thought. She clipped the first melon, but over a slow and patient two hours she obliterated all four of them; progressing to smaller, and more distant, targets.

Light was fading when she spotted the Hare. It sat upright preening itself. She estimated the range at three-hundred and eighty-five metres, and settled in the prone position to take the shot. She was about to squeeze the trigger when an extraordinary occurrence made her freeze. The woodland was descending into twilight, but an armoured beam of sunshine pierced the canopy and clothed the Hare in all his wonder.

"Live, my friend, you do no-one harm."

She moved away so stealthily that the Hare never noticed her departure.

*

Nations move on meandering journeys. Their traces oscillate between footpaths of peace, and highways of conflict. Malcontent young men infest social media with the notion that webs of intricate conspiracy control the destiny of their citizens. Such thoughts are asinine.

History is a womb; an unalterable fecund bowl, from which charismatic homunculi are spawned every so often. From the disabilities of their emotional lives obsessive disorders evolve. Benefitting from their personal attraction they draw to themselves a coterie of likeminded misfits. Together, they coerce the world into accepting their dogma and control. Oh yes, they plan and design the blueprint for their particular form of order, but ultimately they are driven onward by the instinct that tells them they are right; they alone are right. The homunculus is an emotional midget in perpetuity, but his power can grow exponentially to become a giant of destruction.

Julian Marlborough possessed instinct. He was highly intelligent, but the course he had chosen was sired by the twitching of his nose. He sniffed the air, divining the prevailing wind.

A perimeter fence guarded his country retreat near Saintbury. That portion of Special Forces who rallied to his side watched over the Prime Minister.

He liked to stroll in the garden before lunch. It was an opportunity to digest and reflect upon the latest news from his generals. Today his nose scented the first buds of Spring. For the one and only time, he dwelt upon where and why this had all started. He realised, with self-satisfaction, that he had gauged the temperature of the people correctly, way-back. Brexit! Yes, that was where it all began, long before he came on the scene. Nevertheless, that was what impelled him to stride the neural boulevards that led into the blind alley of conflict.

Julian yearned for the certainties of old England, and seventeen million people clamoured for the same chimera. What the chains of dogma prevented him, and them, from understanding was that the mores of another time can only be reclaimed through enforcement. Take that route, and you must march along it for ever. Once the imposition is made upon a nation, it can only be sustained through compulsion. It's a bugger when people won't think as we do. How can they not see that we are so much superior to them, and they must defer to our absolute wisdom? Prosaic omelettes and eggs came to his mind.

"Sir Kenneth Burke, sir. In the drawing room."

"The bearer of glad tidings I trust, Dominic?"

Julian and his acolyte strolled to the house.

"Spring flowers, Dominic, are you a fan?"

"Concrete would improve them, sir."

Julian's laugh had assumed a grave note in recent times. It was like a blast of halitosis that could make flowers wither.

"A witticism worthy of Ken. Let's hear what the old bugger has to say. Ken, old cock, we'll have a sharpener before lunch. Get pouring."

The Home Secretary's unctuous smile presaged his conjuring trick. Two pieces of cut glass emerged from behind his back.

"Hey presto!"

"Let's hear it then, warts and all."

The location of the Prime Minister was known to the opposition. It had been received from inside his coterie. The 'Crown' forces relied, principally, upon earthbound technology. Julian's team retained control of the satellites.

Her briefing was thorough. A cottage in Saintbury had been on the rental market for some time. She signed the lease, and integrated herself into the community. A tale of divorce and new starts was peddled to the neighbours. She attended church, and was pleasant to all and sundry.

After-church fellowship was the best time for intelligence gathering. Sifting the gossip wasn't difficult. Julian's compound was well-known. Occasionally, solemn young men, of impressive physique, appeared in the village shops. They were polite, but avoided conversation.

Old Bill Tressider was the most vocal resident.

"Blinkin' great chain fence all around the property. Blocked an ancient right of way, it has. Not on that. Now I 'as to stick an extra half mile on my constitutional. I'm not getting any younger."

"Do you good Bill. Soon 'ave you chasing the girls again. Isn't that right, Mrs. Clifford?"

She was finishing her cup of tea.

"Get yourself a bicycle, Bill, and you can come for rides with me."

A few of the men nearby overheard her remark, and were envious of the invitation.

"How far out of your way do you have to go, Bill?"

"Oh, not too far, Mrs. C. Normally, you come out of the woods, and walk the footpath across the bottom of his garden. I just take a left, about eighty yards before you leave the wood, and that takes you round the property. Course, the place is never out of sight – even in the woods – great big fence, but you still have a clear view."

"You ever seen him, Bill?"

"I have, Ernie. Large as life, and twice as ugly. You can see right the length of the garden into the back of the house. Seen him twice. Once standing on the terrace, and once through the French windows drinking his coffee in the sitting room."

"Go on! Your eyes aint up to seeing 'im over that distance. What? Must be about four hundred yards."

Ernie, my boy, you're quite right. My old 'lamps' struggle a bit these days...but a set of binoculars helps out!"

Knowing looks passed between the ladies at the tea trolley. Old Bill's birdwatching wasn't confined merely to the fields and woods. His net curtains were well-known for twitching.

"My goodness!"

"What is it, Mrs. Clifford?"

"Look at the time. I've a leg of lamb in the oven. It'll be done to a cinder if I don't skedaddle."

Estate agent Jeremy Plumpton offered his services.

"Give you a lift?"

"Awfully sweet of you, but I have my bike. Nice to see you all. Bye."

Bill and Ernie watched the swing of her derriere, as it passed out of the Village Hall. Psychic forces aligned, and they sang together.

"If you go down to the woods today, you're sure of a big surprise...!"

That nice lady, known as Mrs. Clifford, did indeed go home. She ate her lunch, and then wrapped up warm. A bobble hat covered her hair, and a pair of unnecessary spectacles clung to her face. The collar on the warm winter jacket was turned up, and off she cycled. It was her Sunday afternoon ritual. She waved to one or two others. They were on foot, engaged in their customary exercise.

The bicycle was left in a dell, and covered with broken branches and leaves that had not yet rotted in the dark confines of the wood. She followed old Bill's footpath, taking the left turn he had described. The fence and house beyond were clearly visible. Cameras hung from the posts of the three-metre-high fence. She scanned the woodland path to see if any cameras had been installed on the trees. None were visible, and with her trained eye she was as sure as she could be that they didn't exist in the gloom of the wood.

Bill was right. You could see the terrace, and the French windows. There was no sign of anyone in the room, and nothing stirred in the garden or near the fence. Yet she knew that she was being watched. On she strolled. The walk was a three-mile circuit. She paused when she returned to her starting point, and knelt down to retie her bootlace. It enabled her to check for any sudden appearances. There were none, so she walked into the wood and reclaimed her bicycle. Another hour on the road was consistent with the time she was usually out.

When she hopped nimbly off her bike, before the cottage gate, there was the inevitable nosy neighbour who declared to her husband.

"There's Mrs. Clifford, back from her exercise. Regular as clockwork. She must be in good trim."

Many a husband had to bite his tongue, and just think to himself.

"She certainly is."

Over a few weeks she increased her distance on the bike, and returned home later and later. Her longest route took her to Bidford-On-Avon. From there she turned towards Salford Priors, and fiddled her way home via Evesham and Broadway. The light was going by the time she essayed the final leg, and a Mercedes pulled alongside her. It was Jeremy Plumpton.

"Hi Kathy. Been out long?"

She described her route.

"Phew! You must be exhausted. Come on, let's sling the bike in the boot, and I'll treat you to a drink in the "Cock."

"That's very kind of you, Jeremy. Can I take a rain check? I want to complete this run. Bye."

He gave her a cheery wave as he zoomed by, satisfied that he was on a promise. 'Kathy Clifford' was delighted with the encounter. A witness to her harmless wanderings.

The meeting with Ken Burke went on all afternoon. They took Sunday lunch off trays. Aides and military men came and went at intervals, and business was concluded at just after seven p.m. It was April 1st. The clocks had gone forward, and the days were longer. Nonetheless, the light was beginning to fade on a heavily overcast day.

Whilst Julian put logs in the burner, Ken refreshed their drinks. Then they settled into the cosy armchairs.

"Seen that delicious lady friend of yours lately?"

"To whom do you refer, Kenneth dear boy?"

Julian smirked, he knew quite well who Ken was talking about.

"Your sub-continently named passion."

That pulled Julian up short.

"Why do you call her that?"

"My dear fellow, no need to bristle. I envy you. She's quite delightful in every aspect, and I wish you both the very best of luck. About time Julian, my boy, do you the world of good."

Ken's over-familiarity would normally have caused deep offence. Julian was so warmed by his words, and the thought of India, that he forgave him instantly.

"You sound like my old pa', Ken. I've noticed that you take more than a passing interest in mother. You're out of luck there, she's already spoken for."

Ken flipped an eyebrow.

"Really, who's the lucky chap?"

Julian couldn't find a good reason to keep it a secret.

"She is to be wed next week to the redoubtable Guy Grosvenor."

Ken recalled what his lubricious eye had gawked at through the keyhole at Chequers. He feigned surprise.

"What! Your Head of Counter Terrorism?"

"Former Head. Can't employ him now. It would be like having a tradesman for a step-father."

"Lucky blighter. I say, Julian, we must toast their health. Let me top you up."

Ken moved out of view from the French windows. Julian was silhouetted beautifully by the glow from the table lamp beside him.

She had a clear and uncluttered shot. The line of sight was narrow through the higgledy-piggledy layout of the trees, and the gaps of the chain link fence. 'Kathy' had lain there since before dawn. She had put it out the day before that she wouldn't be in church. Family affairs to address first thing, and then out for the day on her bike. In fact, she'd left the cottage in pitch darkness, walking her bicycle beside her until she was out of the village. Not a soul stirred at that hour, and no-one witnessed her going.

Now she had him. His companion had moved to another part of the room. She inhaled deeply, and then exhaled slowly. Just as she squeezed the trigger Ken Burke shot into view proffering Julian's drink. He stumbled over the rug. Drink flew all over his master, and Ken fell on top of him. The bullet hit Ken in the shoulder, and spun him to one side. Sound was minimal, but the old soldier in Julian was instantly aware that he was under fire. He fell to the floor, and scrambled towards the alarm.

Kathy Clifford was already gone. At the edge of the wood she slipped out of her one-piece jump suit, and crushed it into a pack, along with the balaclava. The rifle was abandoned beneath the leaves and branches from which she retrieved her bicycle. It would be discovered, but it wouldn't tell them anything they didn't already know.

She was on the bike in a trice, and heading for the village. The lights of a car illuminated her before she heard the engine. It raced past, and disappeared round a bend. She heard a crunch of gears, and then its rear end appeared. Kathy was down on one knee beside the back wheel. The air was let out of the tyre post haste. Her heart raced, opposing her effort to focus on staying calm. She glanced upwards, and smiled with relief. Jeremy Plumpton strode towards her.

"Trouble Kathy?"

"Second bloody puncture of the day. That's why I'm so late home. God, I need a drink."

"It will be my pleasure, my dear. Car's open. Climb aboard while I stow the bone shaker."

She luxuriated in the comfort of the leather, and heard the slam of the boot lid.

"To the 'Cock'?"

"To the 'Cock', Jeremy!"

It was almost a toast.

*

The Prince of Wales led a battalion in the Crown forces. His father had overruled the protests of his generals. Leicester had been taken, and they intended to move on Oxford next, to relieve it from the besieging forces.

Regimental structures remained in place, but there had been considerable integration, by necessity. None knew the mind of each individual soldier, and desertion from one to side to the other was commonplace.

The civilian population suffered, as ever. They had one thing to be thankful for, and that was that the commanders of both forces enforced strict discipline on their troops. Looting by soldiers, and more horrific depredations, were dealt with severely and summarily. Neighbours were a different kettle of fish. Towns and cities were split. Before long they resembled Northern Ireland during *'The Troubles'*. People fled their homes, and went to reside amongst those who shared their point of view.

Without air support, both sides had to rely upon armour and the poor bloody infantry. Skirmishes and battles alike regressed to a time when men stood toe-to-toe and slaughtered each other.

All thoughts of relieving Oxford were dismissed. Oxford had been relieved, by the Parliamentary forces abandoning the siege, on Julian's orders. It was the Prime Minister who had named his forces thus. A misnomer, if ever there was one. They marched north-east towards Leicester. Reconnaissance found the Crown forces arrayed south of Market Harborough It was an ill omen for someone.

The April morning was foggy. It was not easy to sight the Royalist army, occupying a strong position on a ridge. General Roland Vaughan had taken the field at the head of the Parliamentary army. Chief of Staff he may be, but something told him that they must win this battle, or perish. He too had located a nearby ridge on which to station his forces.

London was still held by the Crown. The King had assessed the situation correctly, during his flight from Windsor. Two-thirds of the Household Division had remained loyal. A political decision was taken, however, that depleted his forces elsewhere. It was agreed that Scottish troops should not venture south of York. Those who supported the King, throughout the country, understood readily why troops from the far north had first taken to the field on English soil. To see them engaged in battle in the heart of England might jeopardise that acceptance.

The stand-off couldn't last forever. Royalist tanks made the first move, with infantry support. Laurence Merrill had been promoted from colonel to Brigadier. All custom went out of the window, and he was at the forefront of the infantry, as they sought shelter behind the armour. Vaughan had stationed his tanks on the left. It was from this outflanking position that they fired upon the Royalist armour, and inflicted substantial casualties. Such was their superiority that they were able to turn their attention to the Royalist artillery positions, and silence them. Parliamentary infantry advanced, and fell upon their ravaged opponents. The Prince of Wales was ordered to engage, and his battalion raced forward on foot. Englishmen stood toe-to-toe with one another. Bayonets sank into screaming flesh, and rifle butts smashed teeth from skulls.

Both commanders committed all of their troops to the battle, and the savagery of another age stained the fields of England. Major John Welbourne came face-to face with Laurence Merrill, his former commander, and shot him down like a dog.

On they fought for three hours. God alone knows how, but a runner found the Prince of Wales in the midst of a tumult. He and his personal bodyguard were defending the regimental colours. He knew his duty was to obey. The bugle pierced through the din of battle. It was a fighting retreat, with what little armour was left to protect them. The destination was Leicester, from where they hoped to reorganise. Vaughan called off the pursuit after two miles. He was convinced that he had inflicted a grievous defeat on the Crown forces.

"We'll billet in and around Market Harborough for forty-eight hours. Find me a comfy spot, Henry."

"Already taken care of, sir. Rather nice property in a nearby village, with a boozer just round the corner. They do a rather fine fish and chips, or so I'm told."

"Excellent Henry. Oh, what's the village called?"

"Naseby, General Vaughan."

*

The Prime Minister was cock-a-hoop, His convoy charted a course for Chequers on Good Friday. A resounding victory, and now he was going to see his 'girl'. India was once more resident at Desmond Claymore-Browne's. She would join him on Easter Sunday for a very special occasion; the nuptials of his mother and Guy Grosvenor in St. George's Church, Banksmore.

Julian woke, refreshed from a nap after lunch. It was good to be back at Chequers, and within touching distance of London. A ring of considerable steel surrounded Buckinghamshire. Eight thousand troops were on high alert, in case the Household Division tried for an incursion into, what he regarded as, his fiefdom.

He lifted the telephone receiver.

"Call for you, sir. Miss Woake."

India's husky tones breathed down the line.

"Darling, good to have you back were you belong."

He thrilled to her voice, and especially to the sobriquet, 'Darling'.

"Darling!" he rejoined. "Wish you were here. Have you heard the news from Northamptonshire?"

"A great victory for you, darling."

Julian possessed the unique capacity to strut whilst lying down. He took ownership of Roland Vaughan's battle plan.

"Like clockwork. My strategy was perfect."

"What next?"

"Oh, I don't mind telling you. This is a secure line."

He could not see the wintry smile on her face.

"We're assembling my army for a push on the Capital. Once we've taken London it will all be over. Anyhow, enough 'shop'. Looking forward to seeing you on Sunday. At the House for eleven. Has Desmond agreed to escort you? After the service he can hand you over to me, for good."

"That will be delicious, darling. Sadly, Desmond is indisposed. Gippy tummy for the last twenty-four hours. Don't think he'll be up to feasting. You'll have me all to yourself. Oops, got to go, Desmond needs assistance."

Julian heard a distant cry.

"Till Sunday, darling. Love you."

She was gone, and his pitiless eyes shone brightly. She loved him.

Desmond poured them a drink.

"Beautifully done, India."

"Gives me a ready-made excuse to escape his clutches. Hopefully, for the last time. Cheers."

The Prime Minister entered the Operations Room in high good humour.

"All well, chaps and chappesses?"

A dapper young man in civvies moved to his side.

"Would you care to take a look at this, sir?"

The new Head of Counter Terrorism handed him a note.

Julian frowned, as he read the information.

"Where did this originate, Jerry?"

"An intercept by Intelligence. You can listen to the phone call, if you like sir."

"That won't be necessary. Reliable?"

"Absolutely sir. It's as kosher as a rabbi."

"Right, this is what we'll do."

Easter Sunday dawned, and sunlight warmed the land. Whilst he shaved, Julian had the television on. The BBC was still functioning, far and wide, in the hands of the Crown.

He could just about see Arthur Cantwell's bearded face in his shaving mirror. The service was coming from Canterbury Cathedral. Julian switched off from most of it, as he had done throughout his life. When the Archbishop declared *"Christ is Risen!"*, and the congregation in the cathedral and Trafalgar Square responded with, *"He is risen indeed!"*, he waved his cut throat razor at the screen.

"And when I'm back where I belong you can take his place in the tomb; you hirsute fuckwit."

It really wasn't the done thing to attend your mother's wedding accompanied by a platoon of Special Services troops, backed up by paratroopers. They arrayed themselves as discreetly as possible around 'The Manor'. Inside the small party was gay and effusive. Julian pumped Guy Grosvenor's hand.

"You know Jerry Tomlinson, your replacement, don't you Guy?"

The petite man was shiny in his morning dress.

"Good to see you Guy. Feel I should apologise for stepping into dead men's shoes, if that's not an inappropriate thing to say."

The three of them laughed heartily. Julian went to greet his mother.

"Ma, you look ravishing. He's a lucky man."

"I'm fortunate too. Finding true love is next to impossible in youth. To receive it at my age is a miracle. Are you happy for me, Julian?"

"Quite ecstatic, as you should be for me."

She followed his eyes across the room to where India was providing drinks for Ken Burke, and listening to his tale of derring-do. He was making the most of his gunshot wound, and India straightened his sling for him.

"India is everything I would want for you, my darling boy. Pity we couldn't make it a double wedding."

"A charming thought, Ma, but we're destined for a glorious day at the Abbey."

An officer in dress uniform stepped into the room. Julian nodded.

"Got the all clear, Ma, we'd best make tracks."

He proffered his arm, and escorted her from the room. They waited in the Library until the Bridegroom and sundry guests had departed.

"Give them a head start, eh Ma. Then we can make a grand entrance. Sorry about my escort, but at least they're in full fig."

When Lady Deborah and her son stepped from the limousine the small crowd of villagers was held well back. An eerie silence dwelt over the village green. The nation now knew what had really happened in the Church on Christmas Eve, and the remnants of the shattered village population looked on in condemnation. Derek Fisher could not contain himself, and he bellowed at the back of his wife's killer.

"You murdering scum, Marlborough!"

Commander Jerry Tomlinson made a move towards the old man. Julian hissed at him.

"No!"

Mother and son collected themselves in the porch, where Padam Gurung had been found by Marjorie Whitlock, prostrate and barely clinging to life. Mendelssohn's 'Wedding March' cried plaintively from the organ, as they proceeded down the aisle.

The tame Vicar led them through the customary offices, and came to that moment usually reserved for the proud father of the Bride.

"Who brings this woman to be married to this man?"

Julian's face positively glowed.

"I do."

The Vicar gagged on his next word, at the unexpected interruption.

"But not to this traitor!"

A gasp escaped from the congregation, and Lady Debs swayed on his arm. Only Ken Burke was unsurprised. It was not that he had been forewarned, merely that nothing his boss did could surprise him.

"He really is a star performer," he thought.

The Head of Counter Terrorism stepped forward. Two formidable soldiers accompanied him.

"Guy Alan Grosvenor, you are charged with complicity in the assassination attempt on the Prime Minister of the United Kingdom. In times of war this is a treasonable act punishable by death. The sentence will be carried out immediately."

Terror gripped Deborah Marlborough, and bludgeoned her into silence. She watched her beloved walk out of the church. A sepulchral silence dwelt upon them. The single gunshot cracked the air, and she buried her face in her son's chest. He did not mind the fingernails cutting into his flesh. Reclamation, yes, he had reclaimed his beloved mother; she would become a picturesque adjunct to the adornment of his India. He could not see the hatred that disfigured her face.

Ken had wanted to make himself scarce, but Julian wouldn't hear of it. Having his 'Fool' at his side was essential to his ego. On the short trip back to 'The Manor' he reflected that old Ken might be just the right chap to pen his memoirs, when the final battle was won.

He felt snug and smug, seated between his Mother and India. Ma would understand, of that he was confident. She had supported his every move in life, triumphs and indiscretions, with supreme calm and aplomb. India looked pale, so he took her hand and manufactured a sympathetic smile.

Deborah Marlborough stood outside her front door staring into space. Unbidden, India wrapped her arm around an old lady, and led her indoors.

"Ken, old boy, entertain India for me, there's a good chap. Need to have a quiet word with Ma."

He hopped up the steps, and twisted around to look down on his servant.

"Never know your luck, Ken, you might be in the frame to take that bastard's place."

Ken Burke couldn't conceal the look of horror that leapt to his face.

Julian roared with laughter.

"Don't look so bloody worried, old cock. I meant with Ma, not the firing squad. Nearly dragged you up to the altar there and then, after we polished Grosvenor off. All that food going to waste. Still, I'm sure we can make inroads into the booze."

The chameleon charm of the man changed gear, as he mounted the stairs to his Mother's bedroom. He knocked lightly, and entered. Deborah sat before her dressing table, trying to recognise the woman in the mirror. She couldn't quite fathom who the desiccated and ravaged old lady was, looking back at her.

Her son, the killer of her beloved Guy, placed his impenitent hand on her shoulder.

"It had to be done. That bullet in Ken's shoulder was meant for me. I received irrefutable evidence that Guy gave them my whereabouts."

She wanted to scream at him not to soil Guy's name with his unspeakable lips. The legacy of breeding and training kept her spine straight, and her mouth closed.

"When this is over you must come and live with me and India. Tell you what, you shall have entire control over our wedding preparations. What a lark to see you bossing the Dean of Westminster about. Everything Ma'! Dresses, flowers... Every- thing. No expense spared."

She rose from the stool, and examined her wedding outfit in the mirror. The creases would never come out.

"Do we have guests, Julian?"

"India, and old Ken."

"Then we must join them."

"Why don't you rest, Ma?"

"That would be awfully ill-mannered on my wed..., towards our guests. Come."

Three of the foursome in the Library drank heavily. Lady Deborah insisted that the champagne must not go to waste. She sipped a single glass fastidiously, whilst watching and listening. Julian dominated the conversation.

"We've got them on the run. My success in Northamptonshire depleted their resources. I think another few weeks, and we'll be ringing the church bells the length and breadth of the land. What say you, Lord Cranborne?"

A startled Ken blinked furiously.

"I beg your pardon!"

"First task when the curtain comes down is to elevate you to the Lords."

"Isn't there already a Lord Cranborne, sir?"

"Is there? Oh well, think of an alternative. Anything but Clapham!"

India sat nervously. Tollard Royal was located on the Cranborne Chase."

"What made you think of that name, Julian?"

"Oh, nothing special. It just popped into my head. I was down that way not long ago. Looks a lovely part of the world. Oh my God, of course, that's your midden, isn't it? You get looking for a parcel of land down there. We will build the most fantastic house, when we're married."

Deborah's face never altered from its neutral repose. Marriage, weddings and victory – he went on and on, as if nothing had happened. For the first time in her life she lifted the skirts of his superficial charisma. She discerned that it shifted and changed according to who he was addressing. His face was a yawning cavern, revealing the hideous and bestial violence that lurked within. If it were possible, she would have ripped her womb open in hopeless penance for the Neolithic creature she had brought into the world. She was ashamed of herself; mortified that recognition had only come when the pain and suffering was inflicted directly upon her.

"Goodness, look at the time. I'm overdue at Chequers – big pow-wow. Got a spot of exciting news, before I go. No, you tell them Ken. After all, you organised the glittering occasion."

He shook Ken's hand, and kissed his rigid Mother on the cheek. Taking India's hand, he led her into the hallway.

"You can come with me to Chequers."

"Oh darling, I'm so sorry. Desmond is pretty bad with food poisoning, and I've promised to nurse him back to health."

A sigh escaped him, but then he perked up.

"No matter. Might work out better. Go and have a listen to what old Ken has to say. You will laugh. See you on April 23rd, in your best frock."

He looked at her expectantly.

"Can't you guess?"

She shook her head, bemused.

"Not to worry. Lord *'Whatever to be'* will fill you in."

He pressed her to him, and kissed her deeply.

"Bye. The 23rd, don't be late."

India steadied herself, before entering the Library. The kiss had been vile. His lips pulsated in her mind. They were like the flabby breasts of an aging charlady. Without the slightest knowledge of his schoolboy nickname, she said under her breath,

"Titty lips that's what they are; 'Titty Lips'.

32

"What country have we reached?"
'Oedipus at Colonus'

They were not perturbed by the roadblock. It wasn't the first they had encountered. The corporal examined the pass, returned it, and saluted her and the Brigadier seated beside her. He had cast an eye over a very rare beast indeed; one of the few official passes signed by the Prime Minister. Julian hadn't thought twice about issuing one to his fiancé. India simply said that she couldn't abandon Desmond Claymore-Browne who, according to her, was going downhill rapidly. Besides, she would need it to join him at Chequers.

"Bloody hell, Sarge, they're making Brigadiers young these days."

"Strange times, Harry, strange times."

"What about the kid in the back?"

"Not for us to ask, Harry; not when you get one of those passes flashed at you. As rare as rocking horse shit. Her daughter, I expect."

The Audi Q8 S line left the M3 at the junction for Basingstoke, and had passed through two roadblocks already. The third, and last was when they came off the M4 for Maidenhead and High Wycombe.

"Home and dry, Jack, home and dry."

Jack Preston was not entirely convinced by India's assertion, but he had placed his life in the hands of the Lord and that was sufficient. It was Isa who gave voice to his thought, from the rear seat.

"Some way to go yet, India, so let's be cautious. We follow the narrow path, and that is always perilous. It would be foolish not to be on the lookout for snares and pitfalls."

Jack lightened the mood.

"I must say, your father's old uniform fits me like a glove." Then he laughed. "Vanity, vanity, all is vanity."

St. George's Banksmore was packed for Sunday morning service. The Reverend Justin Ambler, the House for Duty priest, led the faithful and not so faithful in worship. When it came to the only reading for the day he paused. Jack Preston emerged from the Vestry, not in military uniform but in cassock and surplice, with the blue stole of the lay preacher around his neck. He strode purposefully down the aisle of the Nave, and mounted the steps to the pulpit.

"The wicked freely strut about when what is vile is honoured among men."

He shut the Bible with a clap that made the congregation jump.

"I see that some of you recognised me straight away. For the benefit of those who didn't, I am Jack Preston one time lay preacher of this parish."

A syncopated hum disturbed the tranquillity, until it reached a crescendo and transformed into a uniform crooning of his name. Those who had never seen him in the flesh knew him from his underground broadcasts shown on social media.

"My time with you is, by necessity short. In this place, your church, I witnessed the most monstrous and sacrilegious act. Some of you may say, "What is that to me? I have only come here because I am fearful in these dark times. I have no certainty in faith; I am unsure if God exists. I am frightened, and I look for comfort." So be it! Sacrilege – an offence against all that is sacred. Whatever the condition of your faith, do you not regard human life as sacred? Yes, you do. You believe in the sacred right to life for yourself, and for those whom you love. What about everyone else? Those who disagree with you, and those who you don't like. You cannot live in the light yourself if you condemn your brothers and sisters to darkness."

He leavened his words with a humorous interjection, and as he sang he remembered Marjorie Whitlock.

"Love and marriage, love and marriage, go together like a horse and carriage. Ask the local gentry, and they will say it's elementary..."

Deborah Marlborough was mesmerised by the compassion that fell upon her from his eyes. She sat in isolation in her old pew. Peace passed into her, as she felt her hands held on either side. She looked first at the serene young girl on her right, and then in surprise at India on her left.

"That was sung by *'The Chairman of the Board';* for the benefit of the younger generation, Frank Sinatra. The real Chairman of the Board is with us now, and He's asking each one of us a question. Will we do our duty? Will we act honourably towards our neighbours; like them or not?"

Jack opened his Bible.

"Love must be sincere. Hate what is evil; cling to good. Be devoted to one another in brotherly love. Honour one another above yourselves."

When he spoke he did so without knowing that an old man had once taught his granddaughter the very same lesson, in the Nilgiri Hills of India, an eternity of pain and joy ago.

"Honour is not to be found in institutions. Its source is not exclusive to the school or university you went to, or the regiment you joined. The wellspring of honour, and the dutiful life that leaps new born from it, is within us. We must drill down into ourselves to release the geyser which washes away the destructive forces of selfishness and hatred towards others. I will not speak long of Christ. It is sufficient that you know I stand here, because I believe He lives in me, and in you also."

He gave them a brief time for reflection. Lady Deborah saw that India was videoing the proceedings on her mobile phone. What she didn't know was that it was going out as a live transmission across numerous networks. Archie Woake was making sure of that, down in Wiltshire. The GOC South-West stood at his shoulder approvingly.

At Hughenden, on the outskirts of High Wycombe, a ‘watcher’ called to Jerry Tomlinson, Head of Counter Terrorism.

“Sir, sir! We’ve got a location for the transmission. It’s being routed out of Wiltshire.”

Tomlinson looked at the screen.

“Never mind fucking Wiltshire. That’s Banksmore, St. George’s Church, Banksmore. I was only there last Sunday!”

Within minutes, three Land Rovers burst out of Hughenden, jammed with men and women armed to the teeth. The old home of Queen Victoria’s Prime Minister had never seen such a fuss and to-do. Benjamin Disraeli might have quoted from his novel, “Sybil.”

“Two nations, between whom there is no intercourse and no sympathy...”

Jack pressed on to take hold of that for which Christ Jesus took hold of him. He smiled, as he heard Marjorie’s voice say, “Philippians 3:12.”

“A time of decision is upon us; not tomorrow, not next week – now! When we return this nation to peace, and only then, will we be able to say, in good faith:

“Pray for us. We are sure that we have a clear conscience and desire to live honourably in every way.”

The Reverend Ambler administered a blessing, whilst Jack hurried to the Vestry. Isa and India stood, and Deborah looked up at her son's fiancé. India's hand was outstretched; it was taken without hesitation. The three of them strode out of the church, and got into the car parked adjacent to the gates. Debs did a double take at the military gentlemen seated beside her.

"Lady Deborah."

"Jack."

They sat back in comfort for the return journey to Wiltshire. The counter-terrorism convoy paid them no heed when they raced past, heading in the opposite direction.

There was a nervous moment when they reached the roadblock that guarded the entrance to the M25. Alerts had gone out rapidly, to stop and detain a wanted priest. Deborah took command of the situation.

"Young man!"

Her stentorian cry brought a young lieutenant scuttling to the car window.

"Do you know who I am?"

She gave no time to answer. Debs was a galleon in full sail.

"I am Lady Deborah Marlborough. You may have heard of my son – he's the Prime Minister! This lady is his betrothed; my daughter-in-law to be. You've seen the pass."

Lieutenant Roger O'Malley hopped about like a demented and indecisive frog.

"For goodness sake, young man. Here's my driving licence, and a photograph of myself with my son. It was only taken last week."

Her nerve nearly failed, as a gunshot echoed in her mind. The lieutenant saved her.

"My apologies, ma'am. Open the barrier."

When Jerry Tomlinson, and his crew, burst into St. George's they found an almost full congregation still present. A few people screamed with terror when they saw the heavily-armed men. Was Banksmore to have a double dose of infamy?

Most remained silent and watchful, as the officers spread out. Tomlinson began to feel distinctly uncomfortable. He was used to the odour of fear when he and his sort pitched up. There was barely a trace of it in that ancient place of worship. He decided to assert his authority.

"Right! No one is to leave until you've all been questioned."

Derek Fisher stood foursquare in the Crossing.

"Let me save you the trouble, old boy."

Derek's life-long passion was for history. He quoted Speaker, William Lenthall, who faced down Charles I. Sarcasm was in every word:

"May it please your majesty, I have neither eyes to see nor tongue to speak in this place but as this House is pleased to direct me whose servant I am here..."

There can be no doubt that the Holy Spirit dwelt with him. Derek's follow-up, however, was a tad light on sanctity.

"The bird is well and truly flown. Now fuck off, old son, the pubs are open."

*

Archie Woake had set up the laptop on the kitchen table. The assembled company could all see and hear. Closest to it was Deborah Marlborough, and she listened intently whilst the silhouetted figure spoke. The lack of discernible features made her smile. A face didn't matter; even through the deliberate distortion of the voice, she knew who spoke.

"So you see Debs, he was with us from the outset. Guy was not an evangelising sort of Christian, but he'd been brought up in that school, and he adhered to its values. He counts amongst the best of men. Guy knew where his duty lay, and he knew the dangers. Courage is not something that pops out of a bottle. It's when, despite your fears, you put your life on the line anyway. Guy had it in Spades. He loved you, Deborah, he told me so."

She looked inward upon herself. Deborah knew that, because of her age, she and Guy would only have shared a limited number of years. Nonetheless, a cold and dispassionate fury possessed her at the thought of those years lost.

Debs looked at the shadowy figure on the screen.

"What about you...?"

She nearly revealed his name.

"What about you?"

A familiar self-deprecating chuckle reached everyone's ears. Deborah had heard it before, and always thought it false humility. Not this time.

"Been a bit of selfish so-and-so throughout my life, Debs, but..."

He searched for words, and decided to bite the bullet.

"Your son offends my very soul, Deborah, and he offends the history and soul of this great nation. I...I...I'm sorry. Would you believe it; I'm lost for words."

Archie Woake spoke urgently.

"You've been on long enough. Cutting communication now!"

Marion Woake disrupted the still-life painting that they seemed to be sitting for.

"Tea or coffee?"

Abir Hussain initiated a little chit chat whilst the kettle boiled. When they had their mugs in front of them, Deborah decided to cut through any preamble.

"India has put you all in the picture, regarding my son's intentions. I must say, even I'm surprised at his *chutzpah*. Flying off at a frivolous tangent in the middle of a civil war."

She paused, and then retracted her words.

"I apologise for saying that. I'm not in the least surprised. Satisfying his ego has been my life's work."

Debs traced a finger in the spilt coffee on the table, as if trying to read the runes. When she raised her head they saw the unwavering resolve in her eyes.

"I have a new employer. I am with you."

General Matthew Stone, GOC South-West held the floor.

"Thank you, ma'am."

He addressed the room.

"The success of our strategy is dependent upon many factors. Countless men and women will lose their lives before we can bring it to fruition. There is a great battle to be fought within the next few days. I am confident that we will triumph, and then we can execute the plan."

He spoke to Deborah directly.

"Lady Deborah, I assure you that we will give our best endeavours to see that your son, the Prime Minister, is taken into custody alive. From there we will surrender him into the hands of the International Tribunal at The Hague."

Lady Deborah Marlborough did not speak. She gave a gracious nod of acknowledgement, exemplary in its adherence to the principle of *noblesse oblige.*

33

"We breathe on the abyss; we are the abyss..."
'Oedipus Rex'

Leicester Cathedral is really just a big parish church, but it is the resting place of King Richard III. The personal bodyguard of the Prince of Wales obscured 'Crookback's' tomb. They stood to attention, whilst their Prince knelt before the altar. He prayed aloud.

"Almighty God, King of Kings, I lift to you the name of my ancestor King Henry VII. Grant to us, Lord, victory in the coming battle, that we may, like him, bring harmony out of discord, and unite this kingdom in peace and prosperity. I ask this in the name of our Saviour, Jesus Christ, Amen."

The young man faced his officers.

"We have our orders. Our brothers from Scotland are called to arms. We, gentlemen, are bidden to undertake a most interesting task. Tony, the Warwickshire's will have the honour of being our vanguard."

He turned to the altar, and the company knelt with him.

"May the power and wisdom of God be bestowed upon you, and the Holy Spirit walk with you through the travails ahead. May you, and all who live upon these islands, come at last to those shores, where the Prince of

Peace awaits you in love. The blessing of God Almighty, Father, Son, and Holy Spirit be with you now, and always. Amen."

The Dean of Leicester Cathedral watched them march down the Nave in sure and certain hope.

General Vaughan had also set out in high hopes. He might have walked past India Woake on the street, never knowing it was she who put a spanner in his works. Julian had not revealed the precise date for the attack on London, but she was able to report the time frame it fell into.

There was something else Vaughan didn't know. The American President had declared to his military advisers that he wouldn't let the UK, *"Go to hell in a handcart!"* The American people had wisely elected a man, instead of the petulant child they'd foisted upon themselves some years before. At George Holmes' insistence NATO played a stealthy hand. Their boffins took control of the UK's satellite facility, and provided a stream of false intelligence. This led to the abandonment of the Siege of Leicester. Intel asserted that the force within the city was too small to constitute a threat; it could be mopped up later.

The Parliamentary forces advanced from two directions. One division came out of Berkshire and Buckinghamshire, intending to enter London through Twickenham and Richmond. The main body headed for North London. With advance warning, the Household Division took up position, under cover of darkness.

The Life Guards and The Blues and Royals were divided equally to provide armoured reconnaissance on both fronts. The Irish and Welsh Guards were stationed to defend the approaches to South London. Three further regiments of Foot Guards would bear the brunt of the attack from the North; the Coldstream, Scots and Grenadier Guards. Artillery and heavy armour was split two to one between North and South.

Vaughan's troops were caught by surprise on the northern outskirts of St. Albans. When men know that no quarter will be given they become tenacious, and they fought back. Soon the battle descended into street fighting, and the General set up his command post in the Cathedral.

The passage into London, south of the River Thames, had the initial appearance of a cake walk. By necessity, it had fewer defenders, and the fighting moved quickly from Twickenham into Richmond. Kempton Park Racecourse, and Bushy Park are adjacent to one another. At the pivotal moment in the battle, The Royal Marines emerged from those confines, and fell upon the rear of the Parliamentary forces. The trap worked beautifully, and within five hours the rapidly-promoted Major-General John Welbourne was surrendering his forces to the Crown.

To the north of London, the sun went down on a stalemate. Roland Vaughan sat long into the night with his senior officers. They added and subtracted; multiplied and divided. The odds didn't look good, especially with the losses south of the river. Still, their armour and artillery remained relatively intact. He was reluctant to shell the ancient city of St. Albans, and send tanks crashing through its streets, but needs must when the Devil drives.

"05:00 hrs gentlemen. Full scale attack. Thirty-minute artillery barrage at 04:30, then armour with infantry support."

The attack never materialised. At 03:30 hrs the Scottish regiments fell upon their rear. Vaughan found himself under fire from two sides. He sent an urgent signal to the Prime Minister. The reply came within five minutes.

"Surrender not acceptable. Employ TNWs."

The order was circulated amongst the assembled officers. Everyone blanched upon reading the instruction. British troops ordered to use tactical nuclear weapons against their fellow citizens, on British soil.

"Gentlemen!"

The general's firm tone brought them to attention.

"Gentlemen, this is the signal I intend to send. Please read it. If anyone wishes to demur they may do so without fear of retribution. It is my intention to gather what is left of our forces, and fight our way out of this trap. Our destination will be..."

He traced a finger over a map.

"Banbury. Yes, Banbury."

A mirthless laugh echoed around the Chapter House.

"Oh look what's nearby, Edgehill! 1642 wasn't it? Who won that one, Freddie?"

Colonel Freddie Richards stroked his chin.

"Mmm? No decisive result, sir."

Vaughan's eerie laugh penetrated their souls again.

"A draw is always unsatisfactory, but on this occasion it might be the best we can hope for. Alternately, we may be riding a cock horse to Banbury Cross. Come gentlemen, let us depart, before we are all hung on one."

34

"Time, which sees all things, has found you out."
'Oedipus Rex'

Sauron is the Dark Lord in Tolkien's *'Lord of the Rings'*. The Royal Shakespeare Theatre, in Stratford-Upon-Avon, has a tower that might well be mistaken for his; from whence the *'Evil Eye of Sauron'*, or anyone else, could cast a baleful look upon the surrounding countryside.

Julian Marlborough did not stand on ceremony. He sat in the Director's office, at the top of the tower. In fact, he occupied his chair, and had his feet up on his desk.

The Artistic Director of the RSC, Michael Moran, stood before him like a recalcitrant schoolboy and quivered. His flowing locks, and bird's nest beard gave him the appearance of Gandalf the Wizard. Sadly, he did not bear himself with the dignity of Gandalf the White, or even Gandalf the Grey; he was more ashen.

Julian was laying into him.

"Why? What's the fucking point of that?"

Moran burbled something about gender and ethnic equality being company policy.

"An all-woman cast, you say, apart from me. Hmmm? Suppose it might work. Showcase my finer qualities.

Okay, I'll go with it, but they'd better be good-looking...and no lezzers! Come on."

Whilst the lift descended, Moran composed himself. The last time he'd heard such offensive language was when he was a teenager. It was rife in the Northern working men's club he'd drink in with his father. Dear God (not that he believed in such an entity)! How had they come to find themselves in this position?

Sir Ken Burke had made a personal telephone call in early April, and given instructions. Moran had cast and rehearsed hurriedly. Now it was the morning of April 23rd, St. George's Day (not that Moran believed in such absurdities as saints). The performance would take place that evening, before an invited audience.

Julian made the short hop from Saintbury, accompanied as usual by a bevy of bodyguards. He was in high spirits. The disinformation he had received from London assured him that all was well. He believed that his forces had regained lost territory and were advancing. Even better, at the lunch break he would munch beside his beloved India, and his Mother. The Arden Hotel, across from the Theatre, had already been commandeered by the security services.

At the second roadblock his companion, Ken Burke, was startled by a sudden exclamation.

"Bloody hell! They're on the other side."

"What?"

"The cap badge. Royal Warwickshire Regiment. Aren't they fighting for the opposition?"

Ken was suavity itself.

"No longer dear boy, no longer. Came over to us a fortnight ago. Saw which way the wind was blowing."

Julian turned to Jerry Tomlinson.

"Why wasn't I told?"

"Sorry, sir, military briefings aren't my domain."

Ken patted his boss' arm, and smiled unctuously.

"My dear fellow. The situation has been, as they say, fluid. Can't keep you up to speed with every fart to the ounce. Besides, you have to focus on today. You're going to be marvellous. Best thing ever. Here we are. Eight a.m. Wonder if the luvvies are out of bed yet?"

"Not bad, not bad," Julian murmured under his breath.

The all-female cast, plus the 'Creatives', as the RSC euphemistically labelled the design and technical staff, were assembled onstage in the Main House.

"Right my luvvlies," he pronounced, as he joined them on the stage, "hear this, hear this."

The set designer guffawed.

"Did I say something funny?"

The will-o'-the-wisp young man spoke unwisely.

"You sounded like the captain of a ship."

Julian strolled over to him nonchalantly.

"Oh yeh. Well you'd better not have been thinking of the Titanic; cos tonight this ship sails into port with bands playing, and crowds cheering."

Julian faced the cast.

"Actors, luvvies, fellow thespians. Forget everything you've been told by Mickey Moran."

The Artistic Director winced. No-one had called him Mickey since he left Dewsbury.

"Come to think of it, Mick, we don't need you. Tell you what, have the day off, or help them put the bunting up. This is a great day of national celebration. Off you trot."

Michael Moran mustered as much of his shattered dignity as he could, and departed. He would supervise the preparations from elsewhere (not that he believed in anything so chauvinistic as national celebrations).

"Right, you lot about your jobs. Just me and the cast onstage. Girls, ladies, it's quite simple. We are going to step back to the age of the great actor manager – that's me, in case you hadn't guessed. Throughout the entire performance you will distribute yourselves decoratively, and keep out of my way. Nobody, I repeat NOBODY, comes downstage."

He swivelled to face the auditorium, and shouted.

"Who's on the follow spot?"

A disembodied voice squeaked acknowledgement.

"It follows me, and me alone. Every minute of the performance. Now then guys and gals, now then, now then..."

Julian's rather fine impression of Jimmy Saville made his company wince in disgust.

"We are going to do a tech dress rehearsal; lunch, and then a dress. Okay, just before we begin I'd like us all to get down on our knees to pray together."

Never before, and not since, has a group of left wing actors fallen so swiftly to its knees. A febrile air wafted outwards into the wings, and beyond.

Julian broke the silence. Rocking back and forth on his heels, whilst shrieking with laughter.

"Only kidding! To work, to work. *'My kingdom for a horse', 'The play's the thing!'*"

His random selection of Shakespearean quotes failed to impress, but the attendant ladies thought it wise to essay a thin smile.

Julian enjoyed his lunch with India. His Ma had been quiet. Her parting words encouraged him.

"It will be a memorable evening, Julian."

The Rooftop Restaurant was reserved for the Prime Minister's personal guests. The *hoi polloi* was distributed around the various bars at ground level. Front of House staff sensed a discernible difference in the punters. Conversation was subdued, as they sipped their drinks. In normal times the chattering middle classes aired their theatrical opinions for all to hear.

Bells rang, and the mass of the audience took their seats in the auditorium. Honoured guests, and critics, were escorted to the best seats in the House. Ere long the house lights went down, and a spartan stage was illuminated. The set designer had gone minimalist. Upstage the Capitol of Rome was arrayed in a state of crumbling disrepair. The stage floor was a tiled vortex, with distorted eyes looking upwards. Centre stage stood a great marble catafalque, its sides engraved with the numbers one to six. It looked like a giant die.

So it was that, apart from military characters, actors clothed in togas took to the stage. A curiosity of the costume design was that the togas had hoods, which masked the performers features.

Act one, scene one of Shakespeare's tragedy, *'Coriolanus'*, sent a frisson through the audience.

First Citizen: *"First, you know Caius Marcius (*Coriolanus after*) is chief enemy to the people."*
All: *"We know't, we know't."*

When Coriolanus' friend, Agrippa, spoke of "...rivers of blood..." the entire audience held its breath. It was Coriolanus' mother, Volumnia, who made the greatest impact in scene three. She trumpeted her son's praises.

Volumnia: *"...If my son were my husband, I would freelier rejoice in that absence wherein he won honour than in the embracements of his bed where he would show most love..."*

Lady Deborah Marlborough felt every eye in the House bearing down upon her, and the eyes painted upon the stage floor seemed to swivel and seek her out.

Julian's first entrance, resplendent in golden armour, was met with disbelief by the critics. He strode downstage, and rooted himself to the spot until he received the applause he demanded as his due. A humourist had seated The Guardian and Daily Telegraph critics beside one another. The latter whispered.

"Dear God, what have we let ourselves in for? I believe the last person to do that was Todd Slaughter in 1923! That evening did not end well."

The critics were puzzled, as the play wore on. Julian's performance was no more than that of a good sixth form student. Yet the audience was still and attentive. No-one was restless.

There were to be two intervals, and the first came at the end of Act two. The keen observer might have noticed that the front of house staff had undergone a complete change. Muscular young men and women manned every station.

When the performance resumed it was still a 'full house', but certain changes had occurred. A few people sat in unfamiliar seats, whilst their former occupants were otherwise engaged.

Coriolanus' great speech comes at the end of Act three, scene three. The senators and patricians of Rome were assembled. Their mouths spat fury; speaking of death or banishment for the tyrant they believed Coriolanus to have become.

When Julian entered he was caught off-guard. The robed and hooded figures were in pale blue. It reminded him of something he couldn't quite recall. He sallied forth to the edge of the stage.

Coriolanus: *"The honour'd gods keep Rome in safety, and the chairs of Justice supplied with worthy men! Plant love among us! Throng our large temples with the shows of peace, and not our streets with war."*

He turned upstage, and became rigid. The actors, excepting one, had pulled back their hoods. Arrayed around the catafalque were Fatima, Abir Hussain, the girl Isa, and his beloved India. He felt the houselights rise behind him, and he swung round. At the foot of the stage stood General Stone, GOC South West, and by his side the Prince of Wales.

Julian shielded his eyes, and peered into the distance. In the aisles he saw men in uniform. Their distinct cap badge pulsated. The proud antelope of the Royal Warwickshire Regiment.

His head sunk to his chest, and then a low rumbling came from his throat.

"You common cry of curs! whose breath I hate
As reek o' the rotten fens, whose loves I prize
As the dead carcasses of unburied men
That do corrupt my air, I banish you;
And here remain with your uncertainty!
Let every feeble rumour shake your hearts!
Your enemies, with nodding of their plumes,
Fan you into despair! Have the power still
To banish your defenders; till at length
Your ignorance, which finds not till it feels,
Making not reservation of yourselves,
Still your own foes, deliver you as most
Abated captives to some nation
That won you without blows! Despising,

For you, the city, thus I turn my back:
There is a world elsewhere."

The power of the stage lights blinded Julian. He peered into the depths of the auditorium, expecting thunderous acclaim. Silence and solemnity reigned, but deference was cast into the gutter when Ken Burke called from the *'gods'*.

"My dear boy, if you really want the play to be a success...join the audience!"

Laughter rippled through the House. It grew like an ominous east wind. An initial breeze rapidly became a gale; it magnified into a storm.

Julian stood downstage clenching and unclenching his fists. His makeup could not disguise the ashen pallor of his shocked features. He spoke under his breath at first.

"Don't...don't...don't laugh at me..."

His howl of humiliation was tossed about as worthless flotsam, unheard amidst the hurricane force of mockery and derision.

"DON'T LAUGH AT ME!"

The stamping and hooting resonated like the bells of freedom, but Julian saw every devil in Hell chasing him. Only those onstage could hear him.

"Mummy, mummy, make them stop. Mummy, mummy, where are you?"

A hand touched his arm. He looked sideways, and beheld his Mother; her disguise abandoned. Deborah embraced him tightly. The song she crooned was familiar, from a world elsewhere.

"Then pealed the bells more loud and deep:
God is not dead, nor doth he sleep!
The wrong shall fail,
The right prevail,
With peace on earth, good will to men!"

Julian felt the pressure of the muzzle she placed against his heart. Deborah Marlborough looked into her son's eyes. The explosion was muffled.

He carried her dead body, and laid it on the catafalque. When he lowered his head, to kiss her goodbye, an audible 'pop' echoed in the silent theatre. Julian fell dead at his mother's feet.

High above, in *'the gods'*, Ken Burke remarked whimsically to the follow spot operator.

"Apart from that, how did you enjoy the show?"

'Kathy Clifford' had already packed the rifle away. She looked at the old man ruefully.

Epilogue

Mother and child knelt before the stone in the churchyard; it was Late-May. They planted summer annuals on the grave. Salvias, Peter had always liked salvias.

"Let's go Sophie. We'll come and see daddy again next week."

"Can I carry your case, mummy?"

"It's rather heavy darling, and it's not mine. That gentleman at the gate is going to return it to its owner."

She handed the sniper's rifle to the sharp-suited man, without a word being exchanged.

The New Forest looked lovely at this time of year. England was free and peaceful again, and Jane Standish had redeemed the past.

in lumine tuo videbimus

"In your light we shall see light"

St. Katherine of Alexandria

Printed in Great Britain
by Amazon

66290644R00187